A Very Mersey Murder

A Very Mersey Murder

Mersey Murder Mysteries Book V

Brian L. Porter

Published 2019 by Next Chapter
Cover art by http://www.thecovercollection.com/
Back cover texture by David M. Schrader, used under license from Shutterstock.com

Dedicated to the memory of Enid Anne Porter
1913 – 2004

Acknowledgements

For the fifth book in the Mersey Mystery series, I have to say a big, big thank you to Debbie Poole. As my one-time proof-reader, Debbie has moved on to fulfil not only that role but has grown into her new role as my on-the-spot researcher in Liverpool. I've been away from the city for a long time, so it's obvious that not everything is as it was 'in my day' and Debbie is able to first of all, correct me if I try to include locations or buildings that no longer exist, or sometimes, corrects my faulty geography when it comes to local geography.

Debbie also throws herself into the research role and has driven many miles around the city and its environs, seeking appropriate locations for scenes in the books. For example, she recently drove around, looking under railway bridges for a perfect 'body dump' site. Thank God the police didn't pull up and ask what she was doing examining railway cuttings, bridges and tunnels. *"You see officer, I'm just looking for a perfect place to dump a body,"* wouldn't go down too well, I think. Debbie has recently been joined in my 'research department' by Dot Blackman and these two fearless and intrepid ladies can often be seen in some of the most unlikely places as they delve into parts of Liverpool that others may shy away from as they go in search of locations, background stories and interesting information for use in current or future books, (hence the search for a body dump). So, thanks to Dot, too.

On top of all that, Debbie has become a great friend and the Mersey Mysteries owe much to her help, her guidance and her critical eye on the words I write. I couldn't do it without her.

Of course, I have to thank Miika, my publisher at Next Chapter, for his vision in having first seen the potential in a series based on my original Mersey Mystery, *A Mersey Killing*, which set the whole ball rolling.

And of course, my dear wife Juliet always rates a big thank you for her patience as I take over the dining table, constantly fail to hear her talking to me, such is my level of concentration while writing, and for always supporting me in my efforts to produce the next book in the series.

As always, my thanks go to the people of Liverpool, and Merseyside in general, without whom, the Mersey Mysteries couldn't exist.

Finally, I have to say a big thank you to all my readers around the world who have helped the Mersey Mysteries on their way to success. I appreciate you all.

Introduction

Welcome to the fifth book in the Mersey Mystery series. Those who have already read the earlier books in the series will already be familiar with Detective Inspector Andy Ross, Detective Sergeant Izzie Drake and the rest of the team that make up the fictional Merseyside Police Specialist Murder Investigation Team. For new readers I hope you will enjoy meeting the chief protagonists in this, their latest investigation, which begins before most of the team were born, on the day the England football team won football's world cup in July 1966.

A young woman is brutally raped and murdered, her body left close to the old disused lighthouse at the local beauty spot of Hale, near Liverpool, her killing being followed by two more in the coming weeks. With no arrests being made the case is consigned to the cold case list and over time, virtually forgotten about. When a similar case occurs thirty-nine years later, with two identical killings taking place, it takes an intervention by the retired, former detective who investigated the original 'Lighthouse Murders' to inform the police that they may have a copycat killer at large. Worse still, there is a chance that the original killer may have resurfaced after all these years have passed.

With the prospect of a third murder strongly suggested, the case is passed to the Specialist Investigation Team, who under the overall leadership of Detective Chief Inspector Oscar Agostini, find themselves with one week to find the killer. Why a week? Because if the current murders follow the same pattern as the original killings, in one week's time the third murder will take place, and, following the pattern of the '66 murders, the next victim will be a female police officer!

With no clues, and not a suspect in sight, Andy Ross and his team face a race against time to try to identify and apprehend the vicious killer of young women. With a fresh-faced new detective joining the team, and with one of their number still on sick leave as a result of gunshot wounds suffered in a previous case, the team find themselves being assisted by a couple of unlikely citizens, and, for previous readers of the series, there is a fond return for criminal profiler and forensic anthropologist, Doctor Christine Bland.

Glossary

Author's note: Some of the dialogue used in this book includes certain regional accents that might be unfamiliar to readers in the USA and other nations around the world. For those who may be confused by some of the idiosyncratic speech found in the following pages, I have provided a short glossary of terms to help to explain some of these odd sounding words and phrases.

Tanner, popular term for a sixpenny piece, a small silver coin, used in pre-decimal times, equivalent to 5 pence in today's money.

La' a contraction of the word, 'lad' popularly used in the local Liverpool dialect.

Babycham and Cherry B two popular drinks in the UK in the 1960s, the first a perry, resembling champagne, but made with pears, the second a form of cherry brandy, both popular with female drinkers of the time.

Lead – Leash
999 – UK equivalent to 911
S.I.O. – Senior Investigating Officer
D.C.I. – Detective Chief Inspector
D.I. - Detective Inspector.
D.S. - Detective Sergeant
D.C. - Detective Constable
Tights – Pantyhose
Knickers - Panties

Scally: Local Liverpudlian description (from the word scallywag), used to describe a ne'er-do-well, a mischief maker or small-time thief or hoodlum.
On the 'never-never' – On credit.
Up the duff – pregnant (slang)

There may be a few words I've failed to mention, but I think you'll get the hang of the 'Scouse' accent after a while. Speaking of the word 'Scouse'

Scouse/Scouser, a common term to refer to the natives of Liverpool, derived from the once popular dish 'scouse,' served in Liverpool households for many years, though not so much nowadays.

In the case of Albert Cretingham senior, he is from the neighbouring county of West Yorkshire and does not have a Liverpool accent. Instead he speaks with a broad Yorkshire accent and has a habit of dropping the letter 'H' from the beginning of his words, e.g. 'is instead of his, 'er instead of her etc. I'm sure you'll soon catch on. The phraseology and grammar are also different and though not correct English, I have written it as it spoken by the people of that part of the country.

Prologue

Hale, Liverpool, 30th July 1966

The 30th July 1966 had proved to be a landmark day for English football, a day that began with hope and expectation among the fans of 'the beautiful game' and ended with joyous celebrations all over the country. Not only did England triumph in the World Cup Final, in a thrilling 4 -2 encounter with West Germany in a game that needed extra-time to separate the two evenly matched teams, but England's Geoff Hurst became the first player in the history of the game to score a hat-trick in a World Cup Final, the final goal scored and accompanied by the now famous words of commentator Kenneth Wolstenholme, as Hurst's shot rocketed into the net, *"And here comes Hurst. He's got…some people are on the pitch, they think it's all over. It is now! It's four!"*

Celebrations began all over the country as those who'd watched the game on television, listened to the radio commentary indulged in impromptu parties and revelry. Victory over the Germans had been the perfect excuse for unprecedented scenes of delirium and togetherness among fans and non-fans of the game as it became a matter of national pride that England for the first time, had been crowned kings of the game that, after all, they had invented.

Nowhere were the celebrations more pronounced, more fervent, than in and around the city of Liverpool, a hot bed of football fanaticism and home to two veritable giants of the English First Division, in the forms of Liverpool and Everton Football Clubs. That year, Liverpool had won the First Division Championship and Everton had won the F.A. Cup with a thrilling comeback victory over Sheffield Wednesday at Wembley, after being two-nil behind, eventually winning 3 goals to 2. For that day, and especially in the evening, all thoughts of partisan rivalry were forgotten as fans of all teams joined together to celebrate England's triumph. The people of Liverpool could feel extra pride as two of the England team that day played for the city's teams, Inside Forward Roger Hunt of Liverpool and Ramon (Ray) Wilson, the Everton full back.

As the night drew towards a close, the customers in the Traveller's Rest public house on the outskirts of the village of Hale, some six miles from the city of Liverpool were enjoying themselves, a spirit of bonhomie and good humour being the order of the day, or night, to be more precise.

Closing time was drawing closer as 19-year-old barmaid Stella Cox made her way through the loud, happy throng of drinkers, tray in hand, attempting to clear the tables of empty glasses. In the packed, crowded bar, more than one stray hand would reach out, trying to grab a cheeky feel of Stella's shapely rear as she tried to navigate the obstacle course of happy, mostly slightly inebriated drinkers.

"Get off, you lecherous old bugger," Stella laughed as she good naturedly fought off the semi-drunken attentions of more than a few of the bar's regular punters.

"Oh, come on, Stella. You look good enough to eat, girl," old Billy Riley said with a grin as he 'accidentally' allowed his hand to encounter the fabric of her softly pleated skirt. "Give us a feel for England, eh?"

"The only feel you'll cop, Billy Riley, is the feel of my fist as it connects with your chin, you old dog," shouted Micky Drummond, the landlord of 'The Travellers' as it was known to the locals. "Leave my sodding staff alone, you bloody pervert. Stella's young enough to be your bloody daughter."

"Aye well, I s'pose I did go to school with yer old man, Stella, so I guess old Micky's right," Riley hiccupped as the effects of the locally brewed Higson's Bitter induced a distinct slurring of his words. "Sorry love."

"I think you ought to be getting off home, Billy," Stella laughed, unperturbed by Billy's fumbling. "Sheila won't be best pleased if you roll in drunk as a lord, now, will she?"

The thought of his wife standing in the hall, rolling pin in hand seemed to have a sobering effect on Billy Riley, who quickly downed the last of his eighth pint of the night, placed his glass on Stella's tray, almost missing entirely as his eyes failed to focus properly, and made a lurch towards the door, calling out a hearty "Goodnight all," as he set off on his drunken walk to his home a few hundred yards away.

"The way he's weaving around, I reckon it'll take him half a bloody hour to get home," Micky Drummond laughed as the door swung shut behind Billy Riley. A wave of laughter accompanied Micky's words and Stella completed her penultimate collection of empty glasses just as Drummond called 'Last orders. please," ringing the bell over the bar to back up his announcement. She'd clear the final lot after the final customers had left the premises. His wife, Dora, took the bell as her signal to leave her place behind the bar and she quickly walked across the room to turn off the jukebox in the corner, that was currently playing the new number one in the charts, *Wild Thing*, by *The Troggs*, for what was probably the twentieth time that night.

"Oy, Dora, love. I paid a tanner to play that song," Bobby Evans protested as the music died and the lights of the juke box faded away to nothing.

At twenty-two, just under six feet tall, with a shock of unruly blonde hair, Bobby was one of the younger regulars at The Travellers, and was the pub's star darts player, captaining the darts team in the Liverpool and District Licensed Victuallers Darts League. By day he worked as a postman and was only in the pub till closing time because it was Saturday, and there was no delivery service on Sundays.

"For Christ sakes, Bobby Evans, you must have played it a dozen times at least this evening. You tryin' to wear the grooves out lad?" Dora cajoled him.

"Right, I'm off then. Youse lot don't know good music when you hear it. Place is like a bloody morgue without the jukebox," Bobby replied, draining the last of his pint, and banging the glass down on the bar in protest.

"Hey, la' break that and you'll be paying for it," Micky said, sternly as Bobby held a hand up in apology and made his way to the door, followed closely by the last of the die-hards who'd stayed till closing time, England's World Cup win being the perfect excuse for a good night out and maybe a drink or two more than usual.

"Thank God for that," Dora exclaimed as a momentary silence followed the exit of the last of night's patrons.

"Don't knock it girl," Micky responded. "That World Cup win has boosted our takings by about fifty percent tonight. He quickly poured himself a large scotch from a bottle of Johnnie Walker Red Label he kept under the bar, for his personal consumption, as well as a gin and tonic for Dora and a Babycham for Stella. As they were joined by Ann Rolls and Pete Donovan, who'd staffed the small lounge bar that evening, he added a pint of Higson's bitter for Pete and a Cherry B for Ann.

For the next ten minutes, landlord and staff enjoyed a convivial drink together before calling it a night. Before the staff left to make their way to their homes, Dora pulled Stella to one side.

"Just wanted to tell you how nice you looked tonight, Stella. That skirt new, is it?"

"Yes, it is," Stella replied, running her hands down the fabric of the navy blue, pencil pleated skirt, that was beautifully complimented by her white satin effect blouse with ruffles at the neck. With her flowing auburn hair, Stella Cox could easily be mistaken for a model, though she would be the first to tell anyone who asked that such a job just wasn't for her. In fact, Stella had ambitions to succeed in a less lucrative but more stable business and had recently gained an interview for a position as a clerk in the Littlewoods Football Pools offices on Walton Hall Avenue, where she hoped to one day become an office manager or something similar. She'd promised Micky that she'd continue to work at the pub at weekends if she got the job, a decision that greatly please the landlord of the Travellers, who knew that Stella's good looks and permanently cheerful disposition helped trade enormously. Everyone loved a pretty barmaid, and they didn't come much prettier than Stella Cox.

"I bought it this afternoon at C & A," Stella continued her conversation with Dora, who, at forty-eight, had retained her own youthful figure, much to the delight of her husband, a former Liverpool City police sergeant, who'd taken early retirement in order to fulfil his lifetime ambition to run his own pub one day. He and Dora had now run the Traveller's Rest successfully for three years.

"You're a very pretty girl, Stella," Dora went on. "Still no lad in your life yet?"

"No, not yet, Dora. You know me, still young and fancy free. My Mam says I've plenty of time ahead of me to get tangled up with boys, as she puts it."

"She's got a sound head on her shoulders, that Mam of yours," Dora smiled in agreement with Lucy Cox, her friend, Stella's mother, who she'd known for as long as she could remember.

"Yeah, well, me Dad agrees with her," Stella replied. "And it could put any lad wanting to be my boyfriend off if I tell 'em me Dad says he'll kill any scally that so much as lays a finger on me, never mind tried to kiss me or anything."

Dora laughed, as did Stella, and a few minutes later Stella, Pete and Ann all made their way to the door, which Micky unlocked to allow them out of the pub, ready for home, and bed.

Pete and Ann both lived on Church Road, about a ten-minute walk from the pub, and Pete, as was customary, would walk Ann home before heading to his own house, a few doors away, not far from St. Mary's church. Stella lived in the opposite direction, her family residing in a neat detached cottage not far from the disused Hale Lighthouse, from where her father, Terry, ran his own small business, making items of bespoke hand-made furniture, much sought after by many of the local city retailers, as well as making individual commissions for discerning customers.

"You going to be alright walking home alone, Stella?" Micky asked the same question he posed every night that Stella worked in the pub.

"Stop fussing, Micky," Stella laughed as she replied. "You're like an old mother hen. What's gonna happen round here? This is Hale, not flippin' London or Manchester, or even the city centre. Besides, everyone round here knows me and my Mam and Dad. We're all one big happy family in the village, right?"

"Aye lass, I suppose you're right at that. Just be careful, okay?"

"I'm always careful, Micky, you know that. Now get yourself in there with Dora and get a good night's sleep. I'll see you tomorrow night as usual."

"Right you are, Stella," Micky replied, bending his six feet three-inch frame enough to allow him to plant a fatherly kiss on Stella's right cheek. "Good night, girl. Take care."

Micky Drummond didn't know it, but those would be the last words he, or any of her workmates at the Traveller's rest would ever speak to Stella Cox.

* * *

Stella was almost home. Turning off the main footpath onto the narrow unpaved track that led to her parent's cottage, she sensed, rather than heard, the soft footfalls approaching from the darkness behind her. A tiny frisson of fear ran the length of her spine, but, seeing the lights of the cottage ahead, she tried to dispel any thoughts of impending trouble. After all, she'd be home in a minute. The sound of someone breathing close by eventually forced her to quicken her pace a little, not easy in her three-inch heels on the unpaved, rough surface of the track to the cottage. Stella whirled round, ready to confront the apparition in the dark.

"Oh, it's you," she gasped, as a familiar face came into view.

"Who were you expecting, Stella?" the voice asked.

"Nobody of course. I'm going home and I'm going to bed. What are you doing down here anyway?"

"I wanted to see you, of course."

"Me? Why?"

"You looked so nice tonight in the pub, so pretty."

"Thank you, but why follow me home?"

"Because I wanted to see you. I already told you."

A ripple of fear made Stella turn towards home again. Something wasn't right here, and she knew it."

"Look, I'm very tired and I want to get to bed. You can see me in the pub again tomorrow, okay?"

She walked two paces in the direction of home when she felt strong arms around her waist, strong enough to lift her off her feet, and throw her to the ground. Before she could scream a hand pressed down across her mouth, silencing her, as the weight of her attacker held her pinned to the ground.

"Scream, and you die," the once friendly voice commanded, and Stella nodded, as he removed his hand and stuffed an old piece of rag in her mouth, choking and gagging her at the same time. She felt herself being flipped over onto her front, and in mere seconds, her hands were pulled behind her back and tied together with a rough length of rope.

Rough hands pulled at her beautiful new skirt, exposing her legs to the attacker.

"Now, I can see you," the voice said, as tears stung Stella's eyes. She felt herself being lifted and was soon hoisted over the shoulder of the man, who, she now noticed, was dressed in black from head to foot. No wonder she hadn't seen anyone behind her as she'd walked along the dark path towards home.

A few minutes later, Stella felt herself being tossed like a sack of garbage onto the rough ground. Rough hands pulled at the buttons of her blouse as the man spoke again.

"I only want to see you, Stella."

Despite the foul-tasting rag that effectively gagged her, Stella Cox did her best to struggle, and behind the gag, she screamed into the night, but her screams went unheard.

* * *

Postman Bobby Evans discovered the body of Stella Cox at three a.m. the following morning. Bobby walked his dog Max, a young Bedlington terrier, along the old farm tracks near the disused Hale Lighthouse, early every morning before heading off to work. He had to be at the local sorting office by four a.m. so made sure Max had a good run before having to leave him at home with his widowed Mum, Edith for most of the day. Despite the fact he wasn't working the following day, he stuck to the usual routine, as Max had no concept of days off and his built-in body clock demanded he be walked at the same time every early morning. Bobby never minded his early morning walks with Max. The village and its surrounding area always exuded a feeling of peace and tranquillity late at night and first thing in the morning, just before dawn, and now, it gave Bobby, after just a couple of hours sleep, an opportunity to walk off some of his slightly drunken feelings, after celebrating England's victory with his mates in the pub. He planned to get his head down for an afternoon nap after one his Mother's gargantuan Sunday roast beef dinners.

He'd let Max off his lead, allowing him to run free and as usual, Max was running well ahead of Bobby, until he seemed to pull up with a start. From thirty yards away, Bobby saw his dog, standing still, whimpering as if he'd hurt himself.

"Hey Max, what's the matter boy? Have you found something?"

In the darkness, Bobby could just about make out a form on the ground in front of where Max stood. Hoping his dog hadn't come across the rotting corpse of a dead animal, he increased his pace until he was almost upon the spot where Max still stood, stock still and whimpering incessantly.

"Oh my God, no, please no!" Bobby Evans gasped in shock as he finally saw what Max had found. Futile as it was, he fell to his knees, trying to find some sign of life in the inert body that lay before him. When he realised who he was looking at, and the enormity of his discovery hit home, Bobby turned away from the body of Stella Cox just before depositing the contents of his stomach on the ground at the side of the path where she lay. Bobby ran over a mile, with Max at his side until he came to the nearest public telephone box, from where he dialled 999 and summoned the police.

* * *

Despite a massive police inquiry at the time, no charges were ever brought in the case of the murder of Stella Cox. As one of the last people to see her alive and also being the one to report the finding of her body, Bobby Evans at first came under close scrutiny as a possible suspect, but he was eventually cleared of any involvement. The investigation was hampered by the fact that between her death and the finding of her body, there'd been a light rain shower, which had potentially destroyed any trace evidence that may have been present at the scene or on Stella's body.

Every man in Hale was interviewed, and many from the surrounding areas. Sadly, in 1966, there was no such thing as DNA testing, so the semen found at the scene of the murder and during the autopsy couldn't be tied to any one man.

Although the case remained on the 'open' file for many years, it would eventually find itself into the archive of 'cold cases,' those for whom a resolution seemed as likely as a snowfall in hell, the longer the passage of time since they were committed.

Chapter 1

Liverpool, August 2005

The squad room of Merseyside Police Force's Specialist Murder Investigation Team was unusually quiet for once. The team of detectives led by Detective Inspector Andy Ross had enjoyed a successful year so far. Their latest case, the so-called 'Frozen Lamb Murders' had recently been solved and the killer, Byron Cummings was now behind bars, awaiting trial. His use of joints of frozen lamb as his weapon of choice in dispatching his victims had been ingeniously simple and at first, the police had found it impossible to identify exactly what the murder weapon had been in the cases of four almost identical, apparently motiveless murders. Who would have suspected the mild-mannered family man of being guilty of such heinous crimes? Using frozen leg of lamb joints, Cummings had bludgeoned his victims to death, cleverly disposing of the murder weapons each time by simply defrosting and cooking them in the oven, then serving them up as a tasty meal to his wife and two children.

Ross and his team had finally latched on to the killer by establishing a link between him and the four victims, all of whom had been customers at the barber shop Cummings owned in Speke. Precisely why he'd selected them was still a grey area, but it was thought they were all vegetarians who had somehow managed to offend their barber while sitting in his chair. That would be one for the psychiatrists to argue about, but for Andy Ross, it was another case closed.

The aftermath of the case involving multiple murders and kidnapping that revolved around the cargo liner *Alexandra Rose* had left its marks on Ross's team. Although Detective Constable Derek McLennan had recovered from his gunshot wounds and returned to work, D.C. Keith Burton hadn't been so lucky. His shoulder muscles had been badly damaged by the bullets that had ripped into him aboard the ship, and he was still undergoing a protracted period of physiotherapy. Whether he would eventually be declared fit enough to return to work was a matter for the doctors, though Ross wasn't too hopeful.

On a positive note, Acting Detective Constable Gary, (Ginger) Devenish who had originally been seconded to the team from the Liverpool Port Police, had been confirmed as a full-time member, much to his and Ross's delight. His position as a full D.C. was now pending and he would soon be able to drop the 'Acting' from his rank.

"When are we going to get a new case?" asked Detective Constable Sam Gable, as she and the others gathered in the squad room on a sultry August morning.

"Good question, Sam," D.C. Lenny (Tony) Curtis replied. Nobody ever referred to Curtis by his given name any more. He would be forever Tony, a result of his remarkable likeness to the old movie idol of the same name.

"Yeah, I hate bloody office work," D.C. Nick Dodds joined in.

"We should perhaps be careful what we are wishing for," said Sofie Meyer. The German detective sergeant, on loan from the police force in Hamburg for two years had assimilated well into Ross's team and now felt perfectly at home with her new, British colleagues.

As the conversation began, so it was brought to an abrupt end by the entrance of Detective Inspector Andy Ross, closely followed by Detective Sergeant Clarissa (Izzie) Drake, his trusted right hand and long-time crime busting partner.

"Morning all, "Ross began. "Did I hear some mumblings of discontent in the ranks as we walked into the room?"

The smile on his face gave away the levity of his comment.

"We were wondering when we might be gainfully employed in our primary role again, Boss," Curtis responded.

"Funny you should say that, Tony. As it happens, D.C.I. Agostini just handed us a nice juicy new case. Anyone know where D.S. Ferris is?"

"I'm here, sir," Paul Ferris replied, as he and D.C. Devenish entered the squad room, loaded down with files that they proceeded to deposit on Ferris's desk. "Still bringing the system up to date, adding some of these older files to the computer records."

"Ah yes, good man, Paul. Now, all we need is Derek and we can get on with this briefing."

D.C. Derek McLennan, who'd now been with Ross's team for five years, had grown in that time, from a young, naïve newcomer to a seasoned trusted part of the team, and only recently had been honoured with a Chief Constable's Commendation for his bravery in attempting to foil a jewellery store robbery during his off-duty hours. A bullet wound to the chest had landed him in hospital where he met and fell in love with his fiancée, Debbie Tate, who'd been one of the team of dedicated nurses who had helped him in his recovery and wedding plans were already underway.

"He was here a few minutes ago sir," Sam Gable commented, "I never saw him leave."

The door to Ross's office at the far side of the room opened, and the man in question appeared with a smile on his face.

"I was under the impression that was *my* office, Derek," Ross said, wondering why McLennan would have been in his office first thing in the morning. McLennan held his hands up in a gesture of surrender.

"Ah, you've got me, sir. I confess. I was trying to steal your supply of paperclips... no, really, I've left something on your desk. It's a surprise, so I hope you'll forgive me creeping around, all furtive, like."

"I'm intrigued," Ross replied. "I'll check out your surprise shortly. For now, I have some news for you all. It's time we got back to doing some work folks. Pull up a chair and listen."

The team members all complied, each taking a seat and waiting expectantly for Ross to begin. As he prepared to outline the latest case the squad room door opened to admit Kat Bellamy, the team's civilian administration assistant.

"Come in and sit down, Kat," Ross urged her and waited a few seconds as Kat, looking flustered, sat at her desk and nodded to him that she was ready to take notes of what he had to say.

"Okay people," Ross began. "The boss seemingly got a call from D.C.I. Mountfield in C.I.D. Three weeks ago, the body of a young woman was found not far from the old ruined lighthouse at Hale."

As he spoke, Izzie Drake moved behind him and began attaching a series of photographs to the whiteboard on the wall.

"I'll let D.S. Drake tell you the basics. Please, Izzie, tell 'em."

"Right, everyone. This is Cathy Billings, aged twenty," she indicated the photo of a pretty blonde with long, wavy hair, positioned at the top left of the whiteboard. "Cathy left her job as a barmaid at The Travellers Rest in Hale at closing time and was never seen alive again. Her body, as the boss said, was found not far from the old closed down lighthouse the next morning. She'd been beaten and raped. The local lads handed the case to C.I.D. who weren't getting far, when, last week, there was a second murder, an almost identical crime scene to the first, the body being found on the beach, close to the car park, again, near the lighthouse."

"That's tragic, sir," Tony Curtis spoke from the back of the room, "but it doesn't really sound like one of our cases does it?"

Ross provided him, and the others, with the answer to his question. "Under normal circumstances, I'd agree Tony, but then, most cases don't have the strange connections this one has."

"What kind of connections, sir?" Curtis continued probing.

"I'm coming to that, in a minute. Now, as I just said, under normal circumstances this would be handled by C.I.D. It's not a case for us, or so you'd think. Sergeant Drake, carry on, please."

Izzie pointed to the second photo on the board, another young woman whose life had been tragically cut short by violent death.

"Victim number two," she began, "was twenty-two-year-old Hannah Lucas, a trainee veterinarian nurse. Again, she'd been beaten and raped, but here's where things began to go a little screwy."

As she paused for breath, a hush fell over the assembled detectives in the room. A sense of anticipation spread through the team. Drake continued.

"As luck would have it, or maybe bad luck, I don't know, when the second murder took place, and was reported in the press, a retired detective inspector who handled an unsolved case back in the 1960s got in touch with the S.I.O. a D.I. Morris.

Apparently former D.I. Stan Coleman had investigated a series of murders in 1966. The first victim was a barmaid at The Traveller's Rest, and the second one was a student at Liverpool University. Anyone want to hazard a guess at what she was studying?"

"Veterinary medicine?" Ginger Devenish piped up.

"Quite right, Ginger," Drake confirmed. "Stan Coleman was able to tell Morris so much about the old case that Morris felt something must connect them somehow. Without telling Coleman a single fact about the new murders, Coleman was able to give Morris chapter and verse on the original killings that exactly match the current ones. D.I. Morris is no fool. She took Coleman's information to her boss and well, to cut a long story short, as nobody was ever convicted for the 1966 killings, the case has ended up in our lap, and, this is important, everyone. Remember that the original killer stopped his spree of killing after three murders. So far, we've only had two."

Sam Gable wasn't the only member of the team to feel a tingle running through her body as she took Izzie Drake's words on board. She spoke in response to the information received so far.

"You said the original murders took place in 1966, Sarge? Surely nobody suspects that the same killer could have suddenly started up again after thirty-nine years?"

It was Ross who supplied her with the answer.

"We just don't know, Sam. It seems highly unlikely and yet the current murders are perfect carbon copies of the earlier killings, according to D.I. Morris. She was upstairs with D.C.I. Agostini when we were handed the case a few minutes ago and she seemed genuinely unnerved by the similarity between the current murders and the original ones. According to her, ex-D.I. Coleman has carried the case around in his head for all those years. It was his one big failure, in a career spanning thirty years. He hasn't forgotten a single detail."

It was Sofie Meyer's turn to speak up, and she was her usual direct self in her words to Ross.

"Sir, I can see why we have been handed this case but there is one thing you have yet not told us."

"Go on, Sofie."

"Sergeant Drake has told us there were three murders in 1966. so far there have been two in the most recent ones. As we know the identities and occupations of the original victims, I think we should be made aware of the age and occupation of the third victim in 1966 and how long you think we have before the third killing will take place, assuming the killer is following the identical timetable as the original killer."

"I was about to come to that," Ross replied. "If the killer of Cathy and Hannah is indeed following the exact timetable of the 1966 murders, we can expect another murder one week from today and that, people, gives us a very precise time frame in which to identify and apprehend this bastard."

"Sir?" Tony Curtis said, questioningly. "What was the occupation of the third victim in the original set of murders?"

Ross looked at Izzie Drake and nodded and she now took a third photo from the folder in her hands and attached it to the now rapidly developing murder board. As she did so and stepped back so they could all see victim number three clearly, there was an audible gasp from the assembled team members. Smiling at them, in the stark black and white photograph was a young and extremely attractive woman police constable.

"Oh, bloody hell," Nick Dodds exclaimed.

"Shit," Curtis added.

"Sick bastard," said Sam Gable.

"This is not good," Sofie Meyer added.

"Who was she?" Derek McLennan asked.

"This, ladies and gents," Ross replied, tapping the photograph added by Drake, "was W.P.C. Elizabeth Warren, known to everyone as Liz. She was just twenty-one years old when the killer beat and raped her before killing her. Like the others, she was dumped near the old lighthouse at Hale. In her case, the original investigating officers were able to positively determine her movements up until a few minutes before she disappeared. She had been at a party in a friend's house in Hale, but she lived in Huyton. Her car was found a few hundred yards from the friend's house, and D.I Coleman concluded she must have stopped, possibly to offer help to someone, maybe her killer, who had possibly set up some sort of trap to lure her into his clutches. I don't have to tell you, we need to move fast on this one. D.C.I. Agostini is adamant there isn't going to be a dead woman police officer on his conscience so it's up to us to make sure we catch this bastard quickly."

Murmurs of agreement rippled through the room as Ross fell silent. Nick Dodds finally broke that silence as he asked the question that was on most minds at that time.

"Sir, you've told us these women were raped and beaten but what was the actual cause of death?"

"Good question, Nick. D.I. Coleman's original investigation in 1966 showed that all three women had been strangled with their own tights. The killer either made them remove them or stripped them off the women himself before using them as the murder weapon."

"That's gross," Sam Gable commented.

"Women's tights are very stretchy," Sofie Meyer commented. "He would have needed a high degree of strength to pull them tight enough to produce a killing ligature, I think."

"You're right, Sofie," Ross agreed. "D.I. Coleman and his people on the first investigation came to the same conclusion. The problem is, you can't arrest or interrogate every man in the city of Liverpool or beyond simply based on their strength. Their biggest problem was a total lack of forensic evidence at the crime scenes. There was no such thing as regular DNA testing back then, so even the presence of semen wasn't of any great help to the investigators."

"When did DNA testing first become used here in the UK?" Meyer asked.

Paul Ferris, who had been silent until now, for reasons all too clear to Ross, provided her with the answer. The team's computer specialist said, "The first recorded use of DNA being used in the apprehension of a criminal was back in the 1980s, Sofie. It led to the arrest and conviction of a man called Colin Pitchfork, who killed two girls, three years apart, in 1983 and 1986. They had the ability to extract and store DNA in the earlier murder but not until the second murder was the system perfected to the extent that, following mass profiling of men in Leicestershire, Pitchfork was identified and eventually convicted."

"Great history lesson, Sarge," Derek McLennan said with a smile on his face.

"Just answering Sofie's question," Ferris replied. The team had been requested, at Meyer's behest, to use her first name as she wasn't comfortable being addressed as sergeant and appearing to be senior in rank to the more experienced members of Ross's team, who she saw as being more experienced locally than herself.

"Thank you, Paul. That is indeed interesting to know," Meyer replied.

"And what have you been up to on that computer of yours while I've been talking, Paul?" Ross inquired, having noticed Ferris battering the keyboard at his desk as he and Drake had been presenting the case.

He had a good idea what Ferris was doing, and now the sergeant, his resident computer expert, replied.

"Thought I'd look up that old case as you were talking, sir."

"I thought that's what you were doing, and…?"

"It's pretty much as you and Izzie laid out, sir. D.I. Stanley James Coleman was the senior investigating officer at the time. He was backed up mostly by a Sergeant Dennis Megson. From what I can see, it was a good investigation. D.I. Coleman did all he could under the constraints of the day, regarding lack of forensics, no DNA testing etc. They must have questioned around a thousand men in the six months following the first murder, and though they were focussed on a local man, Bobby Evans for a while, there was no evidence against him whatsoever and his alibi held up, so they hit a brick wall quite quickly with that line of inquiry."

"What was his alibi, sarge?" Nick Dodds asked.

"Well, it seems he'd been in the pub that night, talked to Stella, but left early while she stayed behind with the other staff for a drink with the landlord and his wife after closing. Evans and Stella were friendly with each other but lived at opposite ends of the village, and nobody ever provided any kind of evidence that placed them together after Stella left work that night.

Now, although there were no witnesses to the crime, there was a rain shower that night, and it was a fairly simple task for the investigators to narrow the murder time down to before it rained, because of the state of the ground below the body. The pathologist was clear on the point that the girl had been murdered on the spot she was found so there was no question of the body being dumped after being killed elsewhere."

"I wonder why D.I. Coleman never advanced beyond Detective Inspector," Sam Gable wondered aloud.

"Probably an 'old school' bobby," Ross conjectured. "Back then, there weren't the same opportunities for promotion as there are today, and maybe he preferred staying at the sharp end of policing, not fancying being promoted to a desk job."

Izzie Drake looked long and hard at Andy Ross as he spoke. He could, she knew, be quite easily describing himself with those words. Certainly not lacking in ambition, Ross had nevertheless turned down a promotion when D.C.I. Harry Porteous had retired due to him wanting to remain as head of the team on a day to day basis. His refusal to accept the promotion had led to D.C.I. Oscar Agostini becoming their new D.C.I.

"According to his record," Paul Ferris continued, "Stan Coleman carried his failure to solve that case like a millstone round his neck for years. It haunted him, and he retired from the force ten years later at the age of forty."

"So that puts him in his sixties or seventies now then," Tony Curtis said. "Can we be sure his memory is accurate about the original investigation?"

"We'll know soon enough, D.C. Curtis," said a voice from behind him, as D.C.I. Oscar Agostini walked into the squad room, accompanied by a white-haired, six feet tall, very fit looking elderly gentlemen who walked with an upright copper's bearing and who barely needed any introduction as Agostini said, "Ladies and gentlemen, allow me to introduce you to former Detective Inspector Stan Coleman."

Chapter 2

Questions upon questions

Former D.I. Stan Coleman soon had the members of Ross's team veritably eating out of his hand. Despite his age, there was no doubting the acuity of his mind. He seemed to possess an almost encyclopaedic knowledge of policing in Liverpool during his time in service with the old City of Liverpool Police Force. When it came to discuss what he told them were referred to as 'The Lighthouse Murders' it soon became apparent why Coleman had taken the case so much to heart at the time and why he felt haunted by his inability to apprehend the killer.

"You see, people, the first two murders were bad enough, but when that bastard struck a third time, he took the life of someone I knew personally."

As he spoke those words, a collective audible gasp circulated round the squad room. He continued.

"W.P.C. Liz Warren wasn't just any police officer. I'd known her for about six months prior to her murder, not closely, you understand but enough to have a nodding relationship with her. Her boyfriend was Detective Constable Leo Forsyth, one of the lads on my team. They planned to get engaged at Christmas. Bloody hell, I can still remember young Leo's face when he heard the news. It was all he could do to stay on his feet; the shock hit him so badly. I could see him trying his best not to break down in front of his mates, but what the hell, his future wife had just been brutally murdered, not to mention what the poor lass went through before the bastard strangled the life out of her. I went and put an arm round his shoulder and told him to just let it all out, that nobody would think any less of him. That did it. He seemed to shake from head to toe and then just broke down. The tears wracked his body for a full ten minutes, and when he finally pulled himself together, I could have sworn he'd aged ten years in those ten minutes."

"There's nothing about that in the report I read, sir. It just said her boyfriend was questioned and immediately cleared, no name mentioned," Paul Ferris told him.

"No, I don't suppose there would be," Coleman nodded. "They weren't legally related at that point and Forsyth was immediately removed from the investigation because of his relationship with Liz."

"What happened to D.C. Forsyth eventually," Izzie Drake asked.

"You got second sight or something, Sergeant Drake?" Coleman asked, and then continuing before Izzie could reply. "He was a broken man. He did his best to carry on in the job, but as time passed and we all grew frustrated at not catching the murderer, young Leo just grew more and more depressed and his work began to suffer. He tried his best, but his heart wasn't in policing any longer. The thing is, none of us really knew just how much Liz's murder had affected him. Six months after her death, Leo Forsyth was found in the kitchen of his flat in Fazakerley, his head in the gas oven, the doors and windows all taped up. Poor bugger gassed himself because he couldn't live without the love of his life. We were still using coal gas in those days, long before your time," he swept his arm round the room to encompass the whole of Ross's team. It was a common enough method of suicide back then. So, you see, whoever killed Stella Cox, Marian Brown, the veterinary student and Liz Warren, was also directly responsible for the death of Leo Forsyth as far as I was concerned, back then and still am today."

The faces of Ross's team of detectives showed their horror as Coleman came to the end of his story. When he'd mentioned Forsyth's suicide, Kat Bellamy and Sam Gable both threw their hands over their mouths to cover their gaping look of shock. A tear even formed in Izzie Drake's eye and trickled slowly down her face. No matter that these were all hardened detectives who had seen most of the worst side of human nature in their time, this was a real story of tragedy and each and every one of them could fully understand why Coleman had taken the 1966 murders so personally.

"I'm so sorry," Sam Gable commented.

"And you never came up with a viable subject, even months later?" Ferris added.

"Not even a whiff of one," Coleman replied. "And don't think we didn't try hard to come up with one or more suspects, because we did."

"No-one is thinking that, I'm sure," Drake added. "It just seems such a tragedy."

"Well, now you know what's haunted me all these years, and when I saw the reports of these latest murders, it brought it all back to me. They are just too much like the '66 killings to not be connected, and when I contacted the police and was put on to D.C.I. Mountfield and told him all the details of the original murders, he quickly took me seriously and passed me along to D.I. Morris, who, I'm pleased to say, also took my information seriously. One thing led to another and well, here we are today, with you fine people tasked with succeeding where I failed all those years ago."

"From what you've told us and from what I've read about you, you're going to be a hard act to follow, sir," Ferris complimented the old man.

"No need for the 'sir' " Coleman said. "It's a long time since I carried any rank and quite frankly, I was glad to get out of the job in the end. Oh yes, I moved on after the murders. We all did, no choice in the matter, but the case was never closed and I was always waiting, hoping that one day we'd lay our hands on the slimeball that terrorised Hale."

"What did you do after leaving the force, Mr. Coleman?" D.C. Curtis asked him.

"I didn't know what to do at first," Coleman replied. "I just knew I couldn't carry on doing what I was doing. Eventually I settled on something simple and used my savings to set up a small taxi company. Over the years it's grown a bit and you might have seen my cabs around the streets, pale blue with a cream stripe down the side, a bit like the old panda car livery."

"You mean you own Coleman Cabs?" Sam Gable was impressed. Coleman Cabs was a much larger company than Stan Coleman was admitting. His natural modesty had prevented him saying he now ran over fifty cabs around the city and his company was well known for its reliability and punctuality.

"Yes, I do," he replied. "It's kept me out of trouble for a few years now. I don't drive anymore of course, but still run the business side of things."

"Going back to the case," Ross pulled the conversation back on track. "Do you seriously think the original killer could possibly have returned to carry on where he left off after all this time?"

"I honestly don't know, Mr. Ross," Coleman shook his head. "If the 60s killer was in his twenties, say, at the time of the murders, he'd be in his sixties or seventies now, so bearing in mind the physical strength required to carry out the killings and the brutality of the rapes, I seriously doubt it."

"Then, what's your theory?"

"Look, whoever is doing this is managing to perfectly recreate the crimes of almost half a century ago. He must have intimate knowledge of the original killings to be operating with such accuracy in relation to the earlier crimes. Back in the day, we didn't release every detail of the murders, much as I'm sure you hold certain information back from the press today."

Ross nodded to confirm what Coleman was suggesting. The ex-detective continued.

"The one detail we withheld back then was that after killing each of the women, the murderer wrote something on their bodies."

"Wrote something?" as incredulous Sam Gable asked. "Some sick message I presume?"

"Yes, I'm afraid so," Coleman replied. "Just above the women's pubic area, the sick so and so wrote, using a blue ball point pen, *Mine,* just the one word as if he was gloating. But the thing is, we never allowed that piece of intelligence to be revealed. Now this new killer is writing the same thing on his victims."

"So, whoever it is, he knows the exact anatomy of the original killings, down to the finest detail," Izzie Drake commented, and a doleful looking Coleman nodded in agreement.

"Could there be two?" *Bundeskriminalamt polizei* officer Sofie Mayer asked in typical, straight to the point Teutonic fashion. Nobody could ever accuse Sergeant Meyer of beating around the bush.

"Eh?" said Coleman.

"Could there be two killers?" Meyer repeated. "I am meaning, in 1966 could there have been two killers who have now met again and are recreating their earlier crimes. Surely, if they had kept themselves reasonably fit and healthy, they would be strong enough to overpower a young woman?"

"I did consider that possibility at the time," Coleman replied, "but we had nothing to suggest there was more than a single perpetrator and I was told to concentrate on finding the man who'd raped and murdered the three women. Tests had proved the semen we found in each case was from a single individual as well."

Meyer was not so easily put off and countered with,

"But maybe only one of them ejaculated into and on the women. The other may just have been a voyeur, a watcher, or, worse still another woman perhaps?"

"Good God, I never even thought of a female accomplice," Coleman looked shocked, "but I have to admit, when you look back over time and recall all we did at the time, no thought was given to a possible female accomplice."

"Right, listen up everyone," Andy Ross interrupted, taking control of the meeting once again.

"I'm sure we're all grateful to Mr. Coleman for sharing his insights into the original killings with us, but our focus needs to be on the current spree of murders. If they are in any way connected to the 1966 deaths, we're going to find out. There's another thing you could have thought of and that's that if there are two of them, why the hell have they waited all this time to strike again, and what was the motivation for the original killings? It's not improbable that two men or a man and woman, even if they are in their later years, could jointly have the strength to overpower the young women, especially if they managed to hit them in a blitz attack, taking them by surprise and incapacitating them before carrying out the rape and murder. Do we have your telephone number in case we need to contact you again?" he asked Stan Coleman.

"Yes, I've given my home number, mobile and business numbers to D.C.I. Agostini. Feel free to contact me any time if you think I can help."

* * *

Sitting in his office with Izzie Drake after the departure of Stan Coleman, Ross finally saw the white envelope that Derek McLennan had tried to secretly place on top of his grey metallic filing cabinet in the corner beside the door.

"Pass me that envelope up there, would you, Izzie?" he asked and his sergeant duly obliged, handing it to him and watching as he slowly opened it to reveal a beautiful, obviously expensive, wedding invitation.

"Bloody hell," Ross exclaimed.

"What's wrong?" Drake asked, thinking the envelope contained bad news.

"Nothing's wrong. Derek and that lady of his have only gone and set a wedding date already. They're not hanging around. This is an invitation for me and Maria. My darling wife will be complaining she only has three months in which to find a suitable outfit."

Izzie laughed, saying, "Well, when you've been shot and ended up in hospital, it probably focuses the mind and they think there's no time to waste. You never know what might happen from one day to another in our job."

"That's true," Ross agreed. "Wonder why you haven't got yours yet."

"Oh, come on, sir. This is Derek McLennan we're talking about. You're the boss. You don't think he'd even dream of giving anyone else their invitation before giving you yours, do you?"

"Good point," he chuckled. "Now, what do you think about this bloody case?"

"It's a bloody stinker," Drake replied. "How the hell can two cases so many years apart be so alike unless, as Stan Coleman believes, the original killer is back on the scene?"

"Yes, I agree, but for the sake of argument, why can't we assume the original killer is simply leading the current killer along, telling him what to do?"

"That actually sounds the most likely scenario, I agree, but, unless we can narrow down the potential killer from back in 1966, it sort of restricts who we should be looking at for the latest murders, don't you think?"

"I think we need to take a long hard look at what the current investigation has revealed so far, if anything. First. D.I. Morris is due to come and talk to us later today. She was called away as you know this morning so couldn't be here with Mr. Coleman."

Drake seemed to have wandered off into another world for a few seconds, prompting Ross to ask, "Are you still with me, Izzie?" You look miles away."

"Eh, what, oh, yes, sorry about that. A thought just occurred to me, that's all."

"Come on then, out with it. You look as if something's troubling you."

"Well, going back to the Lighthouse Murders, as Coleman called them, I was thinking about the fact that they never revealed the information about the writing on the women's bodies and..."

"And what?" Ross asked as she paused in mid-sentence.

"Oh, never mind, it couldn't be."

"Couldn't be what, Sergeant? Come on now, don't be so bloody secretive."

"Well, the only people who knew about the writing were the killer, or killers, the investigating officers and those involved in the medical and post-mortem examinations of the bodies, right?"

"I see where you're coming from, I think," Ross said, thoughtfully. "You're suggesting that anyone from the police investigating team to the medical examiner or anyone connected to the handling of the bodies would know of that information, and could use it to...to what?"

"Exactly. That's why I hesitated. We're still left with the question. *'Why now?'* Why would someone involved in the investigation of crimes that took place thirty-nine years ago suddenly begin a copycat killing spree in 2005? It doesn't make sense, sir, does it?"

"No, Izzie, it doesn't," Ross agreed, "but one way or another, it's up to us to make sense of it, and fast, before an innocent young female police officer joins the ranks of the dead."

Chapter 3

Fiona Morris

The biggest surprise of Ross's day came with the arrival of Detective Inspector Morris just after 3 p.m. that afternoon. Kat Bellamy, knocked and poked her head round the door to his office, where he was in deep discussion with Izzie Drake, Sofie Meyer and Paul Ferris.

"There's a D.I. Morris here to see you, Mr. Ross," she announced.

"Show her in please, Kat," Ross replied "and do you think you can organise some coffees for us all, please? We're bloody parched in here."

"No problem," Kat replied with a knowing smile on her face as she spoke to the newcomer, still out of sight behind her. "Please go in, D.I. Morris."

"Afternoon all," a female voice spoke, as Ross and the others look up at the attractive brunette, dressed in a very smart two-piece navy blue skirt suit who walked in to the office at Kat's invitation.

"D.I. Morris, nice to see you again." Ross welcomed the woman.

"Pleased to be here. Sorry I had to dash off this morning. I'd have liked to come and met you all with Stan Coleman."

"Call me Andy, please, and don't apologise for missing our meeting with Stanley. He was a fount of information on the old case, that's a fact though" "And I'm Fiona. Nice to see you again, too Sergeant," she nodded in Drake's direction. "I'm sorry if I've interrupted a meeting."

"Not at all. We were just discussing the case as we know it so far." Ross took a minute to introduce Fiona Morris to Paul Ferris and Sofie Meyer. "I hope you can tell us something to help to kick start our investigation into the current killings. I'm sorry by the way, if you feel your case has been snatched away from you, but we don't pick and choose our cases on this squad. We were told we were to take it over and that's what we have to do."

"Hey, don't worry about it. I'm glad to hand it over. My investigation is getting nowhere at present. In short, we don't have a bloody clue. You're welcome to it, Andy, really."

A knock at the door was followed by Kat Bellamy carrying a tray of steaming hot coffees.

"I managed to find a packet of chocolate digestives too," she announced as she placed the tray on Ross's desk. "Oh, good, I see you got Derek's wedding invitation too," she commented on seeing the object of Derek's early furtiveness.

"Thanks, Kat. Yes, I did. I take you've all got yours as well, now?"

"Yes, we have. Exciting news for him, especially after the shooting, isn't it?

"Indeed it is, Kat."

"Right, I'll leave you to it," she smiled at everyone as she departed.

"Shooting?" D.I. Morris asked.

"Yes, one of my D.C.'s was shot trying to foil a robbery in his spare time. Lucky bugger went and fell in love with one of his nurses and they are getting married soon."

"The jewellery store robbery? That was one of yours?"

"Yes, D.C. Derek McLennan, one of my most experienced lads."

"And a brave one too, eh?" said Morris. "I remember hearing about it."

"Salt of the earth is our Derek," Izzie Drake added.

"Got a bravery award," said Paul Ferris.

"Was he out there in the squad room when I arrived? I'd like to shake his hand before I leave."

"Yes, you can't miss Derek," Ferris replied. "Six feet tall, dark brown hair, good looking chap with brown eyes and looks more like a TV presenter than a copper. Comes in useful for undercover work, not being an obvious detective like some of us."

"Okay, everyone. Hero worship time notwithstanding, Fiona, please tell us what you have so far."

Fiona Morris sighed as she extracted her copy of the file on the current murders from the executive style briefcase she was carrying.

"It's not a great deal to be honest," she said lamentably. "When the first murder occurred, we were called in as soon as the local community bobby arrived and realised what he was dealing with. I attended the scene with D.C.I. Mountfield and it was obvious we were dealing with some sick bastard when we saw the writing on the poor girl's body. Her handbag was close by, and we were able to identify Cathy Billings immediately from her driver's license. Robbery was immediately ruled out as playing a part in the murder. The girl's purse was in the handbag, containing almost two hundred pounds. She's been paid that evening, we later discovered, and there were two credit cards in the purse as well.

I had the unenviable task of informing her parents. You won't need me to tell you what that's like."

Ross nodded his agreement. There was probably no worse job for a police officer than having to notify the next of kin of the brutal murder of a family member.

"Devastated was putting it mildly. Cathy was their only child. Mrs. Billings was apparently unable to have any more children after giving birth to Cathy, so they totally doted on her, without spoiling her. She grew up to be a popular and intelligent girl, not academically brilliant but she was intending to do a college course in accountancy eventually. Poor kid worked every hour she could get in the pub to earn a decent wage and not have to ask her parents to subsidise her. Anyway, they could think of nobody who might have wanted to harm her. Same at work. The landlord of The Traveller's Rest, his wife and staff all agreed she was a happy, vivacious and helpful young woman.

She never had any bother with the customers who all got on well with her. When we saw the word engraved on her body…"

"Wait a minute. Did you say engraved?" Ross interrupted.

"Yes, the word *MINE* was etched into her flesh just above her pubic area. It wasn't until later, after the second murder, that we learned of the similarity to the 1966 killings."

"But according to Stan Coleman, in the original series of murders the word was written on the bodies in ball pen."

"Yes, as we later discovered when Mr. Coleman contacted us, and I first researched the archives for the old case files."

"He never said anything about the change in M.O." Ferris commented.

"That's because I didn't inform him of it," Morris replied. "Stan Coleman has been very helpful in coming forward with the information about the 1966 murders, but he is no longer a serving officer, so I declined to give him every detail of the current murders. It doesn't really affect him and anything he can do to help us, while appreciated, doesn't mean we have to bring him fully into our current investigation. Having said that," she looked at Ross, "it's really your investigation now, Andy, so it's up to you if you tell him or not."

"No, I agree with you," Ross said immediately. "If the time comes where telling him seems relevant and necessary, I'll cross that bridge when we come to it. In the meantime, the fewer people who know about it, the better."

Fiona Morris smiled, pleased that Ross agreed with her decision. Ross now asked her, "Did the M.E. have any idea exactly what was used to incise the lettering on Cathy Billings's body?"

"Not exactly. But he did say it wasn't done with a surgical instrument like a scalpel for example. From the rough appearance of the cuts, he estimated the killer may have used something like a penknife, or maybe Stanley knife with a blunt blade. I had to really press him to get that much from him. He hates being pushed into making a guess, even an educated one."

"Aha, so I take it Dr. Nugent was the pathologist who carried out the post-mortem examination," Ross said, guessing it was Glasgow-born Dr. William Nugent she referred to. Known behind his back as 'Fat Willy,' Nugent was the brilliant but rather obese senior medical examiner who rarely made a mistake and who would never be pushed into guesswork, which he regarded as the territory of amateurs.

"Yes, it was. I suppose you and your team have had a lot more to do with him than I have since your squad was formed."

"Him and Francis Lees have been involved in just about every case we've investigated," Izzie Drake replied.

"Oh yes, that assistant of his, Lees, kind of reminds me of someone from a Charles Dickens novel"

"I've always thought that," Drake replied. "Uriah Heap would be a good comparison."

"He is a bit ghoulish, hardly ever speaks," said Morris. "This was the second time I'd met him, and I think he spoke about ten words, if that, to me and my sergeant."

"A man of few words, is Francis Lees," Ross grinned as he spoke, "but damn good at his job according to William Nugent."

"So they say," said Morris. "Anyway, we knew we had something weird on our hands when the second murder took place. Hannah Lucas's murder was a carbon copy of Cathy's. Dr. Nugent again carried out the post mortem and was unable to give us anything more than he could from the first one."

"He found no trace evidence at all?" Drake asked.

"Nothing, nada, zilch," Morris said. "It's as if the guy was bloody invisible."

"Or very clever," Sofie Meyer chipped in, having quietly listened in to everything that had been said so far. "Maybe this killer, he is forensically aware and knows how to eliminate any trace of his presence at the scene and on the bodies of the women. You have not so far mentioned the presence, or lack of sperm in or on the bodies of these two women, Inspector Morris."

Fiona Morris looked at Sofie Meyer and wondered for a fleeting second if the German officer had read her mind, then just as quickly dismissed the notion.

"I was about to say, Sergeant, that the other subtle difference between these murders and those in 1966 is the fact that this time, our killer didn't ejaculate into his victims. He used a condom. Traces of lubricant specific to a particular brand were found on the victims, but that does little or nothing to help the inquiry."

Ross disagreed with Morris on that point but chose to say nothing at the time. As it was now his case, her thoughts could be pretty much discounted once she left the room.

"Does Coleman know about that difference, too?" Drake asked.

"No," Morris replied. "Again, I didn't feel he needed to know that.

Andy Ross nodded thoughtfully but said nothing in response to Morris's reply.

Morris spent the next ten minutes giving Ross and his team a blow by blow account of the steps she and her team had taken so far in attempting to solve the case, which, as she admitted, wasn't much, having had little to go on, and of course, once Stan Coleman had come on the scene, identifying the connection with the 1966 murders, the decision had been made to pass the case on to Ross's Specialist Murder Investigation Team.

With Fiona Morris having little more to tell Ross and his sergeants, Ross soon drew the meeting to a close, and after he'd thanked the C.I.D. detective for meeting with them, Morris left them with copies of her own notes, and left the case well and truly in their lap.

"Any thoughts on our erstwhile colleague from C.I.D. folks?" Ross asked after Morris had departed. A few seconds silence followed before Sofie Meyer became the first to answer.

"She is a nice person but not the most professional of detectives, I think."

"Why do you say that, Sofie?"

"Well, sir, she was happy to accept the information from the former Detective Inspector Coleman but omitted to give him the information about the differences in the current case from the one he investigated. It is possible that Mr. Coleman may have had a theory or some thoughts on why these differences exist. For example, I feel D.I. Morris has discounted the evidence relating to the condoms prematurely."

Ross was pleased he wasn't the only one to have picked up on that point and asked Meyer to explain why she thought as she did.

"It is my belief that different manufacturers may be traced through analysis of the spermicide used on individual condoms. If we can identify the make of condom the killer used it may possibly allow us to find out where they obtained the condoms. For example, if the Traveller's Rest has a machine selling such things and we are looking for a brand not sold in the pub, it might be hypothesised that the killer is not from Hale, but from somewhere else. They do sell condoms in British pubs, do they not?"

"But they could be from Hale, and maybe just bought the condoms from a chemist in town," Drake responded.

"True," said Meyer, "but it is still a potential starting point, yes?"

"Yes, I agree," Ross concurred. "Anything else?"

"I think she was remiss in not telling Coleman about the differences in the writing on the bodies," Ferris added. "The guy comes along, gives her chapter and verse on a series of killings that mirror the ones she's investigating, and she keeps him out of the loop. Okay, he may not be a copper any more, but she could have used his brains and experience and his knowledge of the original murders in 1966. He may have had some thoughts on why our killer changed his M.O."

"Paul, I think that last point is easy to figure out. Almost anyone who's watched C.S.I. or something similar has a basic idea of what forensics can do nowadays. If he had used a pen, a handwriting expert might be able to identify his writing, even on a body. And if it had rained, it might have washed the writing away. Not so easy with a word that's been gouged into the flesh with a knife," said Drake.

As ideas and theories bounced back and forth between them, Ross couldn't help thinking they'd been handed a real hot potato of a case, and the trouble was, with very little to go on, they had less than a week in which to catch a killer before they struck again.

Chapter 4

Heat

The full-scale briefing of the team was in progress when D.C.I. Oscar Agostini walked quietly into the squad room, waved at Ross to continue what he was saying and took a seat at the back of the room, not wanting to interrupt the briefing's progress. Andy Ross realised that his old friend and now boss would be getting plenty of heat from above to reach a conclusion to the case as fast as possible before the almost inevitable murder of a woman police officer added to their woes.

Paul Ferris, aided by Kat Bellamy and Sofie Meyer had by now brought the murder board at the back of the squad room up to date, neatly divided into two sections, one headed *The Lighthouse Killer*, the second simply annotated *Current*. Under each heading were photographs of the victims, taken both in life and in death, with photographs from the crime scenes and in the mortuary being displayed. Every member of Ross's team always felt a sadness when looking at such displays, with the photos of the women in life, usually appearing happy, smiling and carefree contrasting so drastically with those showing the results of the 'work' of a cold-blooded killer with no respect for the sanctity of human life.

"So," Ross spoke after a short pause to allow Agostini to settle himself in a chair, "I want us out on the streets of Hale pronto, talking to people, house-to-house, speaking to everyone in the village in as quick a time as we can manage it. Izzie and I will head straight to The Traveller's Rest to talk to the landlord and staff. Paul," he said to Ferris, "I want you and Sam to go and visit the parents of Cathy Billings. They may not know much but if we can build up a picture of each victim, where they went in their spare time, the sort of things they enjoyed doing, we might be able to eventually get a handle on where their paths crossed with our killers."

"Right you are, sir," Ferris replied as D.C. Sam Gable walked across the room to sit him.

"Sofie," Ross now directed his next order to Meyer, "You and Derek go and talk to Hannah Lucas's parents. Same again, let's find out all we can about these girls. It's unlikely they were randomly selected by the killer. If he's trying to recreate the murders from 1966 he must have formulated some kind of selection criterion. We need to work out what that criterion is and if we can find out how and where, at some point, these women's lives converged, it might give us a clue where to look for this bastard."

Sofie Meyer and Derek McLennan both nodded. Ross had clearly selected his most senior and intuitive detectives to the task of developing a 'pen picture' of the victims. He was taking no chances with this case.

"The rest of you hit the streets. Nick, Tony, Ginger, get a map of Hale and divide the place up between you. Hale isn't that big, so you should get on pretty quickly. As soon as the rest of us finish out initial interviews we'll join you, so I expect we can complete our house-to-house in a couple of days at the latest. D.C.I. Agostini has promised me half a dozen uniformed officers by tomorrow to assist with our local enquiries in Hale. They're under orders to report to the mobile incident room that's being set up as we speak. It's going to be in the car park of the pub. Sergeant Ferris will oversee the incident room, once he's interviewed the Billings girl's parents."

Ross turned to look at Kat Bellamy.

"Is that okay with you, Kat?" he said, speaking to the team's admin assistant, who'd be in sole control of the incident room until Ferris arrived.

"Yes, of course it is," Kat replied, delighted to have been asked to take a more hands-on role in the latest inquiry. "It will be good to get out of the office and assist you all more closely than usual. Thanks for your faith in me, Mr. Ross."

"Don't thank me," Ross grinned. "You might end up wishing you were back here if the heating packs up in the mobile unit. It might turn chilly out there."

"I'll take my coat with me. Don't worry about me. I'm a hardy kind of girl, really."

Ross smiled and nodded at her. Kat Bellamy was proving to be a real asset to the team and he knew this task would only serve to boost her confidence and bring out the best of her abilities. Kat was unaware that Paul Ferris had been singing her praises to Ross for the last few weeks, insisting that she should be given more responsibility within the team. As the person who worked the closest with her, on both the computer and admin side of the squad's workload, Ferris was well placed to comment on her attributes, and Ross was a good enough leader to appreciate Ferris's recommendation and act on it. For now, he turned back to address the rest of the team.

"As you complete your door-to-door inquiries, I want you to all to check in and report to Sergeant Ferris at the mobile unit, okay? Any questions?"

I have one please," Meyer said immediately.

"Yes, Sofie, what is it?"

"I have taken a quick look at Hale on my computer. It is as you say, quite a small place, with a relatively small population. I overheard someone say, *"How can this be happening in a place like Hale?"* while Mr. Coleman was here. Is there something special about Hale that I should know about?"

"Of course, you won't know all that much about the local geography and history yet, Sofie. Hale is quite a historical location, and almost unique in terms of its history in relation to Liverpool. D.C. McLennan is our resident brainbox about such things. Maybe you can tell Sofie something about the place we're going to be concentrating our efforts on, as you travel over to the Lucas girl's home."

"Sure, Boss, no problem," Derek McLennan replied.

* * *

"So, you want to know about Hale, eh Sofie?" said Derek McLennan as he drove the police Peugeot towards the home of Hannah Lucas's parents.

"Only because it seems to have aroused extra interest among the rest of the team, yes, please Derek. Tell me all about it."

"Well, I don't know everything about it, but basically it's a historically old village and probably most famous for The Childe of Hale. You'll see a statue in the village of the man, John Middleton, who grew to be over nine feet tall. He was definitely a tall man because his grave in the village churchyard is much longer than normal. The legend tells that he traced a large figure of a man in the sand on the beach, lay down and fell asleep in it, and when he woke up, he'd grown to fill it."

"That is not physically possible," Sofie interrupted.

"I know, but, it's definitely true that he was very, very tall. Until a few years ago the village was treated as part of Liverpool, but recent boundary changes were made which placed it in Cheshire, though it still has a Liverpool postcode, being in L24. Technically it now comes under the control of Cheshire Police, but they have handed it over to us, because of the special circumstances surrounding this case."

"Ah, I thought it strange that D.I Ross and D.I. Morris were not already acquainted, but if she is from a different force, I understand why."

"That's right, but when the 1966 murders took place, Hale came under the control of the old City of Liverpool Police, so Stan Coleman would have been based somewhere around here. Going back to the village, it's said that Winston Churchill once stayed at the old Manor House but that was knocked down years ago. The lighthouse where the bodies have all been dumped in the vicinity of, was closed down in the 1950s and I think it's now partially a museum and I believe another part of it is a private residence now. In short, Hale is a very pretty village which is a great draw for tourists and locals alike. I can remember my parents taking me there as a child and the one thing I really recall is, when standing on the beach near the old lighthouse, you really do feel as if you are miles from civilisation, and not just a few miles from the centre of one of England's biggest cities. Or, maybe that was just the way my boyish mind thought at the time. It's years since I went there, but we'll soon find out, won't we?"

"Thank you, Derek," Sofie replied. "Good background information is always important when embarking on a new case, don't you think?"

"Yes, of course," Derek smiled as he turned off Hale High Street onto Vicarage Close and slowed and brought the car to a halt outside the home of the first dead girl.

Seeing the curtains of the neat cottage-style home were all drawn closed, Meyer commented, "It appears that they may be in bed, Derek."

"No, Sofie," he replied, unable to suppress a small smile as he spoke. "It's an old British tradition to keep the curtains drawn following a death in the home. It's a mark of respect, and they will stay like that until after the funeral."

"Ah, I see, thank you Derek. It seems I still have much to learn about the intricacies of British culture."

"Oh, don't worry about it. It's an old-fashioned custom and a lot of the modern generation don't adhere to it as their parents or grandparents used to."

The grieving parents of Hannah Lucas, David and Linda, could give the detectives little information that might assist them in the search for their daughter's murderer.

"Please can you tell us if Hannah was acquainted with Cathy Billings?" Sofie asked, as Derek made notes of the interview. Though Linda Lucas was tearful and highly traumatised by her daughter's death and found it difficult to talk through the tears that she just couldn't hold back in front of the detectives, David was more forthcoming, though it was clear to McLennan that his stoicism was proving a difficult façade to maintain.

"Not as far as we know, Sergeant Meyer," he replied. "It's possible of course that she knew that other girl, perhaps from the times she popped into the pub for a drink sometimes. She wasn't a big drinker, and only went to the Traveller's now and then if one of her friends invited her out for a quick drink, and they might have met there and had a drink or two before heading into town for the evening."

"So, they were not friends, to the best of your knowledge?" Meyer asked.

"I don't think so, no," David Lucas replied.

"She hardly knew her."

Both detectives were a little surprised when Linda Lucas spoke up, quite suddenly, though she continued to sob quietly in between words.

"When Cathy Billings was killed, Hannah said what a tragedy is was, and that she'd met Cathy on a few occasions when the girl had been working behind the bar in the pub. I asked her if she knew her personally and she told me they had only exchanged a few words in the pub on a couple of Hannah's visits there. Please, tell me you're going to find the monster that killed my little girl."

"We're going to do everything we can to do that, Mrs. Lucas," Meyer answered as best she could, not wanting to raise false hopes in the girl's parents, just in case they failed to find their daughter's murderer.

"Did your daughter have any boyfriends?" Meyer next asked the couple.

"No, she was too determined to complete her studies and fulfil her ambition of working with animals," David replied. "She said there'd be time for boyfriends later, and I must say, I agreed with her. She was a clever girl, Sergeant Meyer. She was so lucky too, to be able to study locally at the university here instead of having to travel elsewhere in the country like most students do."

That was when the paradox attached to his words struck David Lucas.

"Well, at the time, we thought it was lucky. Now, of course, it looks like it was a curse, a bloody awful, terrible curse."

"Did you both use the Traveller's Rest very often," McLennan asked, trying to change the subject, as Meyer paused in her questioning.

"I'm afraid not," the father replied. "My wife and I are tea-total. To be truthful, I'm a recovering alcoholic. I haven't touched a drop in ten years."

"Thanks for your honesty, Mr. Lucas, and congratulations on your achievement. It can't have been easy for you."

Derek didn't ask what had led to David Lucas becoming an alcoholic in the first place. He didn't think it relevant to their investigation, but Lucas provided them with the answer anyway.

"I used to own a thriving business," he began. "I restored classic cars for a living and a damn good living it was too. Trouble was, when the downturn in the economy took place, small businesses like mine were among the first to suffer. As the work began to dry up, and the business dropped off, the creditors and the bank began to lose patience, until one day, I had no choice but to file for bankruptcy. The drinking began as the work dried up, and just got worse and worse, until it nearly cost me my marriage. Thankfully, Linda stuck by me and we got through it together."

Lucas reached out and gripped his wife's hand as he spoke. Tears were forming in David Lucas's eyes by then and his wife placed a comforting hand on his arm. The couple were clearly still very much in love with each other, and Sofie Meyer nodded to McLennan as if to say the interview was at an end.

They thanked the parents of Hannah Lucas for their time and left them to their grief. As they entered the car once more, ready to head for the Traveller's Rest, McLennan turned to Meyer and said, "Thank God that's over. You could almost reach out and touch the grief in that house, don't you think?"

"I think I know what you mean, yes," Meyer agreed. "I am thinking it will take those poor people a long, long time to get over the death of their daughter, if at all."

* * *

Simultaneously with Meyer and McLennan meeting with the Lucas family, Paul Ferris and Sam Gable found themselves seated in the comfortable lounge of the parents of Cathy Billings. Comfortable that is, except for the fact that both parents of the murdered girl were quite short in stature and had bought furniture accordingly. Sitting on the sofa, next to Ferris, Sam was wishing she'd worn trousers instead of a skirt that morning. The sofa was so low that no matter how she sat on it, her skirt rode up uncomfortably high and she found herself crossing and uncrossing her legs in an effort to prevent herself from displaying too much thigh. Eventually deciding it was mission impossible and much to the amusement of her colleague, she rose from the sofa, and took up a standing position near the bay window that looked at onto a small garden and Hale's main street.

"Is everything alright, Constable?" Ralph Billings asked, completely oblivious to Sam's earlier predicament. His grief was so deep, Sam realised she could probably have been sitting stark naked in front of him and he wouldn't have noticed.

"Oh yes, Mr. Billings. It's just that I've spent so long sitting down at headquarters recently, it's good to just stand here and stretch my legs."

"You were saying, Mr. Billings," Ferris tried to return to the subject they'd been discussing before Sam had risen from the sofa.

"Oh yes, boyfriends. Well now, Sergeant Ferris, our Cathy was a right popular girl, she was. Had a boyfriend, Simon McCardle, but they split up a few weeks ago."

"Really? Was it an amicable split, do you know, Mr. Billings"?

Ralph Billings looked towards his wife, and it was Laura who provided Ferris with the answer to his question."

"Simon wasn't happy about it, Sergeant Ferris. Cathy ended the relationship because she thought he was becoming too possessive. He had started hanging around in the pub when she was working and would sit drinking at the bar and made it quite clear he wasn't happy about her having a laugh and a joke with the customers."

"But that's what barmaids do, isn't it?" Ralph Billings piped up. "You know? Have a bit of banter with the customers, like? Goes with the job, doesn't it?"

"Yes, I agree, Mr. Billings. I've always found the most popular and well-liked bar staff are the ones who can hold a good conversation and enjoy a laugh with the punters."

"Just how possessive did Simon become before Cathy ended things with him?" Sam asked from her position by the window.

"He just wouldn't leave her alone," Laura replied. "He'd follow her home after work and pester her to spend almost all her free time with him. He was even jealous if she wanted to have an evening out with some of her girlfriends. He accused her of 'going on the pull' as he put it, and Cathy couldn't take any more of it. One night, I heard them arguing at the front gate after he'd walked her home from the pub, and I heard Simon call her a whore."

"That wasn't a nice thing for you to hear, Mrs. Billings," Sam Gable said, and added, "Did you hear how the argument ended?"

"Yes, I did. After he called her a whore, Cathy slapped his face and told him she didn't want to see him anymore. Then he got more abusive and accused her, and these were his words, of "opening her legs for any bloke who bought her a drink. I couldn't stand to hear any more and told Ralph what was going on. He was listening to music on his headphones at the time so wouldn't have heard the rumpus outside."

Ralph Billings took over from his wife at that point.

"I went out to sort him out. I told him no little scally talks to my daughter like that and he'd better stay away from her in future."

"How did he respond to that?" Ferris asked.

"He said he wouldn't want to touch her with a bargepole. Repeated she was nothing but a little whore, and then took off like a bat out of hell when I started to walk down the path towards him. He could see I was mad, and if I'd got hold of him I'd have given him a bloody good lamping, I mean it. I'm not too old to sort out the likes of Simon bloody McArdle."

"Had he caused any trouble since that night?" Gable asked.

"Not that we know of, Laura Billings replied.

"And were there any boyfriends prior to McArdle?" was the next question from Paul Ferris.

"Not serious ones, no," said Laura. "Cathy had three of four casual boyfriends, over about three years. Just lads she's meet up with for a drink or who might take her to the cinema or something, you know?

Gable nodded, knowing just what the girl's mother meant.

"Do you know where this Simon McArdle lives," Farris inquired.

"We do, more's the pity," Ralph Billings replied. "You'll find the little toe-rag three doors down the road, that way," he said pointing in the direction of the McArdle home. The two detectives exchanged glances, both certain that the information they'd just gleaned from the parents, plus McArdle's location, probably made him a live suspect for the murder of Cathy Billings. It was time to report their findings to Ross.

With little more to discover about the girl, and having ascertained that as far as they knew, she wasn't a close friend of Hannah Lucas, they left the parents to their unremitting grief, and made their way to rendezvous with the rest of the team. Tempted though he was to call at the home of Simon McArdle on the way, Ferris resisted the urge, knowing that other team members assigned to house-to-house inquiries may already have visited the man, or at least be on the way to his home as part of their sweep of the homes in Hale.

"It'll be interesting to learn what McArdle tells the officers who interview him as part of the house-to-house inquiries," Ferris speculated as Gable drove them towards the Traveller's Rest car park, where the mobile inquiry unit would be waiting for them, together with Kat Bellamy and any of the other team members who might have completed their allocated area of search, though neither of them thought that anyone would have completed their allotted number of houses as yet.

"D'you think the boss and Sergeant Drake will have finished talking to the landlord and staff at the pub yet?" Gable asked him as they approached the pub.

"I'd say they might have finished right about now," Ferris replied, pointing. Gable followed the direction of his finger and as she turned the car into the Traveller's Rest car park, she saw Ross and Drake making their way on foot towards the mobile incident unit. Meyer and McLennan's pool car was already parked next to Ross's. It was almost time to pool their collective information, such as it was.

Chapter 5

Going nowhere

The mobile incident room felt claustrophobic as the detectives gathered to report in to Ross and Drake. The Ford towing unit and its attached incident room filled up most of the car park of the Traveller's Rest, and Ross was grateful for the cooperation of the pub landlord, Ben Grafton, who he and Drake had just finished interviewing as Ferris and Gable followed him and Drake into the specialised unit, containing a bank of computers along one side and an incident board on the rear wall. Two narrow filing cabinets took up space by the entrance and as Ferris and Gable walked in, Kat Bellamy was seated at a computer chair, with McLennan and Meyer seated in the two adjoining seats next to her. Ross and Drake, having just arrived, were looking at the whiteboard that Kat Bellamy had set up while she'd been waiting for everyone to arrive.

"Okay everyone," Ross said as the first two pairs of detectives waited to hear what he had to say. "I want to hear what you've discovered from the parents in a minute, but first, let me tell you what we've learned from the landlord here."

Ross spent a few minutes relating the gist of the interview with Ben Grafton and his wife and staff.

"Cathy Billings was a popular employee. She got on with all the staff, though there are only two apart from Grafton and his wife, Kay.

Betty Laine, barmaid and cook, is fifty-five and had a kind of benevolent motherly attitude towards Cathy. Phil Jennings, the barman is forty, and thought she was a 'great kid' in his words, who he also thought needed a bit of looking after. He thought she was a bit naïve at times and didn't realise how some of the male punters looked on her as a bit of a sex symbol. Grafton also mentioned that she'd had some trouble with a boyfriend recently and that she'd blown the guy out, but he wouldn't take no for an answer."

That of course tallied with what Ralph and Laura Billings had told Ferris and Gable, a fact they related to Ross when he asked for the results of their interview with the murdered girl's parents.

"So, you think this ex-boyfriend could have held a sufficient grudge against Cathy to have done something stupid?" Ross asked Ferris.

"I don't know, sir. He might have what he thought was a motive to hurt Cathy but as far as we know he had nothing against Hannah Lucas, much less any knowledge of what took place back in 1966."

"You didn't think of calling at his home, if it's close by, to see what he had to say for himself?" Drake asked.

"No, because I thought it best to see what, if anything, he tells the house-to-house investigators. If he admits to the break up with Cathy, that will show some honesty. If not, he may have something to hide."

"That's good thinking, Paul. Well done you two," Ross said. "What about you, Sofie, Derek?"

Sofie Meyer spoke for the pair.

"I am afraid our talk with the unfortunate parents of Hannah Lucas was not very productive either."

It took Meyer no more than two minutes to relate the content of their conversation with Hannah Lucas's parents, after which Ross and Drake concluded their information from the pub.

"The barman, Jennings, suggested we 'talk to the cretin,' as he put it," Ross told the others, thinking back half an hour to the conversation with Phil Jennings.

"If you wanna known what happened in Hale all them years ago, you need to go talk to the Cretin," said the tall, lanky barman. Jennings dark brown hair was slicked back with gel, giving him the appearance of a nineteen fifties teddy boy.

"The Cretin?" Ross asked him.

"Yeah, sorry, but that's what folks round here call him. Real name's Cretingham, Albert Cretingham. He's lived in the village all his life and there's a few who says as he's got a photographic memory, remembers everything that's happened here since he were a kid, like."

"Do you know where we can find Mr. Cretingham?" Drake asked.

"Oh yeah, everyone knows where he lives. Go to the statue of the Childe of Hale, stand and look towards the coast and you'll see a house with a bright green door. That's where the Cretin lives."

"Why do you call him that? It's not a very flattering name, Mr. Jennings?" Drake went on, probing further.

"That's not my fault, is it? We was all brought up as kids, knowing him by that name. My Da told me once that old man Cretingham was none too bright when he were a youngster and the other kids in the village used to take the piss out of him, if you catch me drift, like."

"In other words, they bullied him because he was a bit slow?" Ross surmised.

"Yeah, probably," Jennings replied. "Kids can be cruel, Inspector, as I'm sure you know."

"Sadly, you're right, Mr. Jennings. So, they even came up with the cruel nickname, and it's stayed with him all these years. What is he, about seventy by now?"

"Must be, or maybe a bit younger, seeing as he had a son in his early twenties and young Albert is thirty to forty now. I was talking to my Da the other day and we was talking about the Cret…Mr. Cretingham, and Da said as how he thinks the old boy would have been about twenty when the murders of '66 happened and now it's all starting again."

"Does your father have any theories as to who the killer was back then, or who might be responsible for the murders of Cathy and Hannah?"

"Nah, my Da keeps out of such things. Says such matters are a thing for the bizzies to handle, sorry, I mean the police, but Da always calls youse lot the bizzies. Must be his generation, eh?"

Jennings tried to laugh but didn't quite manage it. The old, local name for the police wasn't used as much nowadays but was commonplace back in the sixties.

"So, do you think this old chap might be able to offer us anything new on the old case, sir?" Sam Gable asked.

"I don't know Sam. But if people like Jennings and the rest of the locals are sensing a connection between the recent murders and those of 1966, we might find we're stirring up a bit of a hornet's nest in the village. Kay, take a look and see if this Albert Cretingham has a record, will you? It will be interesting to know, when we go to see him. I'm just wondering if he knows anything our friend Stan Coleman doesn't."

Kat Bellamy turned to her computer and started typing.

Meanwhile, Ferris and Gable had paid a fruitless visit to the home of Simon McArdle. After the constables conducting the house to house enquiries on his street reported that the young man had admitted knowing Cathy, and that they'd broken up prior to her murder, the two detectives also paid McArdle a visit. Paul Ferris found him to be a personable young man who was quick to admit to his break up with the dead girl, but he had what appeared to be a perfect alibi for the night of her murder. He had a new girlfriend, who happened to be visiting him at his parents' house as Ferris and Gable questioned him and she confirmed that McArdle was with her, at her parent's home on the night of the murder. She blushed a little as she confirmed that she and McArdle had slept together, with her parents' knowledge, and that he had 'kept her busy in bed' as she put it, from eleven p.m. until well after two in the morning.

* * *

The team were gathered in the bar of the Traveller's Rest. Dodds, Curtis and the others had returned from their house-to house inquiries, feeling dispirited and depressed at the total lack of information they'd managed to discover about the two recent murders.

"I just found it hard to believe that so many people wanted to talk about the murders from 1966 rather than the two women who've just been killed right on their doorsteps." Nick Dodds commented as they sat round two tables that Ross and Ferris had pushed together. The six uniformed constables who'd assisted the detectives with the house-to-house inquiries gathered round a second pair of tables as the Traveller's Rest took on the guise of a temporary police canteen. At least the landlord could be sure there'd be no trouble in his pub with this lot around!

"Yes, it's like they seem to want to ignore what's going on now, and want to resurrect the old case, even if some of them weren't even born when the original killings took place," D.C. Tony Curtis agreed.

"I think they're scared to admit they might have a killer in their midst," said D.C. Ginger Devenish. "If they refuse to acknowledge it, it's like they can pretend it hasn't happened."

"I agree with D.C. Devenish," Sofie Meyer added. "People are known to react in this way when they are frightened by some event or circumstance. I think in English you would call it 'being in denial."

"You're probably right, Ginger, lad," Ross agreed, "but listen, during your house-to-house inquiries, did any of you meet an old chap by the name of Cretingham?"

"Albert Cretingham?" Curtis asked and immediately added, "I did, but he wasn't an old chap. I'd have put him nearer to about thirty to thirty-five."

"Maybe it's the son," Drake said. "It's not unknown for a son to have the same name as the father, after all."

"Funny though, the Albert Cretingham I spoke to didn't say anything about having a father living with him. I asked him if anyone in the house, his wife perhaps, might have seen or heard anything on the nights of the murders. He just said he wasn't married. Maybe he's shipped his old man off to an old folks' home or something," Curtis concluded.

"Sounds odd, I admit," Drake said, adding, "Maybe we need to have another word with young Albert Cretingham."

"I agree, Izzie," Ross decided. "You and I will go and have a word when we leave here. Anyone got anything else to add?"

"Most of the people I spoke to admitted knowing the Billings girl," Ginger Devenish reported. "But not many knew Hannah Lucas. The general feeling I got was that Cathy Billings was a bit of a party girl type of young woman. Hannah Lucas, according to those who knew her, was a reserved, studious type."

"That fits with what we've learned so far," said Ross, "but none of this is really getting us any closer to identifying a single bloody suspect," he went on, frustration clear in his voice.

"The more I think about it," Izzie Drake concluded, "everything and anybody involved in this case seems to hark back to the murders in 1966. I think we need to start delving back into the past in more detail."

"You know, Izzie, I totally agree with you. Paul," Ross said to Ferris. "You've got Stan Coleman's number, right?"

"Yes, sir, I have."

"Call him. Ask him if it's convenient for him to come down here and talk to me again. Send a car for him if necessary. I think D.I. Morris might not have given the link between the '66 murders and the new ones enough credibility and if we're to stop this bastard before he kills again, we're going to need every bit of help we can get. Coleman probably knows more about the original murders than anyone else. I want to pick his brains, as soon as possible."

"I'll call him now, sir," said Ferris, as he immediately took his new Nokia mobile phone from his pocket and was soon in conversation with the former Detective Inspector.

"How far have we got with the house-to-house?"

"We reckon we've done about half the village between us so far," Curtis replied. "We should get the rest done by this evening, with a bit of luck."

"Some people are out at work of course," Dodds added, "so we'll need to come back another day to speak to them, for what it's worth."

"I know it's a sod of a job, Nick," Ross replied, "but we never know when we might find a witness or a vital piece of evidence from such a search. Meanwhile, we have lists of the murdered girls' friends from the parents. As boring as it might be, we'll need to talk to them, and try to find out if there's anything that specifically links them to each other, and more importantly to any person or event that might help us find their killer and also to identify any possible third target for this maniac."

A collective groan went up from the detectives seated round the tables. They all knew the routine. The legwork was a necessary part of the investigation, as fruitless as it was likely to prove. Ross called across to the uniformed officers at their tables.

"I appreciate your help too, lads, and ladies, remembering the two female officers among them. I've spoken to the D.C.I. and you'll be staying with us to help with the investigation as long as you're needed."

There were nods and a few 'thank you's from the officers who were all, Ross noted approvingly, drinking soft drinks or coffees.

"Stan Coleman will be here within the hour, sir," Ferris interrupted. "I've arranged for a car to collect him and bring him to us. He's only too happy to help. He was working the radio for his cab company and just needed to bring someone in to relieve him."

"Thanks Paul. Maybe being back in Hale will jog a few old memories for him. I hope so, anyway."

"And I've looked up Albert Cretingham," Kat Bellamy added. "There are two Alberts, registered as living at that address, as suspected. The one D.C. Curtis spoke to has to be Albert junior, aged forty. The elder of the two, Albert Gerald Cretingham is in his late fifties."

"Which would have made him about eighteen or nineteen at the time of the original murders," Ross mused. "So, he should have a good memory of those days, as Jennings said. "Thanks Kat. Paul, if Stan Coleman arrives before we get back, you know what to do, the things to ask."

"Don't worry, I'll soon have him taking me on a journey back in time, sir," Ferris replied.

With little more that could be achieved at that point, the team soon split up to continue their allotted tasks, and it wasn't long before Ross and Drake found themselves knocking on the door of the home of the two Albert Cretinghams.

Chapter 6

Albert

"Albert Cretingham?" Ross asked the man who responded to his second knock on the door. Albert Cretingham looked older than his years, standing around five feet ten or eleven, his brown hair cut short in an old-fashioned short back and sides style. There were a few patches of premature grey visible at the sides and back, and Cretingham had a thin, hawkish face, with heavy eyebrows that gave him a slightly demonic look in Drake's mind,

Both Ross and Drake had taken note of the small but pristine garden at the front of the cottage style house, even the concrete path to the door being totally clear of weeds or moss, unusual in this day and age.

"Who wants to know?" the man replied.

Both detectives held up their warrant cards.

"Detective Inspector Ross and Detective Sergeant Drake, Merseyside Police."

"I've already spoke to your lot," the man replied.

"So I understand. But we have some questions for your father too," Ross wasn't going to give the younger Cretingham the chance to deny the existence of his father.

"My father?"

"Yes, your father; the one you forgot to mention as being here when D.C. Curtis called on you earlier."

"Oh yeah, right. Well, Dad's not well you see, and I didn't think he could tell the detective much as he doesn't go out much these days, so he wouldn't have seen anything useful anyway."

"We'd like a word with your father anyway, Mr. Cretingham. We understand he has a very good memory and we'd like to talk to him about the murders of three women in 1966."

"What? I thought you were investigating the recent murders here in Hale, not some shit from all that time ago."

"We are, but it's just possible that the two events might be connected."

"I see, well, you'd better come in then. Dad's in the front room, watching telly."

Albert Cretingham led Ross and Drake along a short hallway and ushered them into the living room of the house, a house that had a strange, musty smell that Ross was familiar with, associating it with the elderly and infirm. The air seemed to hold a mixture of stale food and bodily odour, often, he'd found in the homes of the elderly and neglected. It contrasted sharply with the prim and proper appearance of the garden and exterior of the home, although the room into which they stepped was clean, polished and betrayed no sign of decay or neglect.

Albert Cretingham the elder was seated in a comfortable brown velour covered armchair, remote control in hand as he sat watching racing on the thirty-two-inch television positioned in the corner of the room. Looking at least ten years older than his true age, Cretingham had a head of wispy grey hair, and skin that had the pallor of a corpse. His face possessed similar features to his son and it was easy to see the family resemblance.

"Dad, the police are here. They want to talk to you," the younger man said, picking up the TV remote and turning the volume down so the detectives wouldn't have to shout over the sound of the commentary.

"What for, I haven't done anything wrong?" the old man said, still not looking at Ross or Drake, his eyes fixed on the race unfolding on the TV screen.

"Mr. Cretingham," Ross took over from the son. "We've been told you have a very good memory. We'd like to ask you about the series of murders that took place here in Hale in nineteen sixty-six."

That seemed to get Cretingham's attention. He immediately turned to face Ross.

"And who might you be?"

"I'm Detective Inspector Ross and this is Detective Sergeant Drake, from the Merseyside Police, Specialist Murder Investigation Team. Like I said, I'd like to ask you about what took place in the past. It might have a bearing on the recent murders in the village. I'm sure you must have heard about them?"

"I might have heard summat. Don't really get out much nowadays or watch much news on the telly. Boring, most of it is."

Ross had already noticed that Albert Cretingham spoke slowly and deliberately, each word spoken individually as though he had trouble forming joined up sentences. Izzie Drake, who'd seen something like this before, mouthed the word 'autism' at her boss, who nodded in acknowledgement.

She pulled the younger man to one side and in a quiet voice, asked him if his father was autistic.

"Slightly," the younger man replied in a whisper. Drake quickly nodded to Ross. "Dad was tormented a lot when he was younger, so he told me. They didn't understand things like autism back then, at least, not like they do today. The other kids used to make fun of him a lot and called him names. It didn't stop him holding down a job though or getting married to me Mam."

"What's actually wrong with your father, Albert?"

"Asbestosis mostly and angina and asthma too. He used to work for a company that specialised in demolition. Trouble was, a lot of the buildings had asbestos in the roofs or walls and that were in the days before folks were aware of the danger from asbestos."

"And your mother?"

"Can't say as I ever knew her. Ran off and left us, Dad told me when I were old enough to understand them kind o' things. Probably found another bloke, he reckoned, but anyway, we've done alright together, me and Dad."

Ross, meanwhile, was trying to probe the elder Cretingham's mind.

"I'm led to believe you have almost total recall of the events in nineteen sixty-six, Mr. Cretingham."

"So people seem to think, aye."

"Your accent, it's local, but not quite local, if you know what I mean. Have you lived in Hale all your life?"

"Very clever, Inspector. No; I were born in Wakefield in West Yorkshire. Lived there wi' me parents till I was ten, then we moved over 'ere wi' me dad's work."

"I see, and have you always had this incredible memory people say you possess?"

"As far as I know, yes. Other kids used to poke fun at me when I were little cos' I were a bit slow at learning stuff at school, but I used to do okay when exams and such came around, 'cos I never forgot owt the teacher said to us in class, like. The other kids used to think that were right weird, and some of 'em made fun of me and called me names, like 'Cretin' and 'Shit for brains.' I didn't take no notice like. Later, I were diagnosed with a mild autism, but I didn't know what that meant, at least not at that age. I learned more about it later. But I remember the doctor saying that God had given me an almost photographic memory to make up for whatever else ailed me."

Ross listened carefully as Cretingham gave him a boringly long description of his early years in Hale, finally having to interrupt the man by asking him to come to the point regarding the main subject of his inquiry, beginning with Stella Cox.

"Aye, well, Stella was alright. She were a right pretty girl, and I reckon most of the blokes in the village fancied her. She had a right nice figure and always dressed nice. She didn't have loads of money, you understand? I heard tell as she got most of her clothes on the never

never from Littlewoods catalogue. I once overheard a couple of other girls saying they knew Stella even got her knickers from a catalogue. They was being bitchy like, you know?"

"Yes, I think I get the picture, Mr. Cretingham. Tell me, did you know Stella well?"

"Aye, sort of. She were about the same age as me, see, but she were always nice to me, was Stella, not like some of the others. She'd always smile and have a few words wi' me when I went to the pub, once I were eighteen, especially if I were on me own."

"How old were you when she was killed?" Ross asked.

"I were eighteen, nearly nineteen."

"Did you often go to the pub in those days?"

"No, Inspector. I didn't 'ave much money meself back then."

"Did you have a job, Mr Cretingham."

"Aye, but not much of a job. I worked at Mitchells the grocers shop. I did deliveries on an old bike and looked after the stockroom. Sometimes, Mr. Mitchell let me serve behind the counter, but I weren't much good at working the cash register, so that didn't happen often."

"Were you in the Traveller's Rest on the night Stella died?" Ross asked, hoping for something that might give him a new clue to what had taken place all those years ago.

"Yes, I was, for about an hour, early on, like. I weren't there at the end of the night when Stella left."

"Tell me what you remember about the night please, Mr. Cretingham," Ross said.

With that, Albert Cretingham senior launched into a description of that evening in the pub with such detail, he might have been watching a video replay of the hour he spent there. He recalled with vivid clarity everyone who was present in the bar that night, even remembering the brief conversations he'd indulged in or overheard. His list of those present tallied with the list Ross was looking at in the police report from the original investigation that he'd removed from his briefcase as the man spoke. It was clear to Ross that old Albert Cretingham did indeed have a remarkable memory and a flair for remembering the tiniest details from the events of so many years ago.

"Did anyone have an argument or any kind of disagreement with Stella while you were there?" Ross asked, when Cretingham finally fell silent.

"Not as I heard," Cretingham replied. "Mind you, I can't say what might have taken place after I left."

Meanwhile, in the far corner of the room, Izzie Drake was quietly questioning the younger Albert.

"You say your mother ran off with another man? Did your father ever say who that might have been?"

"Only once, when I was about fifteen. He was drunk one night and feeling sorry for himself. He suddenly shouted, 'Damn that bloody Greek bastard.' I didn't know any Greeks, and there weren't any Greeks living in the village, so I asked him who he was talking about, and he said, 'That bloody Alex Christakos, who else?" as if I was supposed to know who he meant. When I asked him who he was talking about he said something like, "Damn waiter, Pat would still be here if it weren't for him." I guessed he meant my Mum. Her name was Patricia, you see. It wasn't hard to put two and two together. Young as I was, I realised he was saying that Mum ran away with this Christakos guy. I tried to get him to tell me more, but he clammed up and then fell asleep in his chair. I went to bed and tried to ask him to tell me more but he never, ever said another word about Mum and Alex Christakos from that day to this."

"I see. That's sad. I suppose your Dad's led a pretty lonely life, all these years."

"I suppose he has, but he's never complained, and he always looked after me well enough. He worked hard until he got sick. Now he sort of lives with his memories and the TV. He likes to watch the racing, and sometimes asks me to go to the bookies to put a bet on for him. Never anything big, just a couple of quid now and then."

"Does he ever talk about what happened in nineteen sixty-six?" Drake asked, trying to probe a little deeper into Albert the elder's past."

"No, never, at least not until those two girls were murdered recently. After the second one was killed, we were watching the news of TV at tea time when there was a report about the killings on, and he said, ever so quietly, "He's back." I asked him who was back, and he rambled on about the original killer having come back to finish what he'd started. I asked how he could know that and he just shrugged his shoulders and hasn't mentioned again until you lot turned up today."

* * *

Andy Ross had been patiently listening while Albert Cretingham virtually relived the nights when first Stella Cox, and secondly, Marian Brown died. Cretingham's recollection of those events were incredibly vivid and Ross knew, from having read the original murder reports, that the elder Albert's memory was indeed accurate in every detail. The one blank however, appeared to be the night of the murder of the young policewoman, when, according to Albert, he was at home all evening, in bed with a heavy cold, and didn't go out at all. His mother told him about the third murder when she brought him breakfast the following morning. It had been reported on the BBC news bulletin that morning. This was a year before the introduction of the local station BBC Radio Merseyside, so the details reported may not have been as detailed as they would have been by local reporters. Cretingham, did however, relate to Ross verbatim, the report of the murder as printed in that evening's issue of The Liverpool Echo.

Ross also asked if Albert was going steady with his future wife at the time of the murders. This time, he was given a glimpse of Cretingham's temper.

"No, I fucking wasn't, and I wish to hell I'd never met that lying, cheating cow. Patricia Howes her name was, and we met when I was twenty. I don't know what she saw in me to be honest. I weren't that bright as you know, but I suppose I were a bit of a looker, you know? I had a right trendy haircut and when I were off work, like, I always dressed smart, better than some of the no-mark scallys that hung around in the pubs and clubs in them days. I earned a decent enough wage working for old man Mitchell at the grocers, so I suppose she saw me as a good wage earner and able to buy her clothes and make-up and such. A lot of lads my age were out of work at the time. Anyway, she seemed to like me, and we went out a few times and then, I proposed to her. I was slow, as I told you, but not so slow as I couldn't talk to girls or take them out for a drink or to the pictures and the like. You could have knocked me down with a feather when she agreed to marry me."

"She must have seen something in you, Mr. Cretingham," Ross said, trying to avoid the man becoming too maudlin, as he feared he was about to become.

"Aye, money, Inspector, that's all, I swear to it. All the so-called clever buggers in the village were either out of work or already fixed up, and I think Pat were afraid of being left on the shelf if she didn't find a husband soon. Anyway, we got married at Brougham Road registry office in Everton, and Pat got pregnant almost straight away. After the lad were born, she wouldn't let me near her again. Said she'd gone through hell giving birth and weren't about to go through all that again."

"What about…?

"Contraception," Cretingham interrupted. "Pat were a staunch Catholic. Wouldn't hear of it, but I bet she used summat when she started spreading her legs for that greasy haired Greek waiter fella."

"I see, and you knew she was seeing this man for certain?"

"Yes, I knew alright. She started saying she were going out with her mates, but one night, young Albert were fast asleep in his cot and I took the chance and followed her. She met him outside the place where he worked, the hussy. He took her to his flat not far away and I could guess what were happening in there alright. I tried to 'ave it out with her, but she told me she didn't love me and was going to go off with him. I asked about young Albert and she said I was welcome to him and that he'd probably turn out to be a dimwit, like his father. That was a cruel thing to say, Inspector. I were a bit slow, yes, but I weren't no dimwit."

Ross could only nod and wait for the man to finish his story.

"Anyway, it were Billy Riley as first told me she were doin' the dirty on me, like. That's why I ended up following her. Told me in the Traveller's one night he did. Said Pat had been hanging around with that Eyetie waiter fella who lived at the end of Church Road. Said he'd seen 'em smooching down the lane by the old lighthouse, I put two and two together. See, Pat had been goin' out more'n usual and wearing her skirts shorter and shorter, not right for a young married mother, it weren't."

"Did you ask her about her relationship with Mr. Christakos?" Ross asked.

"I bloody well did, and the little tart didn't deny it. Said as how they were goin' to go off together, probably to Greece, I supposed. She never said where they were goin'.

Not long after, they just upped and left. I never saw her or that bastard again."

"Did you report your wife missing, Mr. Cretingham?"

"What the 'ell for, Inspector? She weren't missing. I knew where she was, didn't I? She were with 'im."

Ross could see the simple logic behind Albert's thinking. To his young mind, Patricia Cretingham had run away with her lover, left her husband and child behind, so why report her as missing? He still felt a little uneasy however.

"Where did this man live, Mr. Cretingham, did you know his address?"

"Oh aye, he rented a flat above a shop two doors from his work, and a few days after they buggered off, I went round there, thinkin' they'd be shacked up together in there, and I got told as Christakos had left, done a runner without payin' his rent, and that's when I knew they'd fucked off to Greece like Pat said they was going' to."

"Did you try to find her?"

"What for? She didn't want me, did she? Good luck to the pair of 'em. I 'ope they're rotting in hell, somewhere."

* * *

Heading back to the pub car park and their mobile incident van, Ross and Drake quickly compared notes on the two Albert Cretinghams.

"What did you make of them, Izzie?" Ross asked his partner as he sat back in the passenger seat.

"In one word, weird," she replied. "I know you spoke to the old man, but the younger one seemed odd enough to me. He started off being a bit 'off' with me, and then he suddenly came over all helpful. If I had to make a snap judgment, I'd say he was hiding something. What about you?"

"Well, the father can talk for England, that's for sure. He virtually relived everything that took place during the time of the1960s murders, but denied any knowledge of anything to do with the current murders. He shot off on a tangent when I asked about his wife though. It's difficult to work him out really. He was diagnosed with a mild form of autism in his youth, but they didn't know as much about it then as they do now, so he was a pretty misunderstood kid as far as I can tell, and was probably bullied a bit for being different."

"The son seemed to confirm that, sir. Makes me wonder how the old man ever got a good looking young girl like Pat to marry him."

"From what he told me, she was probably a bit of a gold digger, though he wouldn't have known that, given his mental capabilities back then."

"The son was adamant the mother had run off, sir, but, I can't help wondering, well, you know..?"

"If something happened to her, Izzie? I admit, similar thoughts ran through my mind as the father was talking to me. Maybe when we get through with this case, we might want to take a look at the disappearance of Mrs. Patricia Cretingham."

Before they could take the conversation further, they arrived once more at the car park of The Traveller's Rest. After parking the car, they made their way to the mobile incident unit. Parked alongside one of their unmarked police vehicles was a gleaming burgundy coloured classic 1964 Bentley S3 saloon car, that somehow looked completely out of place beside the police Peugeots and Sofie Meyer's bright yellow Volkswagen Beetle. Ross smiled as he almost reverently stroked one hand along the pristine paintwork of the bonnet of the Bentley.

"Unless I'm much mistaken, our friend Stan Coleman will be waiting for us in the van, Izzie."

"Oh yeah, you think?" she grinned. "You don't think Derek McLennan won the lottery and forgot to tell us, then?"

The two shared a laugh as they entered the incident unit, where sure enough, former D.I. Stan Coleman was sitting chatting pleasantly with Sofie Meyer and Paul Ferris as they worked on their respective computer keyboards. It was time for Andy Ross to probe the mind of the ex-detective and compare his memories with those of Albert Cretingham senior.

Chapter 7

The Diary, Part one

The old, well fingered diary lay just where it had stood all day, left on the dressing table when the time to leave for work had arrived at eight that morning. At four by three inches in size, with a navy-blue plastic cover it was a simple, common mass-produced product that many people would have carried in their pocket or purse back in the nineteen sixties. The corners of the cover were turned up with age, much like most of the pages within, printed a day to a page. Whoever had owned it had omitted to fill in the page for name and address and personal details, so Alex couldn't know who the writer of the diary had been. As always, Alex found the 31st of July 1966 to be the natural starting point.

Why didn't she let me kiss her? I wouldn't have hurt her if only she'd let me kiss her, but she screamed at me to get off her, leave her alone. She knew I liked her. I shouldn't have thrown her on the ground like I did, that scared her so when I got on top of her, she kept twisting away from me when I tried to kiss her. I'm sorry Stella. Why did she kick out at me? That did it, I had to stop her. All I could think of was tearing her new skirt. Knew that would shut her up, the bitch. Lucky I had the length of rope in my pocket. Tying her up was fun. Then I saw her legs and her knickers. Black and smooth, like silk. Never saw a girl's knickers before. Felt funny, but good inside. She went quiet when I slapped her again.

Knew what I wanted to do then. She struggled a bit then lay still till I finished. Then what should I do? If I let her go, she'd tell the bizzies. No, couldn't let her, had to make her stay quiet. So I did, Sorry Stella. Felt good this morning though. I want to feel good down there again, soon. Maybe I can find someone else to like me.

Alex often wondered what might have happened all those years ago if the girl she knew only as Stella had allowed one of the men from the pub to walk her home. Maybe that Bobby Evans, the postman who found her body? He was mentioned a lot in the diary. Everyone seemed to have liked Bobby Evans, according to the diarist. He was a popular young fella in the village. Unlike the diarist, who always felt as though he lived on the outside, looking in, never quite one of the lads. The early months of the diary had betrayed a loneliness about the writer, a feeling of emptiness and isolation. When he'd met Stella, every page carried at least a few words about her, *Saw Stella today, she was walking to work,* or, another time, *Stella said hello to me when I walked into pub tonight. She smiled too.* Not long before Stella's murder, he'd written, My birthday today. *Stella stood at bus stop. She looked good. Red jumper, black skirt with those pleat things in it. Told her it was my birthday and she put her hands on my shoulders and gave me a kiss on my cheek, said Happy birthday. BEST DAY OF MY LIFE, SHE KISSED ME.*

Reading between the lines, Alex had long ago guessed that the kiss the writer referred to had probably been one of those chaste, friendly little kisses young girls and women cheerfully give to almost anyone they know on birthdays, Christmas and so on, but to the writer of the little diary on the dressing table, that kiss could have been the final trigger that effectively escalated his behaviour towards Stella, and ultimately led to the tragedy of her death on that fateful night.

Alex sighed, paused from reading long enough to take a sip from the cup of tea that sat primly on its bone china saucer to the right of the diary, and was about to continue reading the so familiar pages, pages whose words were now burned into Alex's memory like a script from a badly-written horror movie when there was a knock on the front door. Realising how much time had passed and knowing who would be standing at the door and that they wouldn't be leaving in a hurry if nobody responded to their knocking, Alex rose from the dressing table seat, smoothed her skirt down, and adjusted her hair in the mirror, taking time only to place the precious diary in the right hand drawer of the dressing table, being careful to lock it, placing the little key in her purse, which was then deposited in her handbag. Taking one last, longing look at the dressing table, knowing she'd have to wait until her shift was finished and her visitor had left before her reading, her *research* could continue, Alexandra Sefton made her way downstairs, walked swiftly along the hall corridor, her heels clicking on the parquet flooring, and opened the front door, smiling a greeting as she did so. One last check of her make-up in the small gold-framed hall mirror, and Alex fixed a smile on her face as she opened the front door to her friend.

Chapter 8

Division of Labour

"Cretingham? Definitely not a name you forget easily," former D.I. Stan Coleman said as he mused over a mug of hot coffee, sitting opposite Andy Ross in the Mobile Incident Unit. "Young lad, about eighteen I think, or he was back in '66. There was something about the lad, not all there, you know? Suppose they'd call it learning difficulties today."

"Autism, actually Stan. He had a mild form of it, still does."

"Ah, I knew there was something about him," Coleman nodded, sagely.

"Did you ever have reason to suspect him at the time of Stella Cox's murder?" Izzie Drake asked.

"Of killing Stella, or the others? No," Coleman said emphatically. "He was just a kid, maybe a bit besotted with Stella Cox, but in a puppy dog kind of way. I think he wanted her to like him, but I didn't think him a viable suspect, no. I think the lad would have been hard pressed to get any girl to notice him, to be honest. Word was Stella felt sorry for him, and tried to be a friend to him, but nothing more. I was the one who interviewed him initially, when we spoke to everyone who'd been at the pub that night."

"Did you know he'd got married a couple of years later, Stan? Ross asked the ex-detective.

"No, I didn't. Why would I, Andy? Two years you say? He must have grown up a lot in the years after the murders."

"He had a child too," Drake added. "He's also called Albert and lives with his father. The Albert you know is now riddled with Asbestosis, angina and asthma. The son seems devoted to his father, especially as his mother ran off with an Italian waiter when he was still a baby."

"And why are you so interested in Albert Cretingham?" Coleman asked the pair.

"No special reason," Ross replied, "apart from the fact that despite his autism, he seems to possess a photographic memory and was able to give us a perfect recollection of everything that took place around the time of Stella's murder. I want to compare his memories with what you have on record in the original murder file."

"I see, and you think he might remember something we missed during the investigation?"

"I don't know, Stan, but we need to move fast here, because of there is a link between the original killings and the current ones, we sure as hell need every bit of help we can get if we're to prevent another young woman losing her life."

"You don't think the son could be our killer then? Maybe carrying out the identical series of murders as his father did all those years ago? I could have been wrong, but then you already know that don't you?" Coleman looked knowingly at Ross, already sure the younger man had already thought along those lines.

"Yes, Stan, the thought had crossed my mind, Izzie's too, but it's almost too easy for them to be the solution. Father kills women, years later; son carries out copycat killings, why? In some twisted tribute to his father? To show he's as cold-hearted as the older man? Or because his Dad is fed up watching the 3.30 from Kempton Park and wants to hear the graphic stories of how his son is raping and killing women according to his own special blueprint? I'm just not buying it, at least not on what we have so far, which, to be honest is bugger all."

"Then again, they are a weird pair, sir, you must agree," Drake added.

Ross thought for a minute before making a decision.

"Okay, to be on the safe side, let's put a tail on Cretingham the younger for a few days. We'll see if he gets up to anything suspicious. Curtis and Devenish, you two can rotate and keep an eye on him, outside his working hours of course. I can't authorise twenty-four-hour surveillance based on the fact they're a bit weird."

"Right sir," D.C. Tony Curtis nodded, echoed by Gary Devenish. Neither man looked particularly happy with what both viewed as a dead-end assignment.

Stan Coleman asked Ross what he expected from him, having asked him to come and meet him on site at the mobile incident van.

"I'd like you to take Sergeant Drake and Sergeant Meyer on a walk-through of the murder scenes from 1966, please, Stan, followed by a look at the recent murder sites for comparison. I know all the bodies were found around the lighthouse site, but there must have been slight differences in their locations and Izzie, Sofie, I want you to compare them with the first two murders that have just taken place. We already have subtle differences that suggest today's killer is aware of forensic counter-measures,"

"You mean like using condoms?"

"Exactly. I want you try and recall exactly how each body was laid out and my people will compare them like for like. Murder one against the new murder one, and so on. If the killer we're looking for is replicating the original murders so exactly it must be a relative, or the original killer has an apprentice."

"Bloody hell. You think my killer might have actually groomed some sick bastard to carry out the current killings?"

"It can't be discounted," Ross said, grimly.

"Bloody hell," Coleman looked aghast. "That's fucking sick."

"Too right it is, Stan, but that's the world we live in today, I'm afraid."

"Sir," Paul Ferris interrupted from his place at the computer.

"What is it Paul?"

"Funny you should mention that, but I've been doing some research since we got here."

Ross knew that when Sergeant Ferris said he'd been doing some research, it meant his resident computer expert had probably been delving into places other people wouldn't dream of delving.

"Go on, Paul, I'm all ears."

"Well, you know how ex-D.I. Coleman said he was convinced, during the original investigation, that the killer was local to Hale?"

"Aye, I did think that, Sergeant," Coleman agreed.

"What have you found?" Ross asked, growing impatient.

"I thought it might be a good idea to check and see if any of the current residents of Hale have any kind of criminal record, specifically looking for anyone who might be on the Sex Offenders Register, and who was also resident in Hale, however young they may have been, at the time of the first murders."

"Sounds like a lot of work," Sam Gable piped up from her place at the back of the van.

"Not really, Sam," Ferris continued. "First, I pulled up the Electoral Roll, then looked at the current Sex Offenders Register, and cross-referenced names and addresses until I had a list of residents who are on the register. There aren't many, as Hale isn't that big to begin with. Then I checked those on the register with electoral rolls through the years to see who, if anyone, was part of any family that lived here at any time in the nineteen sixties, and I managed to narrow it down to three."

"Bloody hell, Paul. That's great work," Ross exclaimed.

"Great work? Your man's a sodding genius if you ask me," Stan Coleman enthused.

"So come on, who are they?" Ross asked, expectantly.

Ferris handed a sheet of paper to Ross, newly printed from his computer.

"There's a John Blount, thirty-two, two convictions for indecent assault. He pinned a girl against the wall at a college dance and pushed his hand up her skirt to cop a feel. He got six months suspended for that one. A year later did something similar, this time groping a woman's breasts while in a packed bus heading for the city centre.

He tried to make out he fell against her accidentally, when the bus lurched, but the magistrate wasn't having it and he got three months inside this time and placed on the register."

"OK, but it's quite a jump from touching women up to full-blown rape and murder," Ross mused aloud. "Who's next?"

"Billy Fry, aged thirty," Ferris went on. "Did three years for rape. Originally sentenced to five, but was released two years ago on licence, time off for good behaviour."

"Yeah, same as always," Curtis jibed. "They never do the full bloody time do they, perverted bastards?"

"That's the system, Tony," Ferris replied. "Nothing we can do to change it."

"More's the fucking pity," Curtis said, angrily.

"Either of those surnames ring a bell, Stan?" Ross asked Coleman. "Obviously the surnames might apply to people you recall from the original investigation."

After thinking hard for a minute and then consulting the original case notes, Stan Coleman replied.

"Blount definitely rings a bell. I just needed to be sure. Frank Blount was here in sixty-six, living with his parents, Graham and Jean. Graham was a petty crook who appeared to be going straight. He'd not been charged with any offences for the three years preceding our investigation. Frank would probably be this lad's father. We questioned him along with everyone else at the time. He'd have been about seventeen or eighteen at the time. He stood out a bit because he was tall for his age and powerfully built. He certainly had the physical characteristics to have killed Stella and the other girls. Without physical or forensic evidence, and in the absence of witnesses or a stonewall confession, like every other bloke in Hale, we let him go. Billy Fry, now, I do remember him, or rather his father, William, also known as Billy. He was already known to us as a sex offender, but the problem was, once again, we had no way of tying him to Stella or the other victims."

"What's this thing about folks in Hale calling their kids after their fathers?" Izzie asked. "Two Albert Cretinghams, two William Frys?"

"Actually, that's not quite accurate," Ferris replied. "William Fry named his son, Billy, not William."

"Oh, whoopy do, but they're both known as Billy."

"Don't blame me, Izzie. I'm just the messenger."

"Just don't tell me we have a third father and son team," Drake wished aloud as she waited for the third suspect name to emerge.

"Not this time," Ferris smiled. "Eric Young, son of Paul and Deirdre Young, age forty two, attended Prescot Grammar School, married with two children and lives, get this, just three doors from where we're parked. He was interviewed earlier but of course; the interviewing officers knew nothing of his record."

Andy Ross had visibly winced when Ferris mentioned Prescot Grammar School, where he himself had received his secondary education years ago, luckily, he surmised, not at the same time as Eric Young.

"What was he convicted of, Paul?" he asked.

"He was done for being in possession of obscene material, ten years ago, did two years inside, and was then given a five year sentence a year after his release for possessing images of child pornography on his computer."

"Bloody fucking hell," D.C. Tony Curtis exclaimed, "and some poor cow is married to a turd like that?"

"And he has children," Derek McLennan added.

"Sounds a real piece of shit," Ross agreed, "but again, not exactly the type of crimes that we'd normally expect to escalate to multiple rape and murder."

Sofie Meyer, who had been quiet for some time, now spoke up.

"But sir, maybe this person, whoever it is, is someone who has kept his true inner desires hidden for a long time. It may not be a relative of the original killer, but what if our current murderer found or inherited documents detailing what the first killer did? This man may have moved into the original killer's old home and found a record of the killings under a floorboard or behind a wall, buried in the garden anywhere at all in fact."

Everyone fell silent as Meyer's words hit home. Ross eventually broke that silence.

"You think he found a diary, or a journal, something like that, Sofie?"

Meyer nodded as he continued.

"Sofie's right of course, people. We may be barking up the wrong tree in chasing down these men on the register, but we need to check them out. Paul, another little job for you. Do you think that computer of yours can track down anyone who lived in Hale in nineteen sixty-six, who was old enough at the time to have carried out the original murders, who later died and left their house to a relative, or if not, whether the house was sold, and who to?"

"Bloody hell, sir, you're not asking much are you?" Ferris looked aghast as the enormity of Ross's request hit home.

"I never said it would be easy, Paul, did I? Just tell me, can you do it lad?"

Ferris intertwined his knuckles, made a cracking sound as he flexed them, his hands laced together. then smiled as he turned to his screen and began tapping on the keyboard as he replied, "You know me, Boss. I love a challenge."

"Okay everyone," Ross ordered, "Let's get to it."

Izzie Drake and Sofie Meyer were the first to exit the incident van as they left with Stan Coleman to begin their tour of the death scenes, the pair, for a short time, luxuriating in the plush luxury of the former detective's gleaming Bentley.

The rest of the team filtered out soon afterwards, leaving Paul Ferris and Kat Bellamy behind, accompanied by the steady rhythm of the tapping of their fingers as they beat a tattoo across their keyboards in search of the seemingly impossible information Ross had asked Ferris to find. Under normal circumstances, Paul Ferris was confident he could solve the problem of the various incoming and outgoings and changes in the residents of the homes of Hale in a few days of searching, but, as he and Kat were painfully aware, a few days in this case could be a day or more too long. A young woman, a police officer, was likely to die if they couldn't perform the impossible, and fast!

Chapter 9

Off Duty Distractions

"Do you ever regret that we never had kids, Andy?" Maria Ross asked her husband that evening as they sat watching a wildlife documentary on TV. They'd just enjoyed one of Andy's favourite childhood meals, good old sausage, chips and peas, which Maria indulged him with now and then. As a doctor she was well aware of the dangers of unhealthy eating but she also believed in the old adage that 'a bit of what you fancy doesn't do you harm'.

"Why d'you ask that all of a sudden?" Ross asked.

"Oh, I just see so many women of my age in surgery every day, and virtually every one of them has a family, two, three, maybe more children and I got to thinking if you'd ever wished we'd not made the decision to concentrate on our careers instead of having kids, that's all."

Andy Ross reached across the sofa and put an arm round Maria's shoulders, pulling her close to him. Looking deep into her deep, brown eyes, he moved even closer and kissed her passionately before pulling away and answering her question.

"Not for one bloody second," he said firmly. "Apart from the fact that I love you as much today as I did on the day we got married, there's the important point that we both agreed to concentrate on our careers. Neither of us was exactly mad on the idea of having kids then or now.

And with some of the things I see in my job, especially in this case we're working on now…"

"How do you mean?" Maria asked. Andy usually discussed his cases, as much as he was able to, with his wife, who, over the years had been able to give him some quite insightful views on the problems thrown up by some of his most difficult investigations.

"Well, we've been talking to people, parents, who, back in nineteen sixty-six, had to bury their own daughters, and even now, all these years later, the pain and the hurt is still there to see in their faces and in their general demeanour when they talk about their lost children. Then we have another two sets of parents who are only just going through the same thing, and it makes you wonder, you know? Is it right or fair that parents should outlive their children and must experience the pain and grief that comes with their premature loss? For me, it's better to be as we are, and not have to face such bloody awful trauma and psychological pain."

Maria took hold of both his hands in hers and squeezed them gently as she replied.

"Andy, you know damn well that I see death all too often as a doctor, but believe me, I've never yet met a parent of a sick or dying child, of any age, who regretted becoming a parent. You can't allow yourself to think like that. We made our decision based on what we both wanted from life, and as we both seem to feel the same now as we did when I was back in Medical School, it appears I've answered my own question, doesn't it?"

The couple stared at one another for a few seconds, then smiled together and Andy Ross pulled his wife as close to him as he could and kissed her lovingly on the lips. The kiss became more passionate until Andy whispered in Maria's ear, "Fancy an early night?"

"I thought you'd never ask," Maria said, her voice husky as she rose from the sofa, and led him by the hand, out of the lounge and up the stairs to their bedroom, where the advantage of not having children to worry about or overhear their lovemaking soon became clear to them both as they quickly disposed of their clothes and fell, laughing and lovingly, onto the bed.

* * *

A few miles away, Izzie Drake (or, to give the detective her married name, Izzie Foster), were engaged in a conversation of a very different nature. When they'd married, they'd agreed that Izzie would continue to use her maiden name at work, as she'd spent her years on the force building a reputation as a police officer as Drake, and change her name to Foster, they thought, might make it difficult for others on the force to relate to the fact that 'Sergeant Foster' was in fact the 'Sergeant Drake' they'd come to know and respect over the years. Izzie, however was having second thoughts. Much to Peter's mystification, she had just suggested, as they lay in bed almost ready to fall asleep, that she officially become Sergeant Foster at work.

"What's brought this on?" he asked, "I thought you were happier being Drake at work and Foster at home."

"It's just that I feel as if I'm being disloyal to you in a way by not using my married name at work. There are plenty of other married female officers on the force who use their married names, so why shouldn't I?"

"I never thought I'd hear you of all people come out with something like this. Izzie, you're not just any female officer, you're Andy Ross's partner, his right hand man, well, woman, and everyone who's anyone at Merseyside Police knows that Ross's partner is Sergeant Izzie Drake. You two have built up a great rapport and reputation over the years you've worked together and if people are suddenly finding themselves being directed to a Sergeant Foster when they ask for Ross or his partner, you'll find yourself having to keep explaining that you are Izzie Drake but under another name. How many times do you think you'll have to do that over the next few years before everyone knows who you are."

"Bloody hell, Peter. I didn't think you were so protective of my relationship with the boss. I thought you'd be pleased that I want to be Mrs. Foster, full time."

"Don't get me wrong Izzie. That would be great, but let's be honest, you and Ross are so well known, it might put a hex on your success as a partnership if you go changing your name now. After all, it hasn't affected us in two years of marriage, has it, so why should we fix something that isn't broken?"

"Are you sure?" Izzie asked, surprised at her husband's reaction to her suggestion. She'd expected him to be pleased, but apparently, she'd been wrong.

"Look, you know I love you dearly, and I love you being Mrs. Peter Foster, but there are some things in life that are inescapable, and one of them is the fact that you and Andy Ross go together, as far as work's concerned, like Morecambe and Wise, or Ant and Dec. Ross and Drake sounds right, and all your colleagues on the force, even those who don't know you personally will have heard of the two of you, I'm sure. Now, I doubt very much whether Ross and Foster would elicit the same immediate recognition and respect, do you? When we're at home, when we go shopping together, visit our friends, go on holiday, whatever, we're Peter and Izzie Foster, but when you walk into that police station, you become Izzie Drake, part of the best damn investigative partnerships in the Merseyside Police force, and you know what? I'm bloody proud of that. It doesn't make me feel any less of a man, or that you're disrespecting our marriage or whatever it is you thinking, so you just get out there every day, Sergeant *Drake* and do your job the way you've always done it, okay?"

Stunned, Izzie could only stare into Peter's eyes with a look of love mingled with intense respect for the man she'd married. After a few seconds hesitation she leaned closer, kissed him hungrily and then said, "Peter Foster, do you know, I love you more than I could ever possibly tell you? You are the most fantastic man on this whole planet."

"Thank you, Mrs. Foster," Peter replied, laughing.

"Oh good, I'm Mrs. Foster while we're in bed then, am I, just so I know?" she giggled.

"Definitely," Peter laughed in return. "You don't think I'd take on the feared Sergeant Izzie Drake in the bedroom, do you? I could actually get arrested for what I'm thinking of doing to you right now, the parts of you I desperately want to investigate for myself."

"Well, as I'm *merely* Mrs. Foster for now, what the hell are you waiting for?" she asked as she pulled her husband on top of her and with her left hand, quickly guided him into the forbidden territory he was so anxious to explore. "Investigate that! She gasped, unable to wait any longer.

Chapter 10

The Third Day

Detective Chief Inspector Oscar Agostini had the look of a worried man as he sat in on Ross's early morning team briefing. So far it appeared the team's investigations were leading nowhere fast. Having called the gathered detectives to order, Ross and Drake took their positions at the front of the briefing room. Sergeant Paul Ferris as usual sat positioned in front of his computer screen, ready at a moment's notice to access any information required by Ross as the briefing progressed.

"So," Agostini said, after Ross had ceded the floor to him, "We have four days left to prevent another meeting if our killer sticks to the original timetable of the earlier murders. I spoke to the chief last thing last night and she is willing to draft in extra bodies if we need them. I told her I have faith in you people to solve this case, but we will be happy to accept the help of as many uniformed officers as we can get to help with house to house and to put extra foot patrols on the streets of Hale and especially the area around the lighthouse. I want to hear from you all this morning on the results of the interviews and investigations you carried out yesterday. Over to you, D.I Ross."

"Thank you, sir," Ross replied and after clearing his throat, he looked at his team as they sat, waiting to give their reports. He could see frustration in their faces and didn't hold out much hope of hearing anything positive from the previous day's efforts. "Izzie, let's hear from you and Sofie first."

"Right sir," Drake began. "As you requested, Stan Coleman drove us down to the old lighthouse, and that Bentley is some car, I can tell you."

Despite the gravity of the situation there were a couple of giggles from some of the assembled group of detectives at Izzie's remark.

"It's a lonely old place, I can tell you, standing where it does overlooking the water and what was, yesterday at least, a deserted stretch of beach. With the fields behind it, with just a couple of footpaths running between them and the one access road to the lighthouse itself, it made for an excellent body dump site for our killer. We had the crime scene photos from the original murders and from the two most recent killings and as you asked, we compared them with each other and with the actual site itself. I can tell you now, whoever is carrying out the current murders has to be in possession of either photographs or some other blueprint of the original killings, because the bodies were, as far as we could tell, left out in the open in, as near as we could ascertain, the identical positions as those poor girls in nineteen sixty-six."

"Either that, or we are dealing with the same killer," Sofie Meyer joined in at that point. "We realise if it is the same man, he will be almost geriatric by now, but Izzie and I, and Mr. Coleman agreed, that such a killer will probably have a strong and dominant personality, and it is quite foreseeable that he may have influenced a younger man to assist him in carrying out these new murders."

"I see," Ross said, thoughtfully." Whose theory was this, originally?"

"It was mine, sir," Meyer replied. "I began to postulate on this idea after it was mentioned at our earlier briefing that the original Lighthouse Killer could have inspired an apprentice as you described it. I thought, instead of someone simply following the original killer in his methods and execution of the murders, why couldn't the original killer be actually leading the apprentice, if one exists, in actually carrying out the current murders."

"It makes a lot of sense, Sofie. Well done on coming up with your theory, but as with everything we've thought of so far in this case, everything seems to be asking us the same question."

"Why now?" Drake said.

"Exactly. Izzie," Ross agreed. "Why the hell has he suddenly begun killing again, or if it's not the original killer, what's the inspiration or motive that has set off a copycat killer to begin these new murders right now, as opposed to next week or next year for example?"

"Next year would have made more sense surely, sir," said D.C. Derek McLennan. This year is thirty-nine years since his first murder spree. Next year would surely have made more sense, you know, like forty years is a much more rounded figure, if you get my drift."

"I know what you mean, Derek," Ross nodded as he spoke, "but there's nothing that says our killer, or any killer come to that, has to be logical, and for all we know, this guy has an agenda of his own that makes this year significant for him in some way."

McLennan nodded as Ross asked the others for their reports. Before those who'd contacted the men on the Sex Offenders Register could give Ross their findings, D.C. Curtis, who'd been following up on a few of the more promising house to house calls, spoke up.

"Sir, we may have another lead, or at least, a person worth looking at."

"Okay Tony, go ahead, we're listening."

"Well, when I spoke for a second time to Bobby Evans, the chap who was the postie back in sixty-six, he couldn't tell me a lot more, but he was one of those closest to the original investigation and was even a suspect, but only for a short time."

"Oh, come on Tony, we haven't got all day," Izzie Drake urged him.

"Yeah, right, sorry Sarge. So when I saw him again yesterday and asked if he had anything that might help us with the recent murders, he stopped to think for a minute and as he did, he walked to look out of his front room window, and then suddenly said, Of course, why didn't I think of him before?"

"Who, sir?" I asked, and he pointed out of the window to the bus stop across the road from his house. There was a man standing there, maybe about thirtyish, I guessed. He looked a bit odd, I must admit. He was wearing black trousers, a yellow high-vis jacket and had not one but two rucksacks slung over one shoulder. He kept stepping out into the road, I assumed looking for the bus coming. As we watched we saw the bus appear in the distance and chappie immediately stuck his arm out to signal the diver to stop. Trouble is, the bus was still two stops away and I doubt the driver could even see him at that point. I asked Mr. Evans who he was."

"His name is Joey Pratt," Evans told me. "He's not the brightest bulb in the candelabra if you get my drift, sort of Pratt by name, Prat by nature. Most of the women hereabouts tend to give him a wide berth. He tries to engage them, anyone in fact, in conversations about stuff they have no interest in and one or two of the ladies I've spoken to have told me he makes them feel uncomfortable. They don't like the way he looks at them. Some of the younger girls say they can feel him ogling their legs and their tits, oops sorry, I mean their breasts. I mean, just look at him. It's summer for God's sake and he's dressed as if he's going for a weekend backpacking in the Lake District. Thing is, he always dresses the same and why he needs those two shoulder bags of his is anyone's guess. Honest, constable, he's definitely a few pence short of a shilling, to use an old phrase. And he always turns up at the bus stop about half an hour before the bus is due. Nobody in their right mind spends all that time waiting for a bloody bus, now do they? I mean, in my day, I walked miles every day delivering the post. He could just as easily walk to work if you ask me."

"Where does he work, Mr. Evans?" I asked him.

"That's the thing, you see," Evans replied. "He only works at Terry's Garden Centre, less than two miles up the road. Hardly need two shoulder bags and high high-vis jacket to go to work as a waiter, I'd have thought."

"A waiter, at a garden centre?"

"Yeah, they've got a café there for the customers. I heard that Joey originally had a job in the main garden centre, but customers complained that he's approach them and start talking about all sorts of crap, nothing to do with plants or selling them anything, so the management moved him into the café where they thought he'd be less of a pest. He began by waiting on tables and they still got complaints about his banal attempts at useless chit chat, so they moved him behind the scenes and now he does the washing up in kitchens, and any other odd jobs that need doing."

"I asked Evans if anyone could corroborate what he was telling me, and he nodded and said, "Oh, yeah, just ask any of the women you see out there on the street, or go talk to Adnan Singh, manager at Terry's. He was the one who told me about Joey over a pint in the Traveller's Rest one night. He lives in the village too, you see, a couple of doors down from the church."

D.C. Tony Curtis ended his narrative there and waited for Ross's reaction.

"I see what you mean, Tony. *Weird* doesn't always indicate criminality. I suppose you've checked to see if he's got a record?"

"I have, sir. Seems young Mr. Pratt, got into a spot of bother as a juvenile. Bit weird really, which matches what Mr. Evans told me I suppose."

"Come on Tony, out with it," Izzie urged him to reveal what he'd discovered.

"Okay, folks, get this. At the age of sixteen, Joey Pratt was arrested for shoplifting. The arrest was fairly and let's be honest, lots of lads get into trouble as juveniles and still grow up okay, but the interesting part about Joey Pratt's offence was what he stole. Fags? Beer? Drugs? Nope! Our young Master Pratt was caught walking out of Marks and Spencer with two women's bras and matching knickers stuffed under his jumper."

"You've got to be kidding," Tony Curtis chuckled, rather loudly.

"Cool it, Tony," Drake quickly shushed him. "It's not funny."

"Sorry Sarge," he said with a smirk on his face.

"I looked into it a bit more," Ferris continued. "Laddo apparently said he was from a poor family and they had no cash for clothes and he wanted them for his sister."

"I feel there is a twist in this tail of yours, Paul," Sofie Meyer joined in the conversation.

"Yes, Sofie, there is. Joey Pratt's parents both had good jobs, they weren't poor at all and get this, he doesn't and never has had a sister."

As Ferris fell silent, nobody appeared able to control their amusement and the room filled with giggles and a couple of real belly laughs.

"Okay you lot, that's enough," Ross now tried to calm things down.

"Sorry, sir, but it just seems so funny," even the normally reserved Sam Gable was grinning from ear to ear. "Looks like he was either a very young cross dresser or he had gender identity problems and couldn't control his urges to dress up in women's clothes."

"You could be right, but I fail to see why the whole squad find it so hilarious."

"Neither do we, sir," Nick Dodds added, "but it's one of those things that just seems to have triggered a bout of simultaneous hilarity."

"I too have heard of such things," Meyer added, her face a mask of deadly seriousness. Sometimes her Germanic senses could miss the nuances of British humour.

Ross couldn't help smiling. It did the team good sometimes, to spontaneously release their emotions in the midst of a difficult case. The stolen underwear case seemed to have been the release valve in this one.

"Okay, back to business you unruly mob," he smiled as he spoke. "Anything after that offence, Paul?" he asked Ferris, who replied immediately.

"Nothing else was heard about him until just over a year later. His parents were killed when their house caught fire one night, and Joey escaped by jumping from his bedroom window and landing in a bed of lily of the valley, breaking a leg in the process."

"Poor kid," Sam Gable said, her voice sympathetic to the boy's plight.

"Ah, but wait," Ferris went on. "There was speculation at the time that young Joey Pratt was responsible for setting the fire."

"It was arson?" Ross asked.

"According to the fire brigade, yes. The investigators decided that the fire was caused by a firework, a Roman Candle to be precise, being lit and pushed through the letterbox. The police could find no motive for anyone to want to kill Mr. and Mrs. Pratt, but neighbours told them that the couple had been having behavioural problems with Joey for some time and had often hear him shouting at his parents. Problem was, nobody could prove that Joey had done it. Detective Sergeant Lewis Gold speculated that Joey had pushed the firework through the letterbox, then ran around to enter the house through the back door, ran up to his bedroom and waited until the fire caught properly, and flames were licking at his bedroom door before jumping out of his bedroom window. In his statement afterwards, Joey stated that he was asleep, and that 'something' woke him up. He went to his bedroom door but was beaten back by the heat. Smoke was coming under the door and he had no option but to jump from the window. Sergeant Gold was almost certain that Joey was lying but there was no evidence to implicate him."

"Bloody hell, Paul," Ross exclaimed.

"That's kind of what I thought, too, sir," Ferris agreed. "I think Pratt needs investigating closely. If he has some kind of fetish, and if he does possess murderous tendencies that have lain dormant for years…"

"Exactly," Ross interrupted. "Sofie, I'd like you and Ginger to talk to Joey Pratt, but first, go and sound out his boss, this Mr. Singh. See if he's aware of Pratt's past, and if he's ever had any concerns about him apart from the fact that he's already had to move him from direct customer contact to a behind the scenes job. It sounds to me as if he's got his eye on Pratt and the man could be one step from being fired."

"Yes, sir," Meyer replied. "We'll leave as soon as the briefing is finished. We'll take my car, Gary," she said to the young Acting D.C. who acknowledged her words with a nod and a smile. The young Detective was pleased to have been teamed up with the extremely clever and efficient German sergeant, whose loan to the Merseyside Force was so far proving a great success. He was also intrigued by the fact that Meyer was the only member of the team who used his real first name and not his nickname. To everyone else he was Ginger, but to Sofie Meyer, he was Gary. Perhaps he could ask her why as they worked together, he thought to himself. He was looking forward to seeing her at work in close-up.

"That was good work, Sergeant Ferris," D.C.I. Agostini complimented the team's resident 'computer genius' as they all thought of Ferris. "I know a lot of that information must have been sealed, as it would have pertained to Pratt's record while still a juvenile. I won't ask you how exactly you obtained it so quickly, if at all."

"Best not to, sir," Ferris smiled at the chief. "What's the phrase they use a lot in American movies? Oh yeah, *plausible deniability* and all that."

"Hmm, yes, right, of course. So, shall we move on Andy?" he asked as he turned the briefing back over to Ross, who also had a broad smile on his face at the thought of Paul Ferris accessing parts of the judicial database that others might only dream about. For the time being, however, he needed the rest of the reports from the previous day's interviews and investigations. Thanks to Ferris's achievement in bringing to light one potential suspect, they were running behind time, and he needed to complete the briefing and move the investigation forward as fast as he could.

Ferris's news had added a certain charge to the atmosphere in the room and he could feel an almost tangible desire among his assembled team to hit the streets as fast as they could. Never had the team felt the meaning of the term, a race against time, quite as keenly as they did at that moment.

Chapter 11

Bedtime reading

Alex stretched her legs to their full extent as she lounged in her bath, her feet resting on the taps as she surveyed her beautifully manicured nails for a few seconds, before she raised herself from the hot water and stood, admiring her reflection in the mirror on the wall opposite the bath. Her figure was good, she decided, as indeed she decided every time she inspected her naked reflection after bathing. Reaching down, she ran a hand down her legs, annoyed to find a semblance of hair growth on her long, shapely legs. It was time for the depilatory cream again, which she would apply after drying herself. She hated the unseemly hairs, that she felt made her appear less of a woman. Stepping from the bath she wrapped herself in a large pink bath sheet that had been warming on the radiator while she enjoyed her bath. She quickly dried herself, sat on the toilet and applied the cream that would rid her legs of the annoying hairs.

Finally, she removed the top of the bath sheet and took a good long look at her ample breasts in the mirror. Pleased with the results of the last operation to enhance them, she massaged them, one at a time, with both hands, finally removing the towel completely and slipping into her favourite, pink floral satin robe. With her hair wrapped in a towel, Alex moved into her bedroom, where she spent ten minutes at work with her hairdryer and diffuser, ensuring her hair was just right before, eventually satisfied with her appearance, she stretched out on her bed, ready to return to her reading of the diary.

Ever since the diary had come into her possession, she had become obsessed with reading the entries, the self-confessed details relating to the murders of three young women back in nineteen sixty-six. She assumed it was nineteen sixty-six because that was the year printed on the front of the old Lett's diary. Somehow, reading and understanding the intricacies of the mind of the killer, caused her to experience a strange feeling between her legs, a tingling, almost a sexual thrill as she felt as though she was actually listening to the voice of the murderer all these years later. Or, was the diary just a cleverly written fake, a piece of fantasy writing by someone with a perverted mind, a sexual deviant from long ago? Alex knew more than enough about sexual feelings. She'd experienced enough turmoil in her own life based on sex.

* * *

I can't lose the feelings that have taken me over. I know I shouldn't have hurt Stella, I never meant to but she made it happen. Now it has I feel as if I want to do it again to feel that power and see the face as those final moments of life depart and she realises that she can't say no to me and get away with it.

Alex, almost subconsciously, reached down and began stimulating herself as her excitement grew at the chilling words she was reading. This, she had previously realised from reading the diary, was the actual genesis of a murder, and she was being given an insight into the mind of a killer such as few are ever allowed. She was a witness, years after the fact, and she found it excited her. She couldn't help wondering if this all made her some kind of pervert herself. She'd read enough over the years that led her to believe that some women actually fantasised about being raped, but, she thought, *Rape and murder? Does that mean I have some kind of death wish? I don't think for one minute that I want to be raped and certainly don't want to be murdered. Maybe subconsciously I have a need to be taken, to be overpowered. Oh hell, just what am I?*

Shaking herself, she returned to her reading.

If I do it again, I have to plan it carefully, so nobody will ever suspect me. Why should they anyway? But not worth taking chances. How? I know. Make sure it's a stranger. If I pick someone I know they might find out. But not a stranger. But how? Where? Need to think. I know. Stella. Must look like Stella. Make them think I have a thing about girls who look like Stella. They think I'm dumb, but I'm clever. Cleverer than they are. They won't catch me, can't catch me. But where do I find her, one like Stella? go? I know what to do. I'll watch them, pick one from there. They are always in the pubs at night, bound to be one who has the same hair, same shape and looks. I'll be a new sort of Jack the Ripper, that bloke in London they told us about in school and they never caught him, did they? And they won't catch me, will they? Who am I talking to? Who is it that's telling me to do this? I don't know, don't care. Have to go, time for work, bloody boring work. They make fun of me because I'm no good with the girls. Well, they're wrong. I can make the girls do whatever I want.

Alex slowly folded the diary closed, her hands trembling as she did so. Was the writer really being told to commit the murders by a voice in his head, perhaps? That would make him a real whack job, she thought. The thought lasted barely a minute. He couldn't have been. She just knew it, in the same way she knew the writings in those old, well-worn diary pages excited her in ways she couldn't fathom, nor did she really attempt to.

I've found her. She must be the one. Saw her in the Swan last night. Don't know her name, but she is perfect. Long, blonde hair, wearing a white blouse and a blue pleated skirt, short, showing her legs but not tarty. She has a lovely smile, just like Stella's. same height too, and a laugh so like Stella's, made me think of clinking glasses, don't know why, just the thought I had when she threw her head back and laughed at one of the men's jokes. I heard her tell the man she'd be back in two nights. She agreed she'd have a drink with him. I can't wait.

Enough for now. The next bit could wait. Alex put the diary down on her bedside cabinet, her hand trembling slightly as she did so. She cuddled up to her giant, pink, fluffy teddy bear and drew her knees up to her chest, curling up into a tight ball. It was time to sleep.

Chapter 12

Return of The Profiler

Andy Ross and Izzie Drake had just concluded giving D.C.I. Agostini the latest update on the case. Even as the pair delivered the details of their disappointingly negative progress so far, they knew they were facing an uphill task in a race against time to prevent a third murder. Oscar Agostini, knowing exactly how they were feeling, didn't mince words.

"Andy, Izzie, we don't have the luxury of time on this one. After giving it a lot of thought, I've decided we need help, outside help, if we want to catch this bastard,"

"But, sir..." Ross began, only to be silenced as the Chief held a hand up in the universal sign for silence.

"Just hear me out, Andy," Agostini went on. "I think you'll be in full agreement and pleasantly surprised when you hear what I have to tell you. After I'd gone home last night I received a call from D.C.S. Hollingsworth. The Chief Super, as you're aware, is under great pressure from the very top, and wants us to utilise every facility at our disposal to identify the killer. She told me she'd been in touch with the Home Office and has arranged for an old friend of yours to visit us and come up with a profile of our killer to help us direct our investigation in the right... well, the right direction."

"I presume you mean our friend Doctor Bland is coming to visit us once again," Ross replied, referring to the Home Office Profiler, Christine Bland, who'd been instrumental in assisting Ross's team with their investigation into a grisly series of murders in Liverpool's graveyards a couple of years previously.

"That's right, and she should be arriving any time now," Agostini smiled at the pair.

"But won't she need time to get up to speed on the case, sir," Drake asked. "We don't exactly have the luxury of time being on our side, do we?"

"Don't worry about that, Sergeant Drake," said the D.C.I. "The Chief Super had copies of the case files emailed down to London yesterday. Dr. Bland should be well up to speed with the case by the time she arrives."

Ross rose from his chair, and, seemingly in thought, walked across to the large, plate glass window that afforded Oscar Agostini a panoramic view of the city streets below the headquarters building. As though by magic, he was in time to see a pristine, almost vintage, burgundy coloured Vauxhall Carlton pull into one of the visitor spaces in the car park in front of the building. He knew the car to be Christine Bland's pride and joy, previously owned and maintained by her late father.

"If I'm not mistaken, she should be being escorted to your door within the next five minutes or so," he smiled at Agostini. "I just hope to God she can help. Lord knows we could do with some form of inspiration."

"You've seen her car down there," Drake responded to his prophecy.

"Anybody ever tell you, you ought to be a detective," Ross quipped at her observation.

"Ooh, now, there's a thought," she grinned back at him.

Sure enough, within Ross's prescribed five minutes, Doctor Christine Bland, Criminal and forensic psychologist and employed by the Home Office as a criminal profiler, was escorted into Agostini's office by a young constable, whose eyes, Ross noticed, appeared to be strictly focussed on Bland's shapely legs. Dressed as she was in a black two-piece skirt suit, similar to the one she'd arrived in the last time they'd worked together, he thought, the thirty-something, shapely and attractive profiler smiled warmly as she held her hand out to Ross, who quickly dismissed the constable as he shook hands, after which she followed the same procedure with Drake, and finally with the D.C.I. who had risen from his chair and walked around his desk to greet her.

Ross spoke first. "Christine, it's good to see you again,"

"You too Andy, and Izzie too. Shame about the circumstances though. How are you, D.C.I Agostini? I hope you've settled into the job, now. You'd only just taken over, the last time I was here, if I remember rightly."

"I'm doing fine, thanks," and it's Oscar, please," he replied.

"Good," she replied and moved straight into professional mode. "It appears in this case, time is our greatest enemy, apart from the killer himself, of course."

"I'm afraid so, Christine," said Ross, unhappily. "If we can't find this bugger fast, and I mean umber fast, we can expect the death of a young women police officer at the end of the week."

"Then we'd better not waste any time, had we? With your permission, Oscar, I'd like to say hello to the rest of Andy's team and then, I want to talk with the pathologist who carried out the autopsies on the two current victims. I'm presuming it was Doctor Nugent?"

She remembered only too well the obese but brilliant senior pathologist she'd met on her previous visit to the city, a real expert in his field and one with whom Ross had an excellent working relationship.

"Correct," Ross nodded. "As far as the case files are concerned, both crime scenes were virtually trace free and gave the original investigating officers little to go on."

"Even so, I'd like to talk with Doctor Nugent."

"No problem. Will you see if he can see us right away, Izzie, as soon as we're out of here?"

"Sure."

"Then consider yourselves gone," Agostini said quickly. "Now go, people and please, catch this murderous bastard, fast."

* * *

Paul Ferris and Derek McLennan led the welcome for Christine Bland as she accompanied Ross and Drake into the squad room. They remembered only too well the help she'd given them in the past. Paul Ferris who'd been a detective constable on the previous occasion they'd met, quickly introduced her to the German loanee, Sofie Meyer and their new Acting D.C. Gary Devenish, whose Nickname of *Ginger* had already been further shortened, thanks to Tony Curtis, to *Ginge!* While the doctor reacquainted herself with Sam Gable and Nick Dodds, who provided her with a coffee, Ross had been on the phone to the mortuary, where pathologist, Doctor William Nugent, affectionately known in private by the team as 'Fat Willie' due to the ever-increasing girth of his waistline, had agreed to see them right away. Ignoring the remains of her coffee, Christine Bland hastened to join Ross and Drake on a journey to the city mortuary laboratory, located in Pembroke Gardens, close to the Royal Liverpool University Hospital.

With Drake at the wheel, the unmarked Peugeot turned into the mortuary car park and the trio concluded their in-car conversation.

"Well, here we are, once again," said Ross, as he held the car door open for Christine to exit the vehicle, weighed down as she was by her briefcase in one hand and a bundle of case files in the other.

"Doesn't seem that long since we were here the last time, does it?" she smiled at him as she spoke.

"You're right, it doesn't, but as much as it's good to see you again, it's still too soon, if you know what I mean."

"I know exactly what you mean," Bland replied. "But come one, let's see if I can help you find this perpetrator in double quick time. Izzy, I never got chance to congratulate you on your marriage. I presume your husband will be here to let us in today?"

"Thanks, Christine, and yes, Peter is working today, so you'll get to meet him."

"How's the car going?" Ross asked her, changing the subject. In truth, he was trying to avoid talking about the reason for them being here as long as possible, to make sure Christine Bland's first impressions of the killer would come from reviewing the autopsy results. He was hoping against hope that the victims could somehow 'speak' to the attractive doctor in the unique way the dead have of releasing their secrets to those who know where to look, what questions remained to be answered.

After gaining admittance to the mortuary, ringing the visitors' doorbell and identifying themselves, the doors opened as if by magic, and they entered the world inhabited by Doctor William Nugent and of course, Izzy's husband, Peter Foster, the administrator of Mortuary Services, who greeted them and issued them with visitor passes. After being directed to examination room one, they followed the antiseptically clean corridor and none of them could avoid the smell that seemed to permeate the entire building as they neared the entrance to the domain of the pathologist. Antiseptic, formaldehyde, the smell of death!

Chapter 13

Pathology and Psychology

Doctor William Nugent, the city's chief pathologist, showed great delight in welcoming Christine Bland to his domain once more. He hadn't forgotten her previous visit to the city when she'd assisted Ross and his team in solving the particularly brutal slayings of several men in Liverpool's graveyards, which had appropriately enough come to be known as the 'Graveyard Murders'. Her reputation preceded her, and the obese but brilliant Glaswegian took a great delight in seeing her once more.

"Christine, so good to see you again," the rotund pathologist positively beamed at Bland.

"You too, Doctor Nugent," she replied.

"Och, come now, it's William, as you well know. No formality, please. And D.I. Ross and the beautiful Sergeant Drake, welcome as always."

Izzy smiled and nodded in reply.

Ross couldn't help smiling. It wasn't often they saw the obese pathologist quite so expansive in his greeting of visitors to his domain.

"Hello Doc," he said. "I hope we're not interrupting your work too much."

"Of course not, Inspector. Certainly not when you bring the beautiful Doctor Bland to visit me once again."

Ross couldn't help noticing a slight blush appear on Bland's face.

"So, you hope to help our dear detective inspector to solve this conundrum of a case? He directed the question to Bland.

"If I can, I will, William, but, according to Inspector Ross, there's very little forensic evidence to go on, is that correct?"

"Well, yes and no," the pathologist replied. "To say there's *no* forensic evidence is just a wee bit inaccurate."

"How so, Doc?" Ross asked.

"Francis, the file please," Nugent said and his erstwhile assistant, the cadaverous-looking Francis Lees hurried from the far side of the room, file in hand. Lees had been with Nugent longer than anyone cared to mention, and it was often joked that the tall, pale unsmiling man looked deader than some of the 'clients' worked on by the pathologists at the mortuary. Lees was, however, a superb forensic photographer, who seemed to know exactly what angle his photos of the dead should be taken from. He was also an expert in all manner of autopsy procedures and Nugent regarded him as almost indispensable.

Ross, Drake and Bland knew better than to interrupt the pathologist as he opened the file that Lees had passed to him and proceeded to relate the facts to them.

"Before I begin, and far be it from me to criticise one of your colleagues, Inspector Ross, I have to say that I was not impressed with your colleague, D.I. Morris, who oversaw these murders before you took over."

Ross already had his own suspicions that D.I. Morris hadn't been as attentive as she should have been to the details of the two murders but, not wanting to give the pathologist any insight into his own private thoughts and. being surprised at such a forthright comment from Nugent, simply replied, "Why's that, Doc?"

"Well, she is, in my opinion, a police officer who feels very comfortable with her own opinions but may have difficulty in accepting the help or advice offered by those in a position to help her."

Ross nodded, saying nothing, but realised that he wasn't the only person who had misgivings about Fiona Morris's handling of the case prior to it being handed over to his team. Just how it would impact on their ability to achieve a swift resolution and possibly prevent a third murder could only be guessed at for now.

"Please, Doc, tell us what you have. If D.I. Morris has been remiss in her handling of the information you provided her with, you can be sure I will be dealing with it."

"Aye, ah'm sure ye will," Nugent reverted to his pure Glaswegian accent, as he often did when angry or stressed. With an air of gravitas, Nugent slowly extricated the contents of the file Lees had handed him and laid the papers out on an empty autopsy table. Taking one of the sheets in his hand, he began.

"I was responsible for performing the post mortem examinations on both Catherine Billings, (he gave the first victim her full first name), and Hannah Lucas. In Catherine's case, it was clear from my examination that the poor wee girl was killed in the same location she was found. There was no evidence to suggest she had been moved post mortem. So, we had a relatively straightforward examination. True, there was little or no trace evidence present on the body, nor on the ground in the immediately surrounding area"

"You said 'little or no trace evidence," Bland interrupted. "The report that was sent to me led me to believe there was nothing helpful in either forensic examination."

"Ha, report compiled by D.I Morris, I presume," Nugent spoke disdainfully, and Ross and Drake shared a look that Drake knew meant that her boss wasn't pleased with D.I. Morris's handling of the case at all. Without waiting for a response from his visitors, Nugent continued. "My report, as you will see if you look closely, mentions the fact that Catherine was penetrated sexually, both vaginally and anally. Sufficient lubricant remained to indicate that her assailant used a condom. There were also small traces of a second lubricant being used."

"Another condom?" Drake asked.

"Possibly, but maybe not," said Nugent. "Analysis shows traces of a water-based lubricant, the sort used for making lovemaking easier for older women, having gone through the menopause, and needing extra lubrication, or to help with the penetration of anal sex."

"Why the hell would our killer need a sexual lubricant?" Drake pondered aloud. "And was there any evidence to suggest anal penetration had taken place in the second murder?"

"Good question, Izzy," Ross agreed. "Any thoughts, Christine?"

"Not yet, at least nothing specific," said Bland, waiting to hear the rest of Nugent's findings. Nugent continued.

"First of all, there was anal penetration in both cases, but I would say that, in my experience, not many rapists go to the trouble of being considerate enough to use a lubricant to enable them to perform the act of sodomy. But look, there's nae doubt in my mind that young Catherine was killed where she was found, as near as damn it. There were enough scuff marks on the path and in the nearby hedgerow to indicate where her attacker had first waylaid the lassie, and heel marks to show where he'd dragged her off the main path to where the rape took place, before he finally finished her off. However, in the case of young Hannah, ye need to be looking for her murder site. The car park at the lighthouse was simply a body dump in her case. We discovered enough trace evidence to suggest that the girl was killed on a concrete surface. Drag marks on her heels and in her hair contained residue consistent with her being pulled, on her back, across just such a surface. Its ma guess that her killer lured her into a building of some kind, or maybe even took her there in a car, possibly unconscious, before raping and killing the lassie and then taking her body to the lighthouse to be left in the open to be discovered later. It's all in ma report. I'm surprised ye didnae see it for yourself, D.I. Ross."

Andy Ross was fuming inside. He now knew that the murder reports he'd been given by the original investigators had been incomplete, or worse, nothing more than a précis of the facts. He would make sure that Fiona Morris was taken to task over this when he returned to headquarters. *What the hell was the woman thinking?*

"I'll be totally honest with you, Doc, it's beginning to look as if we were only given half the information we should have received when we took over this case. Please, go on, if there's anything to add that is."

Nugent gave Ross a telling look, one that said he knew exactly what the detective was thinking, and that he sympathised with his feelings. There was no need for him to mention it, knowing full well that Ross's wrath would be sure to descend upon the young D.I. before long.

"Unfortunately, there's not a lot to add, Inspector. I wish there was more."

Christine Bland, who had remained relatively quiet in the background so far, now made a comment.

"Doctor Nugent, can you state without a doubt, as a result of your examinations, that both women were penetrated by a male penis?"

A look of shock appeared on the faces of both Ross and Drake as they both wondered just where Bland was going with this. Both women had been raped. That much, they had both taken for granted.

"A strange question, Christine," Nugent replied, "but in the circumstances, perhaps a relevant one."

"Okay, just what are you thinking?" Ross asked the profiler, before Nugent could say any more.

"Just thinking outside the box for a minute," Bland replied. "What if your killer who clearly wants to replicate the murders of nineteen sixty-six, is simply, for whatever reason, unable to achieve penile penetration? William, is there anything, forensically speaking, to suggest that the killer may have used some implement to carry out the rape and sodomy of the two women?"

"Bloody hell," Ross exclaimed, looking expectantly at the pathologist as he awaited his reply.

"Aye, well, now there's a good question," Nugent said, not sure how to reply for a minute, so he deflected the question initially. "What do you mean by the nineteen sixty-six killings?"

"You haven't been told that this is series of copycat killings?" Bland asked, almost accusingly.

"Don't blame me," Ross said quickly. "Don't forget, the theory of the copycat has only existed since Stan Coleman contacted D.I. Morris's boss, after which the case came to us. Doctor Nugent would have carried out the autopsies on Cathy Billings and Hannah Lucas before the possibility of the copycat killer came to our notice.

"Ah think ye'd better be telling me about these nineteen sixty-six killings," Nugent said, as though he'd been the only kid on the block not invited to a party.

Ross and Drake quickly brought Nugent up to speed on the Lighthouse Murders of 1966, and as Drake completed the telling of the tale, William Nugent nodded sagely, and fell silent for a few seconds. At last, he spoke.

"Okay," he began, "If I'd known about the previous murders, I could have looked for comparisons. They may have taken place almost forty years ago, but the autopsy records should still exist on file somewhere and who knows, I may be able to help you in some way."

Andy Ross was beginning to feel as if this case was getting away from him. Nothing gelled, everything was a disjointed mish-mash of information and non-information and the half-hearted investigative work carried out by Fiona Morris was doing nothing for his demeanour.

"Surely, you're not telling me the NHS keeps records going back almost forty years, Doc. I would have thought autopsy records beyond a certain date would have been shredded long ago."

"Och, ye of little faith," Nugent replied, almost smiling in the process. "When it comes to something as personal and private as people's health, or in this case, their deaths, the National Health Service is renowned for its painstaking attention to detail and record keeping, surpassed possible, only by the authorities in Hitler's Third Reich."

Ross was grateful that Sofie Meyer wasn't with him. She might easily have taken offence at Nugent's last remark.

"But surely, if every record of every person ever treated by the NHS was stored for ever, you'd need a building as big as the Great Pyramid to keep them in."

"More like three pyramids," Drake added.

"Ah, but, it's a lot simpler than you think," the pathologist said. "Most hospitals in the country have always had an archives department where records were stored and from the late seventies, as computers began to be introduced, those records were gradually transferred, originally to computer discs, and later, compressed further as technology advanced until they can now be stored on a few external memory drives. If your victims were autopsied here in Liverpool, I can find the records of those examinations, believe me."

"It's true, Andy," Christine Bland confirmed Nugent's words. "You might be amazed at the full scope of the record keeping of the NHS. Now, about that broken finger you suffered as a boy…"

"What?" Ross almost sputtered at the thought of Bland knowing about that minor detail from his childhood, but then smiled. "You almost had me there," he laughed. "I told you about that the last time you were here. You'd noticed how I held my pen and commented on it so I told you about the accident when I was ten."

"But if I wanted to, I could probably find out what you had for breakfast while you were in the Children's Ward," Bland laughed with him.

"Ahem," they were interrupted by William Nugent. "If you'd like me to proceed."

"Sorry Doc, yes, please, go on."

"Aye, well, truth be told, there's not a lot more I can add. There was very little forensic evidence present at either scene, though as I said, you are definitely looking for another murder scene in the case of Hannah Lucas. There was one thing that piqued my interest a wee bit though."

"Aha. If it piqued your interest, then it's sure to do the same for me. Please tell us, Doc," Ross commented with a note of anticipation in his voice.

"A hair. One, single, solitary hair," said Nugent. "But, the thing is, this particular hair, which I found lodged in Hannah Lucas's pubic hair, is definitely not human."

That comment brought a look of amazement to the faces of the two detectives. Christine Bland's face remained impassive.

"So, what kind of hair is it, Doc?" Ross asked, impatiently.

"It's canine." Nugent replied, his face deadpan as he delivered his pronouncement.

"So, what? You're saying she was killed by a bloody Cocker Spaniel?"

"Oh no, of course not, Inspector, and sarcasm doesn't become you, I must say."

Ross's impatience was growing, as Izzie Drake could tell. She did her best to hurry Nugent along.

"We know that, of course, Doctor Nugent, but we are in something of a race against time to stop this killer from killing again. D.I. Ross may not have mentioned it, but the third victim back in nineteen sixty-six was a woman police constable and so far, he's stuck to victims with the same professions as the victims back then."

"Ah, right I see, why didn't you say so?" Nugent rebuked Ross.

"Because it doesn't matter what the victim's occupation is or was, we have to find this bastard quickly, Doc, so, if you don't mind, this hair of yours, please?"

"Very well, nae problem. As I said, I thought it a wee bit incongruous. I mean, finding a dog hair in such a place isn't exactly normal. I asked D.I. Morris if Hannah Lucas had a dog of her own, and the answer was no. Neither did anyone in her immediate family have a dog. So my thoughts are, and of course, I'm not a detective is that at some time, a dog encountered Hannah's body."

"Could the contact not have come before her death?" Drake asked.

"Unlikely, Sergeant Drake. Bear in mind that Hannah was found naked from the waist down, her skirt hitched up above her waist, so the dog must have come into contact with her body while she was exposed to the elements. Or, and this is an equal possibility, the dog hair was already on the ground and was transferred to her body from contact with her killer. I doubt she would have allowed a dog hair to be trapped in her pubic hair in any normal day to day activity."

"In other words, the hair could mean something or nothing," Ross said, impatience still evident in his tone of voice.

"Aye, well, I did say it was an incongruity. Whether it's important or not is for you and your people to decide."

"Wait a minute though," Ross suddenly exclaimed. "Hannah was a veterinary student. The killer had to find a way to lure her into his clutches. What if he used a dog to get her attention and then hit her with a blitz attack before she realised what was happening?"

"That would indicate he had a dog of his own," Drake added.

"Or he'd borrowed one," Bland added.

"Of course," Nugent said, playing devil's advocate, "it's equally possible the dog hair became embedded in her clothing at an earlier time and was then simply transferred to her body when she was dressing."

"So the dog hair might be something or nothing," Ross concluded, slightly disappointed.

"Aye, well, I did say it was just an… "

"An incongruity, I know, Doc."

"Now dinna you go shooting the messenger, Inspector," Nugent bristled.

"I'm not, ok? Listen, Doc, if I get Paul Ferris to send you the details of the historical victims, could you do what you can to find those autopsy records and do a comparison with your latest ones, please?" Ross asked in a more placatory tone.

"Aye, of course. I'll get Francis searching as soon as we know who we're looking for."

"Izzie, get on the phone and ask Paul to send those details across asap, will you?"

Drake already had her phone out and was dialling before he'd finished speaking.

On the drive back to headquarters Ross asked Christine Bland two important question.

"Christine, has your visit to the morgue helped you in any way? Has it given you any insights into who we could be searching for?

Give me an hour to think about it and I'll try and come up with something" she replied.

It wasn't exactly the answer Ross was hoping for. For the first time in a long time, he was getting a bad feeling about a case. If the police had been unable to find one solid lead back in '66, what chance did he and his team have of being more successful this time around?

Chapter 14

A Profile of sorts

Christine Bland spent an uncomfortable evening at the Crown Plaza Hotel in Liverpool's City Centre. Uncomfortable in as much as her mind was racing, trying to put together a profile of the killer of two young women, who, she knew, had a third target in mind, and yet the evidence presented to her so far was minimal to say the very least. Her meal of lamb chops, served with new potatoes, garden peas and runner beans, failed to excite her taste buds, despite being one her favourites. The waiter who came to clear her plate away probably thought the pretty blonde woman in the white sweater and designer jeans was pining for a lost lover, or suffering from a recent bereavement, such was the blank look that greeted him as he asked if she'd enjoyed her meal.

"What, eh? Oh yes, sorry, I was miles away," she responded eventually, and the young man slowly began to clear her half-eaten meal away.

"Was there anything wrong with the chops?" he enquired, politely.

"No, they were just lovely. I'm afraid I have some heavy problems to sort out at work, and I seem to have lost my appetite."

The young waiter nodded as though he was used to hearing such excuses on a regular basis and smiled sympathetically as he asked, "Would you like dessert, at all?"

"No, thank you. Just coffee please."

Soon afterwards, she was back in her room, her bed strewn with every piece of paper she'd acquired, with Christine sitting amidst the apparent chaos with a legal pad and a pen in her hand, occasionally looking up from her reading material to stop and make notes in her attempt to put together a profile that might assist Andy Ross and his team. After a predominantly sleepless night, she rose early, showered and dressed and after a frugal breakfast of scrambled eggs on toast and coffee in the dining room, she made her way the car park where her car sat, waiting to carry her to police headquarters, the gleaming Vauxhall Carlton her own personal reminder of her father. She always thought of him as she sat and turned the ignition key and remembered Sunday afternoons when she would help him to wash and polish his pride and joy. Now, it was hers. Parking in a visitor spot in the car park at Police headquarters, she gathered her briefcase and files and before long, found herself facing the morning briefing called by Andy Ross, and attended by his full team.

"Most of you know me from my last visit to assist your team a couple of years ago," Christine Bland began as she faced an expectant group of murder squad detectives in the briefing room. "Those who've joined D.I. Ross's team more recently will I'm sure have been told about me and what I do. Are there any questions before I begin? No? Good. So, can I just say, in advance, that after studying the case files forwarded to me by your Chief Superintendent, and others since passed to me by D.I. Ross and Doctor Nugent, I must confess that this is one of the toughest cases I have ever come across, in terms of profiling the person we are looking for. The lack of forensic and trace evidence is significant of course, but then again, the circumstances relating to the murders is quite baffling.

It's been suggested that because the original killings took place in 1966, thirty-nine years ago, then the current killer must be someone younger, either a relative of the original killer, or a copycat, armed with the full facts of the original Lighthouse murders. I ask you to consider this, however. If the Lighthouse murderer was in his late teens or early twenties at the time of the murders, he would now be in his fifties or perhaps his sixties. There is absolutely nothing to suggest that a man of that age, if fit and healthy, couldn't be repeating his crimes at this point in time. So, on that basis, your original killer may have begun repeating his earlier crimes, for reasons we are not aware of."

"But Doctor Bland," Derek McLennan interrupted. "Why wait thirty-nine years? Why not thirty, or forty, you know, a nice round figure?"

"Because, D.C. McLennan, the killer has an agenda that we are not privy to. Whether this is the work of the original murderer from 66, or that of a copycat, to him, this all makes perfect sense. It may be that the perpetrator has just celebrated a significant birthday, or maybe has just lost his job and finds himself driven to kill by the boredom of unemployment. At present I have so little to go on it's impossible to say what the exact motive for these killings is."

"So, are you saying we're looking for a fifty to sixty years old man, who has just lost his job or has recently celebrated his birthday?" McLennan asked.

"Or both maybe?" D.C. Curtis added, facetiously.

"Not at all," Bland replied. "I'm just saying that these are potential motivators for your killer. I would need to know more before I can go that far."

"So what exactly can you tell us about the killer, Doctor?" Sofie Meyer spoke with a serious look on her face. The German officer had a particular hatred of men who killed in the act of raping women. She viewed such crimes as being doubly heinous, first, the degradation and humiliation of the woman through the violence of rape, and secondly by the vile and cowardly act of murdering a weakened and already traumatised victim. She was determined that the killer would not get the opportunity to carry out what was undoubtedly the third murder on his agenda.

Christine Bland pulled a wry face. It wasn't like her to be faced with a dilemma such as she was now about to admit to and it didn't sit well with her, from a professional standpoint.

"Sergeant Meyer, I have to be brutally honest here. In order to draw up an effective profile, I would need far more information than seems to be available at present. I'm hoping that by obtaining copies of the autopsy reports from the so-called Lighthouse murders, I may be able to compare the victimology in both sets of murders to arrive at a profile that will help you."

"So, are saying you cannot provide a profile for this killer?"

Sofie Meyer was nothing if not direct. Normally this would be a trait Bland admired but this morning she felt as if the woman was putting her on the spot and she inwardly squirmed.

"I can give you something, but nothing as detailed as I would like to."

"Please, Christine, I don't expect miracles, but give us what you think, so far," Ross spoke encouragingly.

"Very well, Inspector. As I have already stated, it is not outside the bounds of possibility that the killer is the same individual who committed the murders in 1966, though my conclusion is that that is not the case. Why? Well, there are subtle differences in the killer's M.O. from then compared to now. For one thing, there is the lack of sperm present in or on the bodies of the current victims. Yes, it could be a forensic counter-measure by the killer, using condoms to deny us a DNA sample. Now, I believe it is a forensic counter-measure but by a younger, more forensically aware individual. In 1966 there was no such thing as DNA testing or profiling so the fact that the killer back then left no forensic or trace evidence was, I believe, pure luck on his part. This killer is smarter, and also has access to a garage or warehouse type building."

"What makes you say that," Nick Dodds asked.

"Because in the case of Hannah Lucas, the scratches on her heels indicate she was dragged along a concrete surface, not killed either on the lane leading to, or in the lighthouse car park which has an asphalt surface. Whereas the original investigators concluded that their killer used victims of opportunity, this individual is carefully selecting his victims to match those of the Lighthouse murders. There is a level of sophistication here that wasn't present back in '66. There is also a presence of a second type of lubrication here, in addition to that normally present when a condom has been used. I suspect the killer has used a lubricating gel to facilitate the insertion of some form of sex toy, into either the vagina or anus, or both, of his victims."

"Bugger me," exclaimed Tony Curtis, eliciting a frown of disapproval from Ross, echoed by a look of equal ire from Izzie Drake. Curtis shrank in his seat.

"Yes, well," Bland continued, ignoring Curtis's facetious comment, "this suggests to me that we are looking for a white male, possibly in the thirty to forty age range, powerfully built, and who has access to a vehicle for transporting his victims. Another reason for suspecting a new, second killer, is that this killer is more sadistic than the original murderer, as evidenced by the use of sex toys or other objects to inflict pain and humiliation on his victims. This perpetrator is enjoying what he's doing. He's not acting from compulsion or mental illness. He's a sadist, doing it for fun. He also has full knowledge of the original crimes of thirty-nine years ago. This suggests he's either a relative of the original killer who has been meticulously schooled by the older man, or he has access to a written record of the original murders."

"You mean, like a journal or a diary?" Sam Gable asked.

"Yes, perhaps, in which case we also have to realise he may not be related to the first killer at all. He may have simply come across such a document by accident. If the original killer died and his house was sold and passed into new hands, the written record might have been hidden in a cellar or somewhere similar and today's killer simply found it after moving in. Having read it and been turned on by it, he may have decided to recreate the events to satisfy his own desires."

"So, do you think the dog hair meant anything?" Drake asked, and then had to explain to the others what Doctor Nugent had found embedded in Hannah's pubic hair.

"Not necessarily," Bland replied. "Hannah was left naked from the waist down out in the open. That hair might have just been blown by the wind and got caught in her hairs as she lay dead, waiting to be discovered."

"So we forget about it?"

"Not necessarily," Ross interrupted. "There's still an outside chance the dog hair came in some way from our killer."

"She was a veterinary student, sir. Could the hair be from a dog she encountered during her studies?" Curtis asked.

"Unlikely, Tony. Inquiries showed that Hannah was involved in lectures in the week preceding her murder. She would have had no direct contact with animals, except maybe family pets, which the family didn't have, during that time," Ross replied. "Until we know better, let's leave no stone unturned, people, got that?"

A collective nodding of heads and murmurs of agreement followed Ross's direction. Christine Bland, feeling professionally depressed at not being able to provide a comprehensive profile, continued.

"Under normal circumstances I would have been able to give you a better idea of who we're looking for. As it is, unless the autopsy results from the 1966 murders throw up further evidence, it looks as if I haven't been of much use to you this time. I'm sorry,"

"Christine, the last thing we want is your apologies," Ross sprung to her defence. "You drove up here to help us and you have helped us. You've given us an idea of the mentality behind the murders and an idea of what we're up against. In fact, your profile, such as it is, has given me an idea. Listen up everyone. As of now, I want the people of Hale looked at very closely. In particular, let's go back to 1966. The original investigation should tell us who was in the pub on the night of Stella Cox's murder. Paul and Kat," he turned to Ferris and his admin assistant. "I want you two to look into those present in the pub that night, who went on to have children. How many of those kids fall into the age range specified by Doctor Bland, and then subdivide them into those living in Hale today and those who have left the area. I know it's a big job, but with your wizardry on the computers, I'm counting on you to find the information, ok?"

"Ok sir, we're on it," Ferris immediately turned to his screen and began tapping away on his keyboard, Kat Bellamy sat beside him as they devised a game plan.

Turning to Sofie Meyer, Ross now said, "Sofie, you and Nick can look at those who were already in the age range of eight to twenty-five at the time of Stella's murder. Any of them could be our killer but look closely at those of teenage years at the time of the murders."

"Very well, sir. You can count on us," Meyer replied. Nick Dodds nodded to Ross, pleased to be working with the pretty German sergeant.

"What about me and Ginger, sir?" asked Sam Gable, including young Acting D.C. Gary Devenish in her question.

"Okay you two, I want you to retrace the steps of both Cathy Billings and Hannah Lucas going back as far as two weeks before Cathy's murder. Somewhere, there must be some common denominator, some point of reference that brought them both into contact with their killer. Talk to their families again, to their friends, colleagues, workmates, anyone who knew them. I know we've done this already but sometimes people remember things after the passage of time. I can't get over the thought that we're missing something, somewhere. I know it's a pretty thankless task, but it has to be done, and quickly."

"No problem sir," Sam replied. "If there's anything to find, we'll dig it up, right Ginge?"

"Right, Sam," Devenish replied. "We won't let you down, sir."

"Good lad," Ross smiled at his latest recruit to the team.

"Right, let's go. Izzie and I are going to take Christine back to see Doctor Nugent and see if he's located the old autopsies. If he's found them, I want to know how they relate to the deaths of Cathy and Hannah. We need a connection people. Let's find it. I also want to go over the information on those guys on the Sex Offenders Register once more, just to see if one of them might have a historical connection to anyone involved in either case."

In the space of two minutes, after much scraping of chairs, the room was empty, apart from one detective sergeant and an admin assistant, studiously tapping on their keyboards. Ferris and Bellamy shared a look that said they wouldn't rise from their computer stations until they found something, anything, that would help the investigation.

Chapter 15

Sex and Alex

It was late in the afternoon. Alex would be working later that night, so was making sure she had a rest, wanting to be wide awake at work. Sleep, however, evaded her as her mind filled with thoughts of what she'd read in the diary. She had quickly realised that the diary was providing her with a sexual stimulus. For reasons she found difficult to explain to herself, reading the killer's words, sometimes reading the words out loud as he described the things he'd done to his victims, gave her a feeling between her legs that she could only describe as arousal. Arousal, something she hadn't experienced in a long time, until recently. She still didn't know if the diary was a true rendering of a serial killer's murders or a work of fantasy by a warped, deviant mind. But she couldn't deny the feelings of arousal.

Arousal! Now, there was a novelty in Alex's life. She lay naked on top of her duvet, the cover a very feminine floral pink and white design that matched the overall décor of her bedroom. Allowing her legs to fall open, the fingers of her right hand slowly strayed down to her nether regions, where she attempted to stimulate herself to satisfaction, only to fail, as usual.

"Shit! Bloody shit and damnation," she screamed in frustration at the ceiling, throwing her pillow at the wall, watching it bounce and soundlessly fall to the bedroom floor. "Why, why, why?" she wailed as her screams turned to sobs. Snapping her knees together, Alex curled up into a tight foetal position, hugging her legs close to her body as she sobbed quietly into her other pillow.

When the tears subsided, she rose slowly from the bed, and stood before the full-length mirror that adorned the right-hand door of her wardrobe. Her eyes took in every inch of her nakedness, coming finally to rest on the just visible operation scars that she hoped would have disappeared by now. The doctor had promised they would gradually fade, but to Alex, they still appeared raw and easily visible, though to anyone else they would indeed have been almost imperceptible.

Opening the other wardrobe door she reached inside and removed a gaudily patterned satin effect housecoat, decorated with exotic birds in myriad colours. Wrapping it around herself, she exited her bedroom, knowing sleep to be a virtual impossibility. Alex instead made for the lounge, where an already opened bottle of Bombay Sapphire gin stood, on her glass-topped coffee table, beside a couple of yet unopened bottles of India Tonic Water. Ignoring the tonic water, she poured a large measure of gin into a waiting tumbler and gulped it down in one. Coughing, she poured another large one, and drank it a little slower than the first.

"This is no good," she said to herself. "I need that bloody job. Wouldn't do to turn up drunk and get myself fired, would it?"

As she drained the last of her second large gin, sans tonic, she felt a wave of tiredness slowly overwhelm her. Placing her feet on the empty side of the coffee table, she allowed her head to rest against the back of the sofa and closed her eyes. Within seconds, Alex fell into a deep yet fitful sleep, beset by dreams based on the contents of the diary that sat on her bedside table, having been untouched for over twenty-four hours. Alex's fevered mind conjured up images of death, of blood and fear. So much fear that when she woke with a start after just over an hour, she found she was sweating profusely despite wearing only the thin satin housecoat. She hadn't bothered to pull on any underwear when she'd left her bedroom.

Alex sat up, crossing her legs and staring at the gin bottle on the coffee table. Tempted, she managed to resist further risk of intoxication and seeing the top of the bottle lying on the carpet below the table, she reached down and replaced it in its place on the bottle. She rose, carrying the bottle with her to the kitchen, where she placed it carefully in one of the overhead kitchen cabinets, first ensuring she'd screwed the top firmly in place.

A glance at the clock told her she should eat. Her fridge revealed little to tempt her pallet, however. Alex knew she'd been neglecting the basics recently, and shopping had been low on her list of priorities. The salad drawer contained two rather soft tomatoes, a half-used iceberg lettuce, brown at the edges, and a cucumber that had begun to turn to mush. As for the rest, a block of cheddar cheese already had a blue mould creeping along one side, and even the tub of spreadable butter was almost empty.

The freezer wasn't much better, the only item present in its frozen interior being a pepperoni pizza. The rest of the contents comprised various packs of frozen vegetables, peas, green beans, cauliflower and a couple of frozen ready meals that looked decidedly unappetising.

While she waited for the pizza to heat up in the oven, Alex considered reading a couple of pages of the diary, but for once, decided against it. She'd already suffered a bad dose of sexual frustration in her bedroom, so, why compound it by getting all worked up again, and getting nowhere? After devouring three quarters of the pizza, and disposing of the rest in the kitchen bin, Alex spent a few minutes watching a mind-numbing TV documentary about a tribe of 'lost' Amazonian Indians and then decided to take her time in getting ready for work.

After showering, drying her hair and moisturising her skin from head to toe, Alex sat at her dressing table in bra and panties, carefully applying her make up, and then, after casting a covetous look at the diary beside her bed, she rose and moved to her wardrobe. A few minutes later, she stood before the mirror, dressed in her uniform of white blouse with black bow tie effect, lined black knee length pencil skirt, black hold-up stockings and gleaming patent leather heels. Satisfied that she looked the part, Alex felt ready for another night at the Pink Pelican. In the semi-darkness of the nightclub, she felt less conspicuous than she would in a normal day job.

With a few minutes to spare before her friend, Lisa arrived to pick her up in the car, she again contemplated spending some time in browsing through the diary, perhaps giving herself a few moments of temporary stimulation, but decided against it. She went as far as taking it from the drawer before coming to the decision to leave it alone for now. Her own feelings would have to wait until later. For the next few hours, she had to focus on the punters. They were the ones who paid her wages, after all. The sound of a car door closing outside beneath her window signalled her friend's arrival. Lisa was one of the few people who Alex could call a friend, perhaps the only one who respected her as a person. She didn't mind driving the few miles from her home across the river to Alex's house on Falkner Street, to pick her up for work, always dropping her off in the early hours of the morning, saving Alex the expense of paying for a taxi home, as most of the girls at the club were forced to do. Alex suspected that Lisa held some definite lesbian feelings towards her and had even contemplated putting her to the test one day, but not yet. Perhaps when the timing was right, but not until then.

Picking up the diary and carefully placing it in the top drawer of her bedside cabinet, under the neatly arranged collection of open-crotch panties, lubricants and sex toys, Alex sighed and promised herself to revisit her reading source on her return. Then, in a moment of indecision, she changed her mind. Knowing it would be late when she eventually returned home, and not expecting anyone would be breaking in and reading it in her absence, she removed it from the drawer and instead placed it on her bedside cabinet, ready to read a soon as she came to bed later. For now, though, it was time to go to work.

Chapter 16

Division of labour

Golden rays of mid-morning sunshine streamed through the wide expanse of the plate glass window that allowed Detective Chief Superintendent Sarah Hollingsworth a panoramic outlook across the city she helped to protect, with a spectacular view of the Albert Dock, now one of the city's chief tourist attractions. Her top floor office commanded a view that ranked with the finest in the city, but at this particular moment, as she stood staring out at the scene below and beyond the confines of police headquarters, her thoughts were far away from any such consideration.

Turning back to face the small gathering of visitors to her domain, she stepped slowly back to her wide and highly polished mahogany desk seating herself in the plush dark tan leather swivelling chair her husband had bought her for her birthday a month ago.

She looked up towards the ceiling for a moment, staring at a ray of sunshine that split the air in the room, carrying with it an annoying squadron of dust motes. Andy Ross fought back the urge to grin, as he imagined her ordering the dust motes out of her otherwise pristine office. Obviously, his attempt wasn't wholly successful.

"Is something amusing you, D.I. Ross?" Hollingsworth inquired, as she turned to face D.C.I. Oscar Agostini, Doctor Christine Bland, Ross and Izzie Drake,

"Erm, no Ma'am," Ross replied uncomfortably. "Just a random thought about my wife," he lied.

"I see. Well, let's keep to business, shall we? I'm sure none of you need me to tell you about the pressure we're getting from the Chief Constable on this case."

"No, of course we don't, Ma'am," Agostini replied. "D.I. Ross and his team are working flat out, trying to identify this bastard killer, before he gets the chance to strike again."

"And if he does strike again, it will probably mean the death of one of our own," Hollingsworth spoke sternly. "And that is totally unacceptable. The Deputy Chief Constable left my office half an hour ago, with the Chief constable's words ringing in my ears. Just how close are you to identifying a viable suspect?"

"To be honest, we have a few persons of interest in our sights, but no definitive prime suspect, Ma'am," Ross replied.

"I don't mind telling you that the Chief is so concerned with the potential for disaster that he's considering pulling all female officers off the streets and ordering them to stay at home for the twenty-four hours of the seventh day."

"With respect, Ma'am," said Agostini, "I don't see how that would help. If this man is going to strike again it's unlikely he'd go after an officer on duty and if he's already targeted a victim, he'll have worked out a way to get to her wherever she is."

"Which is exactly what I just told the Deputy Chief," Hollingsworth replied. "I also have the Chief's authority to allocate any extra manpower you and your team need."

"We can always use extra manpower," Agostini acknowledged, "but it's up to D.I. Ross how any extra bodies you can provide would be best utilised."

"Well Ma'am," Ross said, after a few seconds thought, "If you can give me another dozen uniforms and a couple of extra detectives, I can flood the streets of Hale with a large police presence, which just might deter the killer from taking any action. The detectives would be a great help in allowing me to give some of my people a few hours to rest and sleep. They are going at it flat out at present and they can work a damn sight better if they're fresh and rested. Tiredness can lead to sloppiness and mistakes and we can't afford that to happen."

"I agree," Hollingsworth nodded. "You won't have two additional detectives though. I will arrange for the temporary attachment of five officers from C.I.D. You can use them as you see fit, until the conclusion of the case."

"Thanks, ma'am."

Hollingsworth nodded to Ross and turned to the profiler.

"Doctor Bland. I appreciate you coming up to help us, but D.C.I. Agostini informs me you haven't been able to be too precise in your attempts to provide a profile of the killer."

"I'm sorry, but yes, that's true. As much as I would like to give your people something more tangible than I've come up with, it just hasn't been possible in the time available, with the scant information and evidence that has been provided so far."

"That's not quite true, Doctor, according to the chief inspector. He tells me you've at least come up with a basic profile of the type of person we're looking for. Please don't think my words a minute ago were in any way a criticism of you r abilities, because they weren't. Every scrap of intel we can garner goes some way towards catching the perpetrator."

Bland visibly relaxed a little. She had indeed thought that the Chief Super's words had carried an implied accusation of failure, something the Home Office profiler wasn't used to experiencing.

"Thank you. I will of course stay and continue to offer my services if I'm still welcome, and perhaps when Doctor Nugent is able to produce the autopsy reports from 1966, we might get a little further in our assessment of the mind of the killer."

"I'm sure we're all happy for you to stay and offer us your valuable insights," Hollingsworth replied, as she brought the brief meeting to a close.

"I won't keep you all any longer. I had to see you to hear for myself how far along you are with the investigation. I won't wish you luck,

D.I. Ross and Sergeant Drake. I know you both well enough to know that you and your team tend not to rely on luck. You are usually quite adept at making your own!"

* * *

"Sir," Sergeant Paul Ferris intercepted Ross and Drake as they returned to the squad room.

"You look excited Paul, what have you found?"

Ross and Drake stood behind Ferris and Kat Bellamy as they sat side by side at their computer stations.

"We've been looking into every aspect of the families who were living in Hale at the time of the first Lighthouse murders and it seems your two friends, the Cretinghams haven't been entirely honest with you."

Intrigued, Ross tapped Ferris on the shoulder and urged him to continue.

"Well, sir, Albert Cretingham senior hasn't mentioned his brother to you at all has he?"

"What bloody brother?"

"It appears that Albert Cretingham had a younger brother. Kat came across this information after cross checking the Births, Death and Marriages Registers. Albert was nineteen at the time of the murders, but he had a brother, Edwin, who also lived at home, but only some of the time. Edwin was five years younger than Albert but unlike his brother, he was a very disturbed child. He had behavioural problems and was disruptive at school. As far as I can make out from the sketchy information available, Edwin wasn't living at home at the time of the murders. He was so disruptive that he was taken into care and spent most of formative years in foster care or children's homes. It may not have any relevance to our inquiry, but it is a small anomaly, and like you've always said, every little detail goes towards building the bigger picture."

"You're right, of course, Paul, and well-done Kat. I think it's worth having another word with Albert Cretingham senior. Fancy a trip out to Hale after we've spoken with Doctor Nugent, Christine? I'd appreciate your thoughts on the Cretinghams to tell the truth."

"I'll be happy to accompany you, of course," Christine Bland replied.

"Good, maybe you can profile the elder of the two for me. Something doesn't seem to sit right with me where the two Alberts are concerned."

* * *

Doctor William Nugent was ready and waiting for them when they arrived at the mortuary. Ross was pleased that for once, they were able to meet the pathologist in his office rather than holding a discussion over an autopsy table containing the mortal remains of some poor soul, in various stages of forensic dissection.

"Come in everyone, please. Take a seat. I've asked Francis to organise coffee for everyone. I hope that's ok. We rarely drink tea ourselves, so we don't really have any apart from a few cheap tea bags."

"Coffee's fine Doc, thanks," Ross replied. Izzie thought it weird that they were about to sit drinking coffee in a place where they were surrounded by the dead. Nothing could ever quite disguise the smell of the mortuary building. She often wondered how her husband, Peter, the mortuary administrator, could work in the place all day and yet arrive home smelling as sweet as a mountain stream. As he often explained, his job didn't bring him into direct contact with the dead, though Izzie still thought the smell was all-pervading, and just blessed the miracle that allowed him to evade it on his clothes and more importantly, on his body.

After Lees had delivered the coffees, he took up his customary stance behind Nugent, hovering, as Drake always thought, like a praying mantis, ready to strike at a moment's notice in defence of his master, the obese but brilliant pathologist.

"Now, please listen carefully," Nugent began. "I have, with much difficulty I might add, located the autopsy reports from what were dubbed 'The Lighthouse Murders' back in 1966. Of course, I was not around in those days and the procedures adopted by my predecessors, although exact enough for the day, were not as meticulous as those we adopt in this modern era of forensic science, or in tune with our current medical knowledge. That is not to say the original autopsies were conducted incorrectly, but let us just say that they were clearly not conducted as I would have done, d'ye catch ma drift?" The Glaswegian accent was slipping into his speech again, a sure sign he was becoming excited about something.

"Okay, Doc, we understand where you're coming from," Ross wanted him to get on with it. "Please, tell us what you found."

"Aye, of course. Well now, let me start by saying that, compared with the two murders you are currently investigating there was far more forensic evidence pertaining to the earlier murders."

"There was?" Ross was surprised.

"Och aye, Inspector Ross. Dinna sound so surprised. It was there, but they just didnae have the technology to do anything with it almost forty years ago. Take the DNA for example."

"You have DNA from the earlier killings?" Drake interjected.

"We do indeed Sergeant. This is what happens in what you call a cold case, I believe. The evidence is stored until such times as you people decide to reactivate the case. With so many cold cases on your files I fully understand why not every case can be regularly looked at, but in many cases, the evidence is there, just ready and waiting to be revisited by your good selves."

"So what have you got for us?" Ross asked.

"The most obvious one is semen samples from all three of the original murders. It's still in existence and if you ever come up with a viable suspect, I daresay we could provide a match for you if it's the same killer."

"And suppose it's a relative, like a son for example?" Drake pushed further.

"Of course. We would be able to confirm a familial match if one existed.

"That's great Doc," said Ross, "but that only helps if we have something to compare it against. What else do we have?"

"In the case of Stella Cox, there was bloodstained clothing. That clothing should still be in your police evidence room. It could be that Stella fought with her attacker and there could be further DNA evidence on the clothing. Not only that, but there was blood under the girl's fingernails and I can't imagine her scratching herself, can you?"

"That's even better," Ross was getting excited. "It's a bloody shame they couldn't test for DNA back then. They'd have probably caught the little scrote in no time."

"They were able to determine the blood group of the owner of the blood found under Stella's nails, Inspector, and we know for sure it wasn't hers. Stella was type O, and the blood under her nails was type A RhD negative, which applies to a much smaller proportion of the population. If you do manage to isolate any suspects, a simple blood test will prove if they are A RhD negative and if you can then add DNA testing as well, then the criminal who, all these years has thought themselves safe from capture will fall into your hands."

"That's a major step in the right direction. Anything else, Doc?"

"My, my, we are impatient today, are we not, Inspector Ross?"

"Sorry Doc, but with time being against us on this one, I'm anxious to see this murderous thug behind bars."

"Aye, I'm sure you are. Now, with regards to Cathy Billing and Hannah Lucas, it's the negatives that lead me to believe you are looking at two different killers."

"You've lost me there, Doc. What exactly do you mean by that comment?"

"Perhaps I can answer for the doctor," Christine Bland interrupted, and the pathologist nodded.

"Looking at these autopsy reports from the original pathologist, a Doctor Lambert, and the conclusions of D.I. Coleman at the time, the 1966 killer was, in the case of Stella Cox especially, an opportunist killer. I don't think he set out to kill her. It could have been a romantic interlude gone wrong, or a clumsy attempt at a chat up that didn't go as he expected and violence ensued out of the killer's frustration. Then, having experienced some kind of sexual 'high' he set out to try and repeat it, hence the following two murders. There appeared to be no sense of him trying to cover his tracks. There was and still is, DNA and blood evidence that could be used against him. The girl's clothing even had semen stains on it and whoever killed Stella must have had scratches on him, somewhere that could have been visible for a few days after the murder. He probably came up with a believable excuse for having them, maybe blaming a cat or something, but I would stake my reputation on the fact that somebody must have seen him with those scratches on him in the days after the killing but for some reason they didn't think anything of them. Of course he might have been scratched on his arms and worn long-sleeved shirts until the scratches faded. But usually, rape victims tend to lash out at their attacker's faces, if they can, maybe at the eyes."

"But," said William Nugent, "this killer was strong, very strong. The way Dr. Lambert described the ligature marks around all three women's necks indicates he used considerable power in tightening their tights around their necks, almost to the point of using them like a garrotte. The women probably never had an opportunity to fight back, especially if the killer struck suddenly, taking them by surprise."

Izzie Drake shuddered at the thought.

"Which ultimately leads us to today's killer," Bland took up the narrative again. Nugent was happy to let her put his findings into words. She was extremely intelligent and seemed to know just what he was about to say to the detectives. "This killer is organised and methodical. The fact he is recreating the earlier murders so exactly, *but* with subtle differences, indicates he knows what he's doing and how he wants to do it. It wouldn't surprise me if this man has been planning this for a long time and has perhaps had his victims targeted almost from the inception of his diabolical scheme." It seemed that Bland was finally beginning to put a more detailed profile together as more information reached them. "Doctor, you identified a second lubricant. According to your reports, traces were found in both orifices of both women. "You identified the second one as being the type of lubricant typical of those used when employing sex toys and so on. Could there be any other use for such lubricants?"

"Ah'm nae sure I follow your meaning Doctor Bland?" Nugent replied, looking a little mystified.

"Well, neither am I, really. I was just wondering, that's all. We may be looking at a man who finds it impossible to achieve normal penetration, either through erectile dysfunction or impotence, and might have to use something other than his penis to penetrate the women to complete his sexual assaults."

Izzie Drake, who'd listened carefully to Bland's words, then threw a curve ball into the mix.

"Hang on a minute. We're all assuming that this is the work of a man. But, what if it's a woman?"

"Of course, Izzie. That's a good point," Ross agreed with his sergeant. "A woman would probably use a gel of some sort to enable her to fully penetrate the victims as quickly as possible."

"That's a totally off the wall suggestion, Sergeant Drake, but one we can't discount, I agree," said Bland.

"I'm glad I don't have tae think like you people," Nugent responded to this latest conversation. "Ah could nae imagine a woman doing such things to another woman. Though I should, I know, with what I've seen over the years."

"That's because of your very laudable but sometimes outdated old world values, Doc," Ross smiled at him. "Don't get me wrong. There's nothing wrong with being an old-fashioned gentleman, which in my book is what you are, but sometimes it just might cloud your thinking when it comes to what people are capable of in this sad, cruel world we live in."

Andy Ross had nothing but admiration for William Nugent, as both pathologist and man. In the years he'd known 'Fat Willie'

"Aye, well, ye're welcome to it, Inspector Ross, if that's what we've been reduced to. A woman, for pity's sake."

"It's just an idea, Doctor Nugent," Izzie Drake tried to mollify the pathologist's bruised sense of values. "We do have to consider all the possibilities, you know."

"Aye, ah no, Sergeant. I just find it difficult to understand what might motivate a woman to do such things to other women. That would be more in your line of thinking, Christine," he said to Bland, who'd been considering Izzie's wild card suggestion since she'd mentioned it.

"It's not as outlandish as you might think," she eventually responded. "There have been precedents in the past, particularly in Norfolk back in the nineteen thirties. A woman by the name of Victoria Maddern, having been spurned by her lover, turned to murdering any woman she thought he might be involved with. In the space of two months, she viciously murdered four innocent women, only one of whom had been on a date, and that was only to a dance, with Maddern's former lover. She cut their throats and then mutilated their genitals in her mistaken belief that the women had enjoyed sex with the man."

"Why not just kill the man?" Drake pondered aloud.

"That would have been too simple. She wanted to make him suffer. The only trouble was, because he didn't even know three of the victims, he didn't immediately realise that Maddern was the killer. The police were looking for a man to begin with, and Maddern herself hastened her own demise in the end by sending the police a taunting letter. Her lover, having been questioned after his dance partner had been murdered, was questioned again and when the Inspector conducting the interview mentioned certain facts in the letter, Mr. Driver was able to identify the writer as his ex-lover. Maddern was arrested, made no attempt to deny the charges against her and was hanged according to the law at the time, which left the judge with no other sentence available. She's just one example. There are plenty more."

"A tragic case indeed," William Nugent said, shaking his head ruefully. "Let's hope you can apprehend your current killer before she strikes again, Inspector Ross. I'd hate to think of another young woman lying on my table in the near future."

"You know," Ross said, thoughtfully. "Perhaps we should be looking at women as potential suspects too, as you suggest, Izzie. It's certainly feasible that a female relative of the original killer might be carrying out these murders under some weird and twisted motivation we're not aware of. Let's face it, we don't even know what the motivation for the murders is anyway, apart from the fact that it appears to be a copycat killer who is determined to follow the pattern of the nineteen sixty-six killings. We are still left with the big question of ... why?"

"If I could help you to answer that question, Andy, I could feel my journey up here was justified. Believe me, I haven't stopped thinking about that one detail for a second."

"I know," Ross tried to sound sympathetic to her plight. As a profiler, she had made some useful suggestions but had been unable to provide what she would have wanted to. "Just keep those brain cells working. I'm sure as we garner more intel, you might just hit on what, or should I say, who, we're looking for."

Ross led them in their goodbyes and thanks to William Nugent and in a few minutes, they were once again driving south towards Hale. They had a house call to make.

Chapter 17

Edwin

"You haven't exactly been honest with us, have you, Albert?"

Ross, Drake and Christine Bland were seated in the small lounge of the Cretingham home. Well, in truth only the two women were seated. Ross deliberately stood in front of the bay window, purposely partially blocking the evening sunshine from penetrating the room. His stance also served to intimidate Cretingham the elder, or so he hoped. The younger Albert Cretingham also stood, behind his father's armchair, hoping to give his father whatever support he could. He already knew, or rather had sensed, that the police were not quite as friendly as on their previous visit.

"How's that then?" the elder Albert Cretingham appeared genuinely puzzled by Ross's firm assertion. "I don't tell lies, Inspector."

"Well, if that's the case, I would suggest that your so-called photographic memory of the past contains certain flaws, because when we were last here you completely forgot to mention Edwin, didn't you?"

Old Albert Cretingham looked as if his face had been struck by a wet towel, such was his apparent shock on hearing Ross's mention of Edwin's name. Ross then found himself even more perplexed when Albert the younger, as Ross mentally thought of him, interrupted by exclaiming,

"Who the hell is Edwin, Dad?"

Izzie Drake instantly answered young Albert's question.

"You don't expect us to believe you've never heard of your Uncle Edwin, surely, Albert?"

"Uncle? What fucking uncle?" he declared.

Andy Ross looked at the elder Cretingham as he sat with a look of shock on his face.

"Well, Albert? Would you like to tell us about your brother, and why your own son apparently isn't even aware of his existence? Just what else have you kept from us?"

Albert Cretingham gave a pretty good impression of someone who had just seen a ghost rise up before his very eyes as he struggled for words.

"I, er, well, you see…"

"I can tell this is proving difficult for you," Ross said, moderating his tone slightly. "Take your time, but for God's sake, tell me the truth."

Albert Cretingham sighed, and his shoulders slumped as he suddenly appeared to age another ten years before their eyes.

"I'm sorry, lad," he directed his first words at his son. "I never thought it'd be necessary to tell you anything about Edwin." Young Albert said nothing but listened intently as his father related the story of his brother to Ross, Drake and Bland. "Edwin were me brother, that's true enough. He were a few years younger than me, but while I had some trouble with my schooling, though I never knew why at first, as I've told you before, Edwin had troubles of a different kind. I swear to you, Inspector Ross, that I never deliberately hid Edwin's existence from you, because I can't see for a minute how he could be owt to do with what's been going on."

"I think you need to explain that, Albert," Ross urged him to continue.

"Edwin were nowt but trouble from the time he learned to walk and talk, Inspector. Me Mam were in tears some days. He'd scream and rant and rave until he got his own way, even as a nipper. If she didn't give in to 'im, he'd throw a tantrum and by God, them tantrums of his was something to behold."

The more he spoke, the more his West Yorkshire accent came to the fore.

"As young as he was, he'd smash things up if Mam didn't give in to him. I were about ten when I remember him throwin' me Mam's best china vase across the room and it shattering into a thousand pieces. Mam cried because it had been a present from her own Mam, my Gran who'd died the year before. Me Dad gave him more than a wallop or two but all that did was make our Edwin even more mean spirited. It were about that time that me Mam and Dad decided they couldn't put up wi' our Edwin no more and as much as they still loved him, they went to see the Social Service people and the next I knew, our Edwin were gone. They told me he'd gone to live with some nice foster parents. I didn't know what that meant but didn't ask in case me Mam and dad thought I were being thick, like, you know? Any road, I found out for meself a couple of years later, at secondary school. Some of the lads telled me our Edwin was crazy and had been sent away because he were a bad 'un. Every so often, our Edwin would come home for weekends, but he were just as bad as before, worse in fact. Soon them visits stopped altogether. I never saw Edwin again, Inspector Ross and his name were never mentioned in our house again. When me Mam and Dad eventually got divorced I heard some rumours that Edwin had been staying at me Dad's new place now and again, but Dad denied it when I used to visit him."

"Didn't you ever stay at your Dad's new home for weekends or anything like that?" Izzie asked him.

"Nah, nowt like that. He weren't great at parentin', me Dad and he didn't live far away. We arranged it that I'd go and see him every two weeks on a Saturday and I'd catch the bus and we'd go to the footie, or maybe to see a film, or we'd go down the Pier Head and watch the ferries comin' and goin'. I used to like that, imagining where the folks were goin' and what they'd be doin' at the other end of their journey. It might only have been the Mersey Ferry, but a kid's mind could invent all sorts of things, different destinations and such, you know?"

Ross nodded and felt a degree of sympathy for Albert Cretingham.

"I wish he'd been a proper brother, one I could have had fun with, but as young as he was, I admit our Edwin scared me, Inspector, he really did."

Ross had by now changed his opinion of why Albert had failed to mention his brother.

"And when did you last see your brother, Albert?"

"Let me see," said Albert, thinking for a few seconds. "I think I would have been about eighteen and was working at the grocers. I had to make a delivery to a house on the outskirts of the village and when the lady of the house opened the door, Edwin was standing in the hallway a few feet behind her. I don't know if he recognised me, but I knew it was him. He looked a bit weird to me."

"In what way, weird?"

"He had a look in his eyes, Inspector, a look I'd never seen before, and he sort of looked right through me as if I didn't exist."

"Did you speak to him?"

"No. I could never forget the heartache and pain he'd brought to our house when I was a boy. I couldn't bring myself to talk to him. Anyway, that was the last time I ever saw him. By the time I got married and young Albert had come along, I had stopped thinking I'd got a brother. Why do you want to know about Edwin, anyway? You don't think he could have anything to do with these murders, do you?"

"You knew him better than us, Albert. I think the more pertinent question should be, do *you* think he could be capable of murder?"

Ross was becoming increasingly inclined to think that Edwin Cretingham could indeed be a viable suspect, if he was still in the area and possessed a violent temper as described by his brother.

"I couldn't rightly say," Albert replied. "It's a long time since I saw him. He were certainly a violent little so and so as a kid, but folks can grow out of things, can't they, Inspector?"

"True," said Ross, "and then again, sometimes they can get worse as they get older. Do you remember the address of the house where you last saw him? If the same family live there, they might know where he went after leaving them."

"I can give you this address, but I later heard someone had seen him living with a Mrs Dixon, who used to live in the village. She moved into town and one of the lads in the pub said Edwin was living with her as a lodger and doing odd jobs for her. You might have more luck there."

Albert Cretingham reached for a notepad and pen that rested on top of the daily paper on the side table beside his armchair. Usually used to write down his choices in the horse racing of the day, this time he slowly and carefully wrote down an address and, tearing the sheet of paper from the pad, he passed it to Ross.

"One advantage of a good memory," he said, as Ross looked at it and nodded his thanks. One thing I do remember," he added. "When Mam and Dad got divorced, me Dad bought another house. That's where I saw me Dad for the last time, not long before the cancer took him. I never went there, and he met another woman not long before he died and moved her in with him. I know her name was Carol Biggs and he left her the house. I can give you the address. She might still live there and if our Edwin ever went to see Dad, she might know where he is."

"So you didn't go to visit your Dad when he had the cancer?" Drake asked.

"He didn't want me to see him like that, so he said, so I never went, like I said. He were me Dad after all, and I just did what he told me."

* * *

"Do you seriously think Edwin Cretingham could be our man, sir?" Drake asked as they sat in Ross's office as the sun set, leaving the room bathed in the glow of fluorescent lights and the last vestiges of daylight.

"I think it's a possibility, based on what Albert told us. What do you think Christine? You were very quiet in the Cretingham's house?"

"I was keeping very much a watching brief. I didn't want to interrupt your interview. I was very interested in Albert. He seems a complex character. I know you told me he had autism but, in my opinion, if he has, it's a very mild form of the illness. He was clearly brought up in a household where the father ruled the roost with a heavy hand.

The mother, as far as I could tell, would have been a typical, down-trodden, servile wife who either couldn't or wouldn't stand up to the husband. The fact that she was also bullied by a child as young as Edwin tells a large part of the story. Albert witnessed all this at close quarters and probably developed an affinity with his mother, seeing her as a victim of oppression and though he wanted to, he felt unable to help her in any way. Watching him today, it wasn't difficult to see him as being a very submissive personality, and even though Edwin was much younger, he was clearly a highly dominant individual. Not many children of such tender years can totally dominate their mother to the extent Albert described or instil such fear in a sibling."

"Seems you learned an awful lot by not saying anything," Izzie grinned at the profiler.

"And if I'm not mistaken," Ross added, "it sounds very much as if you're coming around to producing a profile of a killer."

"Indeed I am, Andy. From what I've learned today I have to say that Edwin Cretingham, at least based on his early years, does appear to have the background that could have led him down the path towards the dark side."

Izzie, thinking on Bland's words, quickly asked,

"But that leads us to speculate on the fact that if Edwin is the current killer, how did he get hold of the details of the original murders, unless…?

"Unless we work on the premise that Edwin and Albert's father was the killer of the women back in nineteen sixty-six," Ross responded without hesitation.

"But, we have no evidence to support either assumption," Bland retorted, "and it would appear that nobody seems to know if Edwin even lives in Liverpool at present."

"Izzie, let's dig out the original sixty-six case reports again. I want to know if Stan Coleman or any of his team interviewed Albert Cretingham's father. What was his first name, did you get it from the younger Albert?"

"Reginald, known as Reg, sir. I'll get on to it right away."

"And give Stan Coleman a ring. He may remember talking to Reg. If he did I want to know his impressions of the man."

"Okay. And what about Edwin?"

"That's one for Paul, I think. Edwin might have done a disappearing act, but he can't hide from the computer skills of our own cyber-boffin."

"And I take it we are going to visit his last known address?"

"Too right we are, Izzie. I think we might just have got ourselves a suspect at last."

Chapter 18

Friends and Lovers

Alex and Lisa arrived at Alex's house within a half hour of finishing work. Alex had not had a good shift. A groper had tried feeling her backside as she'd bent over the table to clear the plates and glasses away and it had taken all her self-control to refrain from slapping him hard across the face. Only the thought of losing her job for striking a client had held her temper in check. Now, unusually for her, she'd invited Lisa in for a drink, as she felt in need of company.

"Nice place," said Lisa as she sat on the small sofa in Alex's lounge.

"Thanks," said Alex. "It's not exactly as I'd like it, but beggars can't be choosers I suppose."

"What d'you mean, Alex?"

"I bought it cheap," she replied. "I knew the old woman who lived here and when she died and had no one to leave it to it went up for auction. I got it for way under market price."

"Well, I'm sure you'll soon have it looking the way you want it to."

Alex merely nodded as she looked intently at her best friend. In truth, she realised Lisa was possibly her only friend. She'd always found it difficult to form relationships and even after the operations, when she'd imagined herself feeling so different, she still found it difficult, especially with men. Thoughts of a happy and fulfilling sex life seemed as far away as they'd ever been for Alex. *Maybe, if Lisa is a*

Lesbian as I imagined earlier, it might not hurt to explore something new, Alex thought.

"Are you okay, Alex?" Lisa asked, sensing Alex was miles away in her thoughts.

"What? Oh sorry Lisa. Yes, I was just thinking about that old perv in the club, grabbing my bum as if he had some right to feel me up just because he'd had a couple of drinks too many."

"I know," Lisa replied, "I suppose it's the only downside to an otherwise well-paid job."

Alex, having made a decision, rose from her armchair and walked across and sat beside Lisa on the sofa.

"You know, you're about the only real friend I have Lisa? I don't know what I'd do without you, sometimes."

Lisa, hoping she was reading Alex's body language correctly, reached her hand across the sofa and gently placed it on top of Alex's hand, intertwining her fingers with those of her friend, who made no objection. Encouraged, Lisa looked into Alex's eyes, and spoke softly, "I don't know how you feel Alex, but I really do like you a lot, you know. It's kind of more than just friendly, the way I feel about you."

"I think I know what you're saying," Alex replied, a little unsure of herself now that she'd relaxed her guard a little. "You know, Lisa, I've never actually slept with a man. I've had some surgery, and, well, I've been afraid to try anything, or even to let a man see me, down there, if you know what I mean. Oh god, I'm not saying this very well, am I? I know you're not a man but, well, I suppose what I'm trying to say is..."

"That you've never even thought about doing it with a woman either," Lisa finished the sentence for her.

The words froze in Alex's throat as she nodded in reply and almost jumped in alarm as Lisa placed a hand on the side of her face and gently turned it towards her own. Before Alex could object, Lisa leaned forward and kissed Alex on the lips, softly, gently, and with a tenderness Alex found surprisingly reassuring.

"Lisa, I'm not sure..." she began, but Lisa ignored her mild protest, and Alex felt a hand gently closing around her right breast, the thin material of her blouse doing little to disguise the fact that her nipple was beginning to swell in her bra.

"Oh, God," she exclaimed as Lisa kissed her again, with greater passion this time, and Alex couldn't resist as Lisa's other hand found its way onto one of her knees and gently began to stroke her stockinged leg as it moved beneath the hem of her skirt, moving inexorably upwards.

Alex's breath began to arrive in short sharp gasps and within minutes she found herself being led up her own stairs towards her bedroom. As the pair entered the room, Alex hesitated for a second as thoughts of how Lisa might react when she saw her naked sent a shiver of fear through her body. Sensing she was holding back, Lisa reached out, kissing her again, with a passion that released Alex from her momentary lethargy.

"What's wrong Alex? Please, don't be afraid."

"It's not that, Lisa. You remember I told you I'd had some pretty drastic surgery in the past? I'm afraid you might not like what you see."

"Shhh," Lisa hushed her as she slowly began to undress Alex, until she was left in nothing more than bra and panties. "Help me, Alex" she urged, her voice husky and expectant, and Alex allowed herself to be carried by the moment as she began unbuttoning Lisa's blouse which soon fell to the floor. "Don't stop, Alex," Lisa gasped as the zipper of her skirt was next, and the skirt slid down her smooth nylon covered legs.

Lisa pulled Alex down on to the bed and as she kissed her once again she reassured her friend.

"If you're that worried, we can turn the light out, but I won't be put off by a few scars if that's all you're worried about."

"Lisa, I…"

Lisa reached across and turned out the bedside lamp, so that with the curtains open, the room was bathed in natural moonlight that streamed through the window, falling almost like a pale spotlight on the bed.

"I've wanted you for months, Alex," she said as she pulled her new lover close to her, and as their bodies finally connected, she let out a gasp of contentment.

"Lisa, I've never…" Alex was almost in a panic which at the same time was mixed with unexpected anticipation.

"It's okay, I told you. I won't do anything you're uncomfortable with. Come here and kiss me again."

Alex suddenly stiffened as Lisa's hand closed around her breast, but soon relaxed as Lisa used all her experience to place her new lover at her ease. By the time Lisa moved lower down her body to the most sensitive of areas, and the site of three previous operations, Alex had lost all her inhibitions and was giving as much pleasure as she was receiving.

The next thirty minutes seemed to fly in a blur of pleasure Alex had never previously experienced. She was floundering in an ocean of previously unknown emotions. She could never have foreseen a situation like this, could never have dreamed that her emotions could be so stirred by the touch of a woman. As the two women basked in the afterglow of their lovemaking, with Lisa gradually drifting off into a deep, peaceful sleep, Alex looked at her friend, tenderly pulled the duvet up to cover her nakedness, quietly left the bed, still naked, and made her way to the bathroom. There, she quickly washed herself all over, ensuring she was scrupulously clean in her most private places, then using a mirror, she examined herself, afraid that her operation scars might have been damaged in some way by her recent exertions. Satisfied that all was well, she tiptoed back to the bedroom where, horrified, she noticed that she'd left the diary in full view on her bedside cabinet, having removed it from the drawer earlier, intending to read some more in bed, never of course expecting that she's be bringing Lisa or anyone else home with her that night.

She checked, carefully, that Lisa remained fast asleep, then quietly and as fast as possible, she removed the diary, placing it in a lockable box she kept on the shelf above her clothes rail. If there was to be any repeat of the events of the previous night, she would need to be more protective of the secrets it contained. If Lisa saw it and read even a small proportion of it, the ramifications could be disastrous, for both of them.

Already used to keeping secrets about her personal life, Alex had now added another very important one. Making her way to the kitchen, she made herself a mug of instant coffee. Not yet wanting to disturb the sleeping woman in her bed, Alex sat at the kitchen table and sipped at the hot drink as the afterglow of their lovemaking began to wear off, to be replaced by an incoming tide of emotional confusion. When she'd gone through the operations, Dr. Pelham hadn't touched on the possibility of a lesbian relationship. Despite her age, Alex had hoped … made herself a mug of instant coffee. … she would finally be able to enjoy a genuine sexual relationship with a man at last. Somehow, age notwithstanding, and after various failed efforts at cementing some form of romantic relationship with a man, Alex had come to the sad conclusion that men were somehow repulsed by her, that her secret past was emblazoned across her forehead for all to see, making any happy ever after hopes she may have harboured a failed dream, and fuelling her anger and frustration. Could she possibly find love in the arms of a woman instead? As much as the thought would have been anathema to her even a few short days ago, Lisa had made her re-evaluate her feelings and her mind now reeled with confusion.

Unsure how to proceed, she drained the coffee mug, rinsed it under the hot water tap, and crept quietly back to the bedroom where Lisa remained, lying on her side in her deep, contented sleep. The duvet had slipped down, revealing most of Lisa's naked body. Looking at the soft, feminine curves of the sleeping woman, Alex felt a surge of emotion. Unable to resist temptation, Alex slipped her housecoat off and slid in to the bed next to her sleeping friend, her back towards her. No sooner had she done so, Lisa's sleeping form turned towards Alex and an arm subconsciously reached across and pulled Alex in close to her, Lisa's hand coming to rest on Alex's right breast. Somehow, that small intimacy gave Alex a feeling of comfort and togetherness she had come to feel would be forever denied to her. In seconds, she joined her new lover in the land of dreams, her worldly cares and tribulations, operation scars and feelings of inadequacy temporarily banished from her mind. Tomorrow would be another day. But for now, Alex was at peace with the world, and more importantly, with herself.

Chapter 19

Confession

"We might just have got lucky at last," Ross said, as he and Izzie Drake sat in the office of D.C.I. Oscar Agostini. "If we can obtain a DNA sample from either of the two Albert Cretinghams, and if Doctor Newton runs a DNA scan in comparison with the alien blood samples obtained from the clothes of the 1966 victims, we'll know that Reginald Cretingham was the original killer. It's a shame that semen doesn't retain viable DNA for more than the life of the sperm, which certainly isn't thirty-nine years, but the blood should be enough."

"And that could mean?"

"That Edwin Cretingham is our killer, sir," Drake responded. "We've already eliminated the two Alberts from our investigation and the only remaining Cretingham is Edwin."

"Who nobody appears to have seen or heard from in years."

"That's true, Oscar, but me and Izzie are heading out to his last known address in a while, in the hope his ex-foster mother might still live there and can give us more information," Ross continued.

"Then let's hope she does still reside there. How come this Edwin character is so elusive anyway?"

"He appears to have dropped off the radar as he entered his teens. He was bad news, by all accounts, parents couldn't handle him, and god knows how many sets of foster parents chucked him out too," Ross replied. "But for some reason, it's believed, by his brother at least, that he got on well with this Mrs. Fox."

"Well, Andy, the clock's ticking, so I suggest the pair of you make tracks and get to this woman's house as soon as you can. I'd like to know why Edwin was easily able to disappear from the system, that's for sure," Agostini said, as he waved them out of his office with a high degree of urgency.

* * *

The house on Falkner Street in the Canning area of the city was typical of many of the older terraced houses that still lined many of the streets in the older areas of the city. The street's one small claim to fame was the fact that the Beatles manager, Brian Epstein, once owned a flat there and at one time he loaned it to John Lennon and Yoko Ono for some time, who were probably the streets most famous previous residents. Some of the current residents had done their best to modernise the old red brick properties, some by adding double glazing, others by having completely new windows and front doors fitted. No other external changes were permitted however as the houses on Falkner Street were classified as Grade 2 Listed Buildings, and as such were protected from any external modifications. Number forty-seven however, didn't fall in any way into the modernised category. It still looked pretty much as it would have done when first built towards the end of the nineteenth or early twentieth century, with its original windows with faded, peeling paintwork on the frames and door. Ross felt depressed walking along the street's narrow footpath, having been forced to park in the next street due to lack of space. Izzie Drake knocked on the door, and the two detectives waited a respectable time before Izzie knocked a second time. Ross was about to step forward and use his added vigour to knock even louder when they heard a bolt being drawn back and a key being turned in the door lock. The door opened a crack and jerked to a stop on the end of a security chain.

"Who is it?" a female voice answered, hoarsely. Sounded as if the owner of the voice had just got out of bed.

"Police," Ross announced, firmly. "We're looking for a Carol Biggs."

"Why?"

"We need her help with an ongoing inquiry. Is she here, Miss…?"

"She doesn't live here anymore," the woman behind the door asserted.

"Look, we need to talk to her. Please can we come in and talk for a minute? It's very important."

"Oh, I suppose so. Just a minute."

The door closed, and Ross and Drake heard the chain being slid back. As the door opened, a tall, but slim and attractive brunette stood back to allow them to enter and led them into the house's small living room, where she invited them to sit down. Dressed in an expensive looking pink housecoat and slippers, Ross's assumption that she'd been in bed appeared to be confirmed. Alex meanwhile was fighting a feeling of panic. What the hell could the police want with her? Did they know about the diary? Surely not, and anyway, it was so old, how could it be important?

Ross and Drake showed their warrant cards and Ross introduced himself and Izzie to the woman, who looked very uncomfortable at their presence, though many of the city's residents might have felt some trepidation at a surprise visit from the police.

"I apologise if we woke you up," Ross said, trying hard to form a rapport with the woman, who he felt was decidedly cool towards the visit by the police.

"Don't bother" she replied. "I work in a club at night, and I was asleep when you came banging on my door."

"We didn't get your name, Miss…? Drake asked.

"It's Sefton, Alexandra Sefton. People call me Alex."

"Right, Alex," Ross spoke again. "You said that Mrs. Biggs doesn't live here any longer. Do you know where we might find her?"

"Toxteth Park cemetery," Alex replied, sarcastically. "She died a few years ago. She had no heirs, and the house was sold at auction and I bought it."

"Did you know her when she was alive?" Izzie asked, already feeling that something was a little 'off' about Alex Sefton.

"Yes, as it happens, I did. She was a very friendly person, and I used to help her out with shopping and odd jobs around the home."

"I see," Izzie replied. "Did she have any relatives you know of?"

"No," said Alex, "that's why the house was auctioned off. What do you want her for anyway? Did she commit a crime or something when she was alive?"

"Nothing like that," Ross rejoined the conversation. "We need to talk to someone who used to lodge with her some years ago. If you knew her maybe you've heard of him too."

"Maybe," Alex replied, still feeling nervous about just what the two detectives were looking for.

"His name is Edwin Cretingham. He'd have been quite a young man when he lived here. He's in his early fifties now of course, but we need to talk to him. Can you help us?"

Alex fell silent. She wondered whether to tell the truth or think of an alternative. Ross and Drake both picked up on her hesitation. To their experienced minds it was plainly obvious that the woman did know Edwin. Why would she deny it unless she was hiding something? Alex came to a decision.

"I'm not sure how much I can help you, but yes, I used to know Edwin."

Alex suddenly had the full attention of Ross and Drake, who both listened attentively as she began her story.

* * *

Meanwhile, back in Hale, Derek McLennan and Sofie Meyer were sitting in the lounge of the Cretingham home. Sent by Ross to obtain voluntary DNA samples from the two Alberts, they explained the reason for their request, and the elder of the two men was sad, but cooperative as Meyer produced the DNA testing kit from what looked like an innocuous woman's handbag and approached Albert senior, ready to take a simple swab from the inside of his mouth. Before she could ask him to open his mouth, Albert spoke to her with what she perceived to be deep emotion in his voice.

"It's a bit hard to get me head round this, lass. What you're saying is that if this 'ere sample you're taking from me and from our Albert, matches blood found on them women's clothes all those years ago, it will mean my dad was a bloody murderer."

"And a rapist Dad," the younger Albert chimed in from his position, standing close to the door that led to the hall and the front door. D.C. McLennan stood close to the man. For some reason he couldn't put his finger on, Derek felt he should remain close to young Albert, in case he decided to do a runner.

"Aye, lad, that too," his father replied. "He was a hard man, me Dad, Sergeant Meyer, but I'd never have had him down as a sex killer. Still, I suppose you need to get at the truth, even after all these years have passed."

"That is very true, Mr. Cretingham," Sofie replied. "Believe me, we do appreciate your cooperation in this matter."

"You know what else it means, don't you Dad?" Albert junior asked his father. Derek McLennan had a good idea what the man was about to say to his father. This, he realised, was the cause of his earlier disquiet regarding the younger man.

"What's that, son?" old Albert asked, as Meyer removed the swab from his mouth, having taken the required saliva sample in a few seconds as the son spoke.

"If it's a match they could try to claim it was one of us killed the women recently and they could try and do you for the killings in nineteen sixty-six."

"I assure you that is not the case," said Meyer. "We merely wish to verify whether your father could have been involved in the earlier killings, and if your brother Edwin could be connected to the recent murders," she addressed the older man. With that she quickly moved across the room to the younger Albert and before he could say another word, she instructed him to open his mouth, and promptly collected the second saliva sample of the visit.

Leaving the two men wondering what the results would be, and how it could affect their lives, Sofie Meyer and Derek McLennan headed back to headquarters, from where the samples would be logged and then forwarded to Doctor Nugent for analysis."

Meanwhile, Alexandra Sefton was relating the story of her connection with Edwin Cretingham to Ross and Drake.

"Edwin was quite a few years older than me, Inspector. I was still a little kid by comparison. He was in his late teens and Mrs. Biggs took him in as a foster child. I knew he had an older brother called Albert, and that was about all I did know about him. She was great like that. I got to know her through a young boy, Eric, who she fostered before Edwin who was about my age. We used to play together after school and at weekends. One day he left, because, so he said, his Mum was better. She'd been ill, and his Dad was dead, and she had been in hospital for a long time. Mrs. Biggs told me when I was older it had been a psychiatric hospital and Eric had been considered 'at risk' until his mother was well again. Anyway, Eric left and soon after, Edwin arrived. If I'm honest, he scared me sometimes. He had what I thought was a cruel streak and took delight in tormenting other kids and animals. I used to go around to see Mrs. Biggs and run errands for her and Edwin used to call me a little faggot. I had no idea what he meant at the time of course, but I learned later. I found Mrs. Biggs in tears once. She pulled me close to her and sat me on her knee and told me that Edwin had stolen money from her. Some people came one day and took Edwin away, but he came back a couple of weeks later. Mrs. Biggs gave him a second chance and to be fair, Edwin seemed to be a changed character. He got a job and settled down a bit. He stayed with Mrs. Biggs for a long time, Inspector. I think she looked on him like a son and for a while Edwin was happier than I've ever seen him."

"Please don't get me wrong, Miss Sexton," Ross interrupted, but would you happen to have any photographs of those days, specifically any that would include Edwin? It's vitally important we contact him."

"I might have one or two, but please, can't you tell me what Edwin's done? There must be something important to make you want to talk to him so urgently, Inspector?"

Andy Ross didn't answer Alex at first. He wouldn't usually give away details of a case to a member of the public, but with time ticking down towards the potential third rape and murder, he was seriously considering giving Alex Sefton a good reason to help them as much as she could. His eyes sought out his sergeant and Izzie Drake, knowing exactly what he was thinking, surreptitiously nodded her agreement with his ultimate decision.

"Have you been watching the news recently? Or reading the *Echo* perhaps?"

"No, I'm sorry. I never watch the news or read the local rag."

"How about local radio?" Izzie asked, and Alex shook her head, another no.

Ross sighed and decided to take the plunge. This woman was the first person they'd found who had first-hand knowledge of Edwin Cretingham, and though it might be old information, it could be helpful to their investigation.

"In the last couple of weeks, the bodies of two young women have been found, deposited on the car park of the old lighthouse at Hale."

For the first time since their arrival, Alex's face appeared to betray some form of emotion. Was it horror, shock or a painful realisation that the news wasn't as much of a surprise as he'd expected it to be. Ross continued.

"The thing is, these women were both raped and murdered in a similar style to three murders that occurred in nineteen sixty-six. The evidence we have so far seems to indicate that Edwin's father may have been involved in the original murders."

Alex now knew who the diary belonged to. Having found it behind a false wall panel when she'd done some do-it-yourself work in her kitchen, her source of continual sexual stimulation was now revealed to be not just some fantasist's creation from years ago but was in fact the real diary of a genuine murderer. She now had to decide whether to reveal its existence to the police.

"Oh my God. You think if his father was a killer, then Edwin could be behind these recent murders you're talking about, don't you?" she asked with a distinct tremor in her voice.

"We're awaiting DNA test results on Edwin's brother and nephew as we speak," Ross said gravely, "and if there's a match to the blood samples found on the clothing of the original murders, we can be pretty certain that Edwin is involved, yes."

"Oh shit," Alex said, and both detectives could almost see the guilt spreading across her face, which had turned almost a bright vermillion red.

"Alex, you know something, don't you?" Izzie spoke softly, not wanting to cause the woman to panic. "Please, if you do, it's important you tell us. Another woman's life is at stake and we need to find Edwin as quickly as possible, if for no other reason than to eliminate him from our inquiries."

Alex seemed to disappear within herself for over a minute. Ross and Drake could almost hear the gears turning in her mind as she wrestled internally with some great load on her mind. The detectives found themselves almost holding their breath as they waited, patiently, for Alex to return to reality. Eventually, Alex sighed, a deep and meaningful sigh that carried a welter of emotion and she spoke, her voice breaking and almost sobbing.

"I saw Edwin for the first time in ages a couple of years ago, and then again last year. Before I tell you anything else, I suppose I need to be honest with you. Edwin isn't Edwin any more Inspector Ross."

A puzzled look crossed his face as he waited, allowing Alex to tell this in her own time.

"First you need to know something about me. My name wasn't always Alexandra Sefton, Inspector. I was born Andrew Berwick."

"You've undergone a sex change?" Ross cottoned on instantly.

"They call it gender reassignment nowadays, but yes, that's what it means. I knew from the age of about six that I wasn't like other boys.

While the other lads in the street wanted to play football or cricket, and play cowboys and Indians, I wanted to play with my sister's dolls, to wear her skirts and dresses, and, well, I wanted to be female. It was an overwhelming feeling, but not something a child could very well talk to their Mum and Dad about, certainly not back then. I would have done anything to get rid of the offending appendage between my legs but had to wait until I was an adult before I could talk to my doctor about it. Luckily, she was very sympathetic, and I soon began the necessary evaluations to see if I was suitable for reassignment. The only person who knew about my feelings when I was very young was Mrs. Biggs. She was sympathetic and understanding and told me to be patient. We talked about a lot and she told me that nobody in the world would agree to a young boy like me being operated on to make me into a girl, but that if it was what I really felt deep down inside and still felt the same when I was grown up, even though it was years away, then it would happen for me eventually. When I was in my early days of hormone treatment until the time of my operation, I lived here with Mrs. Biggs. She was wonderful, and never judged me or said a bad word against me, unlike some of my so-called friends and my family at the time."

Izzie had been listening intently. She'd instantly felt there was something different about Alex and now they knew for sure, she was more comfortable with the woman. Izzie certainly wasn't one of those bigoted people who failed to recognise a transgender person by their new sex.

"So, am I correct in assuming you met Edwin again during your treatment?

"Yes, you are, Sergeant. You see, when I told you a few minutes ago that Edwin was no longer known as Edwin it's because he is also a transgender person now."

"Bloody hell," Ross couldn't help blurting out. "You mean Edwin is now a woman too?"

"Well, yes and no," Alex said, a little hesitantly.

"That's a strange answer, Alex," Izzie said. " Can you explain that for us?"

Alex seemed to drift off into the deep recesses of her mind for a few seconds, as she contemplated how to explain herself to the detectives. Ross was about to try and hurry Alex along. Izzie sensed his impatience and tried to communicate with him via a look that said, *"Give her time. Let her tell it her own way."*

"Before I can tell you about Edwin, please, let me tell you about me and then you might understand what I said about him a minute ago."

Ross nodded and allowed her to continue.

"You really need to know what gender reassignment entails, Inspector. A man can't just go and ask for a sex change on prescription from his G.P. I had to undergo two psychological evaluations and live as a woman for eighteen months before my real treatment began, and it would have been the same for Edwin. All that time, I was taking female hormone tablets to encourage breast growth and to make my body shape, my hips etc, begin to appear more feminine. There's a lot to it, but that'll give you an idea. Eventually, the goal of the process is the removal of the penis and the creation of a vagina and a clitoris, which functions, by the way. My case was routine, I suppose, but more recently I had to have another operation when some of the work on creating my vagina became infected and they had to virtually redo the whole thing. Then, I underwent breast augmentation to make my tits bigger, more attractive to men I thought. I've lived as a woman for over five years now, and apart from visits to the clinic for regular check-ups, and the additional operations, my life has been good. A few months ago I was experiencing some other problems and needed another small operation. So you see, it's a long and often painful process, and not everyone comes out at the end of it exactly as they might have expected. In my case, I have been totally unable to maintain a relationship with a man, and in that respect, I'm still a virgin. Last night a girlfriend slept over and we ended up in bed together and I had the first orgasm of my life as a woman."

The last bit, about Lisa, just seemed to slip out before Alex could stop herself and she realised she might have said too much, become too personal, giving the police more information than she should have done.

She may well have been correct in her thoughts, because, at last, Ross's patience began to grow thin.

"Please, Alex, as interesting as it may be to hear all this, what bearing does it have on Edwin Cretingham?"

"I'm coming to that now, Inspector, but I felt you needed to understand the process before you could understand what happened to Edwin. By the way, one of the first things you must do while undergoing gender reassignment is to change your first name by Deed Poll. I went further and changed my full name, wanting a totally fresh start, a whole new life, and I told Edwin that when we met the first time. You see, one of the reasons for his bad behaviour as a boy and young man was because of his own gender crisis. His problem was in not recognising it for a long time, and when he did, he didn't want to admit it, even to himself. Eventually, he found the courage to approach a doctor, accepted what he was, and he began the process."

"I have a feeling you're going to tell us that something went wrong with Edwin's treatment," Ross said, beginning to see where Alex was heading with her story.

"You're catching on, Inspector. Yes, you're right. At first, he was fine. He changed his name by Deed Poll and began the hormone treatments and lived as a woman for the required period. Edwin's problems began when it came to take the final step, the removal of his penis and creation of the female genitals. He kept putting it off, or so he told me on that second meeting. Remember he was a lot older than me, maybe older than most people who undergo the change. His excuse, or should I say her excuse was fear of going under the anaesthetic and not waking up again. I didn't believe him. As Edwin, he'd never struck me as a coward. I think he was having second thoughts. I'd met one or two others who had similar fears so I just thought that as Teresa, she'd get over it in time and go ahead."

"Are you saying Edwin didn't complete the change?" Izzie asked, wondering if his gender problems were the catalyst for him to turn to murder.

"No, he did have the operation eventually, but I heard there were problems. He had his penis removed but the creation of the female sexual organs produced some complications and she had to go under the knife again. You must understand, once it's been removed you can't just sew it back on, if you change your mind."

Ross had been listening intently, and he was sharing Izzie's feeling that the results of the gender reassignment operation might have tipped Edwin over the edge.

"You still haven't told us what name Edwin is living under now, Alex. We really need to know that," he said, trying to get Alex to move along with her story.

"Oh yes, I'm sorry. Edwin's name is now Teresa Moore. She works for a small import/export company as a shipping clerk. I haven't quite finished her story yet, Inspector."

"OK, I'm sorry. Please go on."

"You see, in most cases, gender reassignment has a positive mental effect on the patient. It certainly did for me, despite me having some initial problems and finding it difficult to form relationships with men. I was lucky though. As far as I know, most people find me attractive as a woman, and there certainly isn't anything about me that would give people an inkling that I used to be a man, but for some, that isn't always the case."

"You mean Edwin, or Teresa, I assume?"

"Yes. Teresa is now all woman, but for some reason, people look at her and her facial features are such that she tends to look like a man in drag, no matter how much make-up she wears. I don't know why, but sometimes that's just the way things turn out. Maybe it has something to do with the fact that Edwin made the step to gender reassignment later in life. Not every transgender person is in their teens you know. Despite knowing she was a woman trapped in a man's body, Teresa took a good few years before finally deciding to go ahead with the change. Anyway, all I can tell you is that the last time I saw her, Teresa Moore was a very bitter and disillusioned person. She's taken all that time, so many years, agonising over her own identity and having eventually taken the big step to do something about it, she feels she's a freak, Inspector. If you think that gives her a motive for murder, that's for you to decide."

Andy Ross was convinced that Alex had just given them exactly what they needed to place Edwin Cretingham, now known as Teresa Moore, at the very top of their suspects list.

"Do you know where Teresa Moore lives, Alex?" he asked, but it was a forlorn hope that Alex could make things that easy for them.

"I'm sorry, no, I've no idea."

Ross signalled to Ozzie. They had probably learned all they could from Alex Sefton. It was time to return to headquarters and launch a serious search for Teresa Moore. Ross was confident that Paul Ferris and his computer would quickly trace the woman.

Alex, however, had been agonising over something else. Should she reveal her big secret to the police officers or not, and if she did, was it going to get her into serious trouble? She finally made a decision, and as Ross was about to thank her for her time and lead Izzie to the door, Alex cleared her throat and gently stopped him by placing a hand on his left arm.

"Detective Inspector Ross?"

"Yes, what is it Alex?"

"Erm, I'm not sure how to put this, but there's something else I think you should see before you leave…"

Chapter 20

DNA

Andy Ross was furious. When Alex Sefton disappeared upstairs, leaving Ross and Drake waiting near the front door, they had no idea what she was about to show them. When she reappeared a minute later, thrusting a small, ageing pocket diary into his hands, without saying a word, he had little choice but to open the little book and begin reading the contents. Within seconds, and Izzie Drake would later swear she could virtually see steam venting from Ross's ears as he read, he virtually exploded on the spot.

"Bloody hell, Alex. Just how long have you been in possession of this damn diary? Don't you realise how significant this could be? Did it never enter your head that this could be the diary of a genuine serial killer? Just what did you think you were hoping to gain by holding on to it? For God's sake, what possible use could it have been to you? Or dare I ask?"

By the time he'd vented his anger, Alex Sefton stood, crestfallen and in tears, no more than three feet from him. Izzie Drake had to admit to herself that she was shocked. She'd never, ever heard Ross harangue a potential witness to such an extent, though she knew exactly where he was coming from and why his anger was so intense. She quickly walked back into the lounge they'd so recently left and picked up the box of tissues she'd seen on the coffee table as they'd listened to Alex's story.

"I'm sorry, OK? Really sorry," Alex bawled, as she gratefully accepted a tissue from the box Izzie proffered to her. "I wasn't to know it was important, was I? It must have been there for years, so how was I supposed to know it had any significance. It could just have been some kid's deranged rantings for all I knew, and anyway, I…I… "

"You what, Alex?" Ross was still in a temper.

"I found it strangely, Erm, sort of, well, a bit of a turn on."

"You found a diary about some bastard raping and murdering women a bloody turn on. For Christ's sake, Alex, if I didn't believe you were telling me the truth, which for some reason I do, I'd run you in for obstructing the police, withholding evidence, anything I could think of to make things very difficult for you."

"Sir," Izzie interrupted, attempting to defuse the situation, "At least we have it now, and it might not help us find Edwin, sorry, I mean Teresa, but it will give us a great insight into the way the Lighthouse Killer's mind worked. If Albert Cretingham has anything in his possession with his father's handwriting on it, it might also help to prove Reg Cretingham's guilt of the original murders."

Ross took a deep breath. He realised that he'd gone over the top in his reaction to Alex's sudden production of the diary, and was grateful for Izzie's intervention. She was right of course, the diary had little or no bearing on the current murders, though he was well aware that the fact it had been found in a house where Edwin Cretingham had lived for a time in the past, added weight to the supposition that it had been in the possession of his father, Reginald, who was looking more and more like the Lighthouse Killer of 1966, though how it came to be in Edwin's possession, Ross had no idea. He was however, well aware that Edwin wouldn't have been the only foster child or lodger who spent time at the house, from what Alex had told them about the kind-hearted Carol Biggs.

"Yes, you're right, of course. I'm sorry, Alex. I may have overreacted a little. I didn't mean to scare you half to death. It's just... well... we're kind of racing against the clock before the killer strikes again, and..."

"Apology accepted, Detective Inspector," Alex replied, feeling relieved that she'd kind of got away with withholding the diary from them until now. "I suppose I never really thought of it as being something that was real, until now of course."

"Yes, well, I'd like it if you'd visit headquarters with us and make a formal statement as to how it came into your possession and about your relationship and knowledge of the life of Edwin Cretingham, now Teresa Moore of course."

Alex could do little other than agree with Ross's request. She felt relieved that the inspector hadn't arrested her for withholding evidence or something like that. Of course, she knew she hadn't deliberately done anything like that. If she had, she'd have handed the diary in right away, or at least she thought she would have done. With a look of bitter apology on her face, she agreed to his request.

"When would you like me to come in and make it?" she asked.

"I'd like you to come back with us now, Alex," Ross replied. "Don't worry, we'll arrange a lift home for you afterwards."

Alex agreed and asked for a few minutes to get ready. She was still dressed in her housecoat and slippers, hardly appropriate for a visit to police headquarters.

Ross agreed, and Izzie Drake accompanied her to her bedroom, where she attempted to give Alex a little advice.

"Does your girlfriend know about your past, Alex?"

"You mean does Lisa know I used to be a man? No, she doesn't."

"I think you should tell her, be honest with her. If you hope your friendship with her might turn into something more meaningful, you need to be truthful with her."

"I know you're right, Sergeant, but I'm scared that, having found someone who seems to like me for myself, I might lose her when she learns the truth about my past."

"If she truly cares for you, she'll understand your situation and if she doesn't, then is she really worth all your agonising and self-doubt?"

As she fastened her navy-blue skirt and slipped on a contrasting paler blue lightweight sweater, Alex nodded.

"You're right of course," she replied as she sat on the stool in front of her dressing table, applying a spot of make-up, enough to make herself look respectable for a visit to police headquarters. "Thank you for your advice, Sergeant Drake."

Within minutes, Alex found herself seated in the back of the unmarked police car, with Izzie Drake at the wheel. Ross seemed to spend the journey exclusively engaged in conversation on his mobile phone. She heard her name mentioned a couple of times as he made arrangements for an interview room to be made ready on their arrival. In no time, they pulled into the car park at Police Headquarters, and with her legs shaking as she walked, Alex accompanied Ross and Drake though the main doors of the building and led her to the lift that would take them to the fourth floor, where their unit was located. Ross, feeling he would probably make Alex feel uncomfortable and less likely to be open and honest, left Izzie to take her statement, accompanied by D.C Sam Gable.

As he entered the squad room, about to instruct Paul Ferris to begin the search for Teresa Moore, aka Edwin Cretingham, Sergeant Ferris usurped him by calling to him as he began to walk across the room.

"Sir," he called, "got some news for you."

"Hope it's good news, Paul. I could do with some, that's for sure."

"I don't think you're going to like it," Ferris replied.

"Oh shit, man, come on, out with it."

"Doctor Nugent rang a few minutes ago, Boss. You're not going to believe it, but the doc rushed the DNA tests through, top priority and the results don't do much for our case."

Ross felt the cold hand of disappointment reaching out to touch him on the shoulder.

"Alright Paul, you'd better put me out of my misery."

"Ok, here goes, and remember not to shoot the messenger."

"Get on with it man."

"Right, well, you'll be as surprised as I was to learn that the DNA markers indicate that Reginald Cretingham was *not* the Lighthouse Killer of 1966, which helps to eliminate Edwin Cretingham as our major person of interest, I'd say, unless he's operating out of some connection to the original killer that we're not aware of."

Ferris of course, wasn't yet aware what Ross and Drake had learned from Alex Sefton. Ross however, had to admit that without a connection to Reginald Cretingham, the likelihood of Edwin/Teresa being involved in the recent murders was receding by the minute.

"Thanks for ruining my day, Paul. Anything else you want to throw at me to make me feel even worse?"

"Well, there is one thing, though I'm not sure if it really has any bearing on the case, as such."

"Okay Paul. You've got me hooked on your little mystery. What's this other info then?"

Ferris looked almost bemused as he looked Ross straight in the eye and replied, "Albert Cretingham junior is not Albert Cretingham senior's son."

Ross's face reflected the shock he felt at receiving Ferris's news. Sitting next to Ferris, Kat Bellamy could almost feel the depth of that shock as, for the first time in her memory, the D.I. appeared speechless, as he stood open-mouthed, assimilating the information. After what seemed an age, but was in fact only about ten seconds, Ross found his voice again.

"So whose fucking son is he?"

"We don't know, sir. All I can think is that Albert senior's wife was having it off with that Greek waiter, or someone else, long before poor old Albert caught wind of it."

"I wonder if young Albert knows," Sofie Meyer interjected. "If he found out by accident, it might have been enough to send him over the edge and uncover the darker side of his nature."

"Good point Sofie," Ross replied. "But, and it's a big but, how the hell did he get hold of the information in that damned diary? And why start killing women just because he found out he's not his father's real son?"

"It was just a thought, sir," Meyer answered his questions.

"It's okay, Sofie. At this point we are going to have to really plumb the depths in this case. We're running out of time and we appear to be going backwards, instead of forwards with this damned investigation.

At that moment, Derek McLennan looked up from his desk, where he'd answered his phone a minute or so ago.

"Sir," he called to Ross, "I have Doctor Bland on the phone. She's with Doc Nugent at the morgue."

Ross took the proffered telephone from McLennan.

"Christine, hello, I hope you have something positive to tell me."

"I can't guarantee it, Andy, but I have an idea. Doctor Nugent invited me to come and witness the DNA comparison tests and even though they haven't produced the results you were expecting or needing, an idea came to me just a couple of minutes ago. I've been kicking it around in my mind and I think we need to change tack a little if we're to solve both sets of killings."

Ross knew that when the Home Office profiler and forensic pathologist had an idea, it would be worth listening to.

"Go ahead, Christine. I'm listening."

"Well, as the results of the DNA comparison were coming through, it struck me that the whole DNA idea could still be instrumental in your search for the original Lighthouse killer, and of course, if you can isolate a suspect for those murders, it's logical to assume you should be able to identify a relative, or some other close acquaintance of the original killer who might be responsible for the current murders."

"That's a good thought, Christine. Any idea how we proceed with your theory?"

"I know time is short, but the only way I can see you being able to test my theory is by DNA testing of the men who were questioned back in 1966. If one of them is the Lighthouse killer, his DNA will be a match to the alien bloodstains on Stella Cox's clothing."

Ross fell silent again. He knew Bland was correct in her assumption but was also aware that with less than forty-eight hours to go before the killer was likely to strike again, he didn't have much time or indeed the resources to DNA test virtually every male who lived in Hale back in '66 and still lived there today. Even then, he had to consider that the Lighthouse killer might not have been a local, and could have come from anywhere in the area, or from further afield, some random psychopath who'd chosen the picturesque, relatively quiet and isolated village of Hale as his killing ground.

"Andy? Are you still there?" Christine Bland asked, in response to his silence on the phone.

"Yes, sorry, I was just thinking, that's all."

"Oh, good, I thought I'd lost you for a minute. So, what do you think?"

"I think you could be right, but whoever this person is, they have to have some connection to Carol Biggs, the house on Falkner Street and the diary."

"Diary? What diary?" Bland asked. She hadn't yet been brought up to date with the details of Ross and Drake's visit to the home of the late Carol Biggs and the discovery of what he now knew to be the diary of a serial killer.

"Sorry, things have been happening at our end too. I'll fill you in as soon as you return to headquarters."

"Sounds as if things are happening. I'll be back within the hour and you can bring me up to date."

"Right, see you soon," Ross replied, and handed the phone back to Derek McLennan who hung up and turned to his boss.

"Everything okay sir?" he asked.

"Maybe, Derek," was his reply.

Soon afterwards, Izzie and Sam Gable returned, having completed taking the statement from Alex Sefton.

"All okay, Izzie?" Ross asked as she knocked and entered his office, where he sat pondering his next move.

"Yes," she replied. "Alex was totally cooperative, though she couldn't tell us much more than we already learned at her house. I asked if she had any idea of other people who stayed as paying lodgers or even foster kids of Carol Biggs, but she couldn't help us at all in that respect."

"At least you tried. Sorry I lost it a bit out there at her house, by the way. This bloody case is really getting to me."

"I'd noticed," Izzie replied. "I don't think I've ever seen you so close to the edge as you were out there. You've got to try and relax a bit. We can only do what we can do, you know."

"I know Izzie, but I can't escape the thought that we might have missed something obvious and that someone could die because of that."

Izzie Drake, having worked with Andy Ross for over five years, probably knew him better than anyone except his wife, Maria, and perhaps when it came to the job, even more than that. She walked behind him and placed both hands on his neck and shoulders and began to massage them, not for the first time during times of extreme stress whilst engaged in a difficult investigation.

"God, that feels good," Ross sighed as Izzie's hands worked their magic and the muscles in his neck and shoulders began to relax, the tension slowly easing. "I hope that husband of yours knows what talented fingers his wife has."

"Oh, I can safely say he's well aware of what I can do with my fingers, thank you very much," she replied suggestively.

"I don't think I want to know any more, thank you, Sergeant Drake," Ross said, a smile appearing on his face at last. The pair shared such a close working relationship, but never had the spectre of romance ever entered into it. They were great friends and worked so well that people often though they were almost telepathically connected, but both were happily married and would never cross the line between work and play, despite their incredible bond.

"Ha, at least I've got you smiling again," Izzie laughed. "Want a coffee?"

"Yes, please," he replied, and Izzie quickly exited the office, returning a couple of minutes later with two steaming coffees in mugs, which she deposited on Ross's desk after moving a pile of papers and files to make space for them.

"So," Ross said, after blowing on the coffee in a vain attempt to cool the boiling liquid down enough to brave a small sip. "I presume you arranged transport home for our friend Alex?"

"Of course. I found Tony Curtis in the corridor as we came out of the interview room so I delegated the job to him. He seemed quite happy to be giving Alex a ride home."

"Did you tell him about Alex being…"

"Are you kidding? I can't wait to see what he has to say when he gets back. That's if he finds out, or if Alex tells him of course."

Ross nodded and couldn't help but smile at Izzie's grinning face.

"You're a cruel woman at times, Izzie Drake."

"I just couldn't help myself. You know how Tony loves to chat up the women, and you must admit, Alex Sefton is a good-looking woman."

"I have to admit, I had no idea she was a sex change patient. If she hadn't told us, I'd never have known she used to be a bloke."

"I just want to hear what Tony thought of her when he gets back," Izzie giggled again.

"Like I said, you have a cruel and wicked sense of humour sometimes. But, getting serious for a minute, you aren't going to believe the results of the DNA comparisons on the Cretinghams."

After he'd spent ten minutes explaining everything to Drake, and she'd expressed a similar reaction to his own on hearing what Nugent had found, and agreeing with Bland's theory, Ross decided it was time to call the team together. With time running out, it was time to come up with a new strategy.

Chapter 21

Briefing

With not much more than a day left to the team to prevent a third murder, assuming the killer kept to the timetable of the original Lighthouse Murders, Ross knew this was probably time for a final roll of the dice. With all the odds stacked against him and his people, the pressure was mounting by the minute as the clock ticked away the minutes. The wall clock in the squad room was loud enough that, as everyone sat or stood silently, waiting for him to begin, the sound of the second hand as it made its way inexorably round the clock face was like the knell of doom, creeping ever closer and Ross could only see it as watching and waiting as some as yet unknown woman police officer's life slowly ebbing away.

It was unusual for such silence to pervade the squad room as they waited for Ross to begin a briefing. There would normally be an incessant low buzz of whispers, the scraping of chair legs on the floor and a few comings and goings as various squad members visited the coffee maker, and some would shuffle papers in their hands as, without exception, an air of expectancy would be present as they all prepared for Ross to speak. For now, though, it felt as if time was suspended, a pall of negative vibes hanging over the team who all knew their inquiries so far had led to one dead end after another. This was proving to be one of the most difficult cases to be dropped in their laps for years.

The door opened to admit D.C. Tony Curtis, the last of the squad members to arrive, having just returned from ferrying Alex Sefton home. Sensing the atmosphere as her entered, the usually cheerful Curtis attempted to lighten the mood.

"Bloody hell you lot. You all jealous because I got to take the lady home?"

Ross and Drake couldn't help it. Both of their faces broke into knowing smiles.

Curtis saw the look on Drake's face and asked, "Was it something I said, Sarge?"

It was Ross who provided the answer.

"I think you'd better sit down and listen to what we have to say, Tony."

"Right, okay, I'm all ears, Boss," Curtis replied as he noisily grabbed a chair and seated himself, waiting for Ross to begin.

As the D.I. cleared his throat, ready to start the briefing, the door opened once more and D.C.I. Agostini entered the room and stood at the back, leaning against the wall.

"Don't let me interrupt, Andy, go ahead. I just want to see where we're at."

For the next ten minutes, Ross and Drake jointly filled the rest of the team in on their visit to the former home of Carol Biggs, now the property of Alex Sefton. Ross left it to Izzie Drake to explain the truth about Alex's sexuality and her tenuous connection to Edwin Cretingham's past, ending with Edwin's own gender reassignment. Izzie couldn't help but smile again as she watched Tony Curtis's face and body language, as he almost squirmed at the realisation he'd almost been on the verge of fancying the transgender woman he'd taken home a short time ago. Curtis regarded himself as a full red-blooded male and held some very old-fashioned ideas about the difference between men and women. Somehow, he knew he'd be in for some light-hearted ribbing from his colleagues later. When Ross announced the results of the DNA comparison tests on the two generations of the Cretingham family and the fact they bore no connection to the Lighthouse killer of '66, there was a stunned silence in the room.

"So does this mean we're back to square one?" D.C. Nick Dodds asked, a look of intense disappointment on his face at the thought of their investigation being 'on the rocks.'

"Not necessarily," Ross replied. "I still want to find Edwin Cretingham, now known as Teresa Moore. She might know how the diary came to be hidden in the home of Carol Biggs."

"And," Izzie Drake continued, "we need to have another word with Albert Cretingham junior."

"What for Sarge?" Curtis asked, having recovered his composure.

"He may have discovered the truth about his parentage, and, if there is a connection between the Cretinghams and the murders, no matter how loose, discovering that he wasn't really his father's son could have pushed him over the edge, turning him into a killer."

"Do you think that's a possibility, Doc?" Nick Dodds addressed Christine Bland, who until now had sat quietly beside Ross and Drake. She didn't hesitate to reply to Dodds's question.

"I think it can't be discounted, D.C. Dodds, though I have another theory which might be more likely to help you identify the man, or men, you're seeking."

With those words, Christine Bland had the total attention of everyone in the room. She looked at Ross, and when he nodded for her to continue, she went on, "Following the DNA comparison tests on Albert Cretingham senior and junior, which were, frankly, disappointing as far as previous theories about the case were concerned, it made me focus on other options. Now, let us suppose that the Lighthouse killer of 1966 is still residing in Hale. That would mean that a simple DNA test on any such members of the community would instantly identify the killer, beyond a reasonable doubt. Secondly, if we can identify that individual, we then have a link on which to seek the current murderer, whether it be a relative friend or indeed the original killer having come out of retirement, so to speak. At the time I was formulating this idea, I was with Doctor Nugent and was unaware of the existence of the diary, as alluded to by D.I. Ross a few minutes ago. Being in possession of that information, I can now firm up my theory by saying that it is highly likely that the Lighthouse killer, or a close connection to him, must have stayed for some time at the home of Mrs. Carol Biggs. It shouldn't be too difficult for a team of expert detectives such as yourselves to seek and find that connection, perhaps before any DNA tests are completed."

Ross spoke as she paused to catch her breath.

"Listen up everyone. We know we're fighting against a ticking clock here, so I want us to start with every male who we can identify as having been in the Traveller's Rest on the night of Stella Cox's murder in '66. Paul, print out copies of the list we were given by Stan Coleman and add anyone mentioned by Albert Cretingham who didn't appear on Coleman's list."

Paul Ferris nodded and mouthed "OK sir." Christine Bland spoke again.

"And this is very important, everyone. You're looking for someone who has undergone some form of recent trauma, what we call a 'stresser,' a trigger that has set this recent set of murders into action. Something has made the original killer, or someone connected to him, kill these women. Find that something and we should find our killer."

Derek McLennan, always the pragmatist, was the first to voice his concerns, standing up and directing his words to Ross.

"Sir, we're all aware of the ticking clock scenario, but let's be realistic. No way are we going to be able to carry out and rush through DNA tests on that many men in twenty-four hours. For God's sake, even if we sent the entire uniform division of Merseyside Police out to Hale with DNA testing kits, some of those men might not be at home, or might not be at work, or might not agree to voluntarily being tested. We can't assume refusal is a sign of guilt either."

"No we can't Derek, but we could see it as an indicator of suspicion on our part. I think even a guilty man would realise that, but I get your main point, I really do, but at the moment, it's the best option we have available to us. I can tell you that the Chief Superintendent will assign as many uniforms as we need to help us. She already gave me that promise in the presence of D.C.I. Agostini."

All eyes turned to the rear of the room where Oscar Agostini stood, still leaning against the wall.

"It's true, we have the Chief Super's assurance of whatever unformed assistance we need, and I'll be taking full advantage of the offer. By the time this briefing is over there'll be twenty uninformed officers waiting for us in the squadroom, plus an inspector, and two sergeants. Inspector Dave Brough is there to act as liaison with D.I. Ross and he'll make sure his people are fully conversant with whatever tasks you require from them. Please, carry on Andy."

"Okay everyone," Ross continued, "Those officers waiting to join us have been fully briefed by Chief Superintendent Hollingsworth herself, so they are all fully aware of the importance of their attachment to the investigation. When we leave this room, Izzie here will accompany you all to meet Inspector Brough. I want at least one or more of the uniformed officers to work alongside each one of you, under your guidance, as you hit the streets again. That is, all except you, Sofie," he said to Meyer.

"You have something special for me, sir?"

"Yes, I want you to take one of the uniforms with you to the Cretingham home. You've already been there so you know what they're like. A uniform might also help to loosen some tongues. Have a word with Inspector Brough and borrow one of his sergeants. Let's try and find out exactly what's going on there. I want to know if the younger Albert knows his father is not his biological dad, and secondly, I want you to try and get the older man to open up and maybe tell us who young Albert's real father is. I have a bad feeling growing in my gut about those two. I won't say any more for now, but I would like you to find out what you can and then report back to me as soon as you've been there, okay?"

"Okay, sir," she replied. "Any guidance on what perhaps you are thinking?"

"No, Sofie. I want to hear what they have to say to you first. If I'm correct in my thinking, we might have opened up a can of worms in that house?"

"A can of worms?" Sofie Meyer looked puzzled.

"I'm sorry. It's an English phrase, probably one you don't have back in Germany. It means there is something hidden under the surface, a buried secret, beneath what appears to be an innocent façade."

"Ah, yes, I see," she smiled her understanding. "I think perhaps there are many of your English phrases I still need to learn."

"You're doing great Sofie. Don't worry if we sometimes sound like we're from another planet."

Meyer laughed and instantly replied. "Thank you, sir. I think so far I am very much enjoying my time on planet Liverpool."

Ross laughed at her reply and was joined by Paul Ferris, who quipped, "Hey sir, be careful. Our Sofie is beginning to get the hang of our Scouse humour."

"God forbid," Ross smiled back at Ferris, a few seconds of light-hearted banter helping to lift some of the pall of gloom that had hung over the room a few minutes ago.

"I will be going now, sir," Sofie Meyer added, "I will pick up a sergeant and be gone in a few minutes."

Ross and Ferris smiled at the way she worded her sentence. "Lucky sergeant," Ferris said, out of Meyer's earshot.

"Behave yourself, now, Sergeant Ferris," Ross said, equally quietly.

"Being serious again, sir," Ferris relied. "Do you really think there's something to find out at the Cretingham house?"

"I'm not certain, Paul. Something keeps nagging away at the back of my mind about the two Alberts. Sofie Meyer is one very perceptive officer. Whether it's a natural talent or a bit of 'women's intuition' whatever that is, or a combination of both, I just think she's the one who might just sniff out what's going on, if indeed anything is, going on, I mean."

"I get your drift," Ferris nodded. "Do you think, despite everything pointing elsewhere, that young Albert might be involved in the murders?"

"D'you know, Paul? At the moment I'm not bloody sure what I friggin' think, but let's hope Sofie can throw some light on the situation, okay?"

"Okay, sir, you're the boss, Boss."

"Oh, shut up, Sergeant," Ross laughed again as Izzie Drake wandered back into the squadroom, fresh from organising the division of labour with regards to the uniformed officers, with Inspector Brough. Seeing the smiles on the faces of Ross and Ferris, she tilted her head to the side, quizzically, wondering what had amused them.

"Have I missed something? she asked, as she walked across to where Ross and Ferris stood close to the sergeant's computer station.

"Not really, Ross replied. "We're just discussing Sofie's assimilation into English culture."

"Yeah, that sounds plausible, I don't think," Izzie smiled at the pair.

"Okay, let's just say she's on her way to pick up a sergeant, and then they are going to look for a can of worms, aboard the Starship Liverpool, boldly going where no German copper has gone before" Ross said, keeping a straight face.

"Have you lot been drinking?"

"Not yet, but we might be if this conversation carries on much longer," Ferris said, turning and sitting at his desk, grinning across at Kat Bellamy seated at the next desk to the unit's computer specialist. Kat, only just over five feet tall, pretty with shoulder length blonde hair, the team's civilian administrative assistant, was almost as proficient on computers as Ferris and as such, was making herself an indispensable part of Ross's team of specialists. She grinned back at Ferris, grateful, like most in the room, to have witnessed those few important moments of levity in the midst of such a serious and soul-destroying case. She could see the strain showing on the faces of every detective in the room, and though not directly involved on the streets with the rest of the team she felt as personally involved as the rest and shared in their trials and tribulations on a daily basis.

"Take no notice of them Izzie," she said to Drake. "They're just acting like big school kids."

"Oh good. For a minute there I thought I'd actually walked into a professional police squadroom." Izzie said, heavy on the sarcasm.

"Take it from me, Izzie," Ross said, fighting to maintain a straight face. "We've been into some real heavy stuff here, girl. Not forgetting that there's a chance that the shit is preparing to hit the fan big time for the Cretingham boys."

Izzie waved a dismissive hand as she walked straight past Andy Ross on her way to the coffee machine.

"Oh, forget it. I'll try to get some sense out of you after I've got my coffee. You might want to hear about the arrangements I've agreed with Inspector Brough on the deployment of his men in tandem with ours."

Ross, switching back into serious mode, turned on his heel and made for his office.

"Make that three coffees, Izzie and come and join me, and we can swap notes. Please join us, Doctor Bland. We are about to flood the streets of Hale with coppers and also find out the truth behind the history of the Cretingham family."

Izzie nodded and a couple of minutes later, she walked into Ross's office, three coffees balanced on a tray together with a couple of KitKats, and pushed the door closed with a backward nudge of her bottom. Ross wasted no time in getting down to serious business.

"Sit down, Izzie. We need to talk."

Chapter 22

Suspicion and Admission

Sofie Meyer was finding life in Liverpool more enjoyable and certainly more exciting than she'd expected it to be when she first took up the offer from her superiors in the Bundeskriminalamt (BKA), the German Federal Police Force, to take up a two-year secondment to Merseyside Police as part of a reciprocal exchange scheme. One of the main reasons for her current feelings of professional satisfaction had been her attachment to the Specialist Murder Investigation Team, and its leader, D.I. Andy Ross. Ross had proved to be the kind of superior officer Sofie not only liked, but totally respected. From the day she'd arrived, Ross had made sure that Sofie received every ounce of help he and the rest of his team could give in integrating her into the team and its way of operating. Although her rank of Kriminalkommissar translated as Detective Inspector, she'd been granted the honorary rank of Detective Sergeant while in England, due to her relative inexperience with matters pertaining to criminal investigation in the UK and the fact that in Germany she was newly promoted to her rank after completing the three years training necessary to attain her position. Sofie didn't mind at all. To her way of thinking, this was a fantastic learning experience, and one she intended to grasp with both hands.

In many ways he reminded her of her boss back in Germany. Dieter Helm, who was her direct superior in the SO, (Serious and Organised

Crime) Division and who worked along similar principles to Ross, both personally and professionally.

Now, she sat in her car beside one of the unformed sergeants appointed to assist in the investigation. Brian Norwood was forty-five years old, with a wealth of experience working on the streets of Liverpool, having served almost twenty years on the force. Sergeant Norwood looked imposing in his full uniform, medal ribbons attached and Sofie was pleased he'd been appointed by Inspector Brough to accompany her on this visit to the Cretingham home. If any trouble transpired, she was sure Norwood would be more than capable of backing her up if she needed it. So far, Sofie hadn't needed to display any of her martial arts skills since joining Ross's team and hadn't felt the need to announce that she was trained in the Israeli art of Krav Maga, the military self-defence system developed by Hungarian born Emrich Lichtenfeld and widely taught to the Israeli Defence Forces.

Would there be trouble from the Cretinghams? Sofie knew Ross suspected something, but his refusal to reveal exactly what those suspicions were, she took as a compliment. He knew her insights and instincts were sound and trusted her to carry out this task professionally, and to report back to him with her findings, which he would probably expect to mirror his own, giving him confirmation of his suspicions.

"You have earned some medals?" she said as she drove towards the Cretingham home in Canning.

"Nothing special, I assure you," Norwood replied. "I spent a few years in the Royal Air Force before joining the Force and they are just campaign medals, that's all."

Sofie nodded, impressed all the same. She'd have been more impressed if the modest Norwood had told her that one of the medal ribbons on his uniform represented the George Cross, Britain's highest civilian honour, awarded to a young P.C. Norwood, who'd risked his own life to save two young children from a burning house, receiving a number of injuries himself in the process that required three months of hospital treatment before he could return to duty. If this visit to the Cretinghams threw up any nasty surprises, the couple who soon exited the police saloon car a few yards from the house were physically well equipped to overcome any potential situation.

"How do you want to handle this?" Norwood asked Sofie.

"I think D.I. Ross has some suspicions that may not be directly connected to the current case. I do not know why, but he seems to think I might be able to figure out why he feels uneasy about these men."

"He's putting a lot of faith in you, Sofie. He must trust your instincts."

"That's true. I took the DNA samples from both men, so they know me, and may let their guards down more because of that. I think your presence in your uniform will make them perhaps a little nervous and might tempt one of them to give something away without meaning to, Sergeant Norwood."

"Okay," said Norwood. "You take the lead and I'll provide whatever back up you need as and when it's called for, and please, call me Brian."

"Brian it is, then," Sofie nodded as she stood to one side as the uniformed officer knocked boldly on the Cretingham's front door.

After five minutes in the company of the two Alberts, Brian Norwood could see why D.I. Ross had a bad feeling about the men. Something just didn't sit right in his mind as they responded like a pair of automatons to Sofie Meyer's initial probing questions. Sofie was about to turn up the heat.

"Mr. Cretingham," she addressed the father. "I have to tell you that the DNA tests we conducted the other day produced some rather disturbing results."

"What d'you mean, disturbing?" senior asked.

This was the moment. Sofie knew she could have separated the two men, asked Brian Norwood to take the younger Cretingham man out of the room while she spoke privately to the father, but she instinctively knew that if she was to find anything along the lines Andy Ross was suspecting, this had to be done with both men present in the same room. Without hesitation, she jumped in with both feet.

"By disturbing, I mean that the samples I personally took from both of you have been analysed and have shown without a shadow of doubt that you, Mr Cretingham, are not the biological father of the man you call Albert, your son."

"*What?*" The younger Albert Cretingham virtually exploded and tool a step towards Sofie, but Norwood stepped forward, raised one enormous hand and Albert stood still, not retreating, but holding his ground. "That can't be fucking true. Tell them Dad. You people have messed up the tests, got it wrong somehow."

Albert the elder was very quiet. Too quiet, Sofie thought, and at that moment, she experienced a feeling of enlightenment, that magic moment when she suddenly realised just what must have given Ross his feeling that something was wrong in this house.

"You knew he wasn't your son, didn't you, Mr. Cretingham?"

Still the man remained silent, and Sofie knew without doubt that she'd hit upon the truth. Albert Cretingham senior had known all along that the boy he'd raised as his own wasn't his child at all. But what would have motivated him to perpetuate the lie for so long, unless…"

"How long were your wife and her lover involved Mr. Cretingham?"

Albert remained tight-lipped, saying nothing, unlike his son, now proved to be not his son.

"Dad, will you say something for fuck's sake?" Tell them this is all a bunch of lies. You and Mum had me long before she took up with that Greek waiter didn't you? You always told me that."

Albert senior didn't speak, but instead, looked long and hard at young Albert and slowly shook his head.

"Why don't you say something?" young Albert asked. Brian Norwood noticed that Cretingham's hands were now balled into fists, held tightly by his sides. Expecting trouble, he took another step towards Albert, cutting off his direct access to his 'father.'

"I think you know exactly what happened to your wife and her lover, Mr. Cretingham," Sofie decided to take a wild leap and see where it led. "Would you like to tell me about it?"

Norwood, who knew the bare bones of the case as briefed by Sofie on the way to the house, was nevertheless professional enough to guess at what the German officer was getting at and he now spoke up, giving her the force of his back up in order to press the elder Cretingham into a possible confession.

"Come on, Mr. Cretingham," he said, his voice, deep and firm, and full of authority. "I think we both know what Sergeant Meyer is saying, don't we? Your wife and her lover didn't really run away together, did they?"

The younger Albert now appeared totally confused, his anger dissipating as uncertainty entered his thoughts. Just what were these police officers trying to say? Were they accusing his Dad of something?

"Can somebody tell me what the hell this is all about? I thought the DNA samples we gave you were for you to do some comparisons with those murders in 1966. You had an idea my grandfather might have been involved, so what are you asking about my Mum for?"

Sofie ignored young Albert for a moment as she addressed the older man again.

"You see, Mr. Cretingham, one of our very clever computer geniuses at headquarters did some checking and we can find no record of a man called Alex Christakos ever leaving the United Kingdom, or for that matter, anyone named Patricia Cretingham. In fact the passport office tells us that your wife never applied for a passport in either her married name or her maiden name, so how could she have left the country?"

Before Cretingham could reply, Sofie Meyer went in for the kill, so to speak.

"In addition, the Greek authorities have no record of Alex Christakos having entered the country at the time you say he ran off with your wife, and they have no record of a man by that name and approximate age living or working in Greece around that time. But, even after all that, we did manage to trace his family. In Piraeus. Seems they lost touch with Alex a long time ago, soon after he told them he had met a woman and was going to bring her home to Greece. When he never turned up they reported him as missing to the Greek police, but because he was a grown man and living in another country the inefficient Greek police at that time did little or nothing to find Alex. So he was listed as missing of his own volition and nothing was done to find him."

"Do you see the picture that's building up here?" Brian Norwood interjected, giving Albert a glare that would melt the polar ice cap. "We can only think one thing, Mr. Cretingham."

"Sergeant Norwood is quite correct, Mr. Cretingham, and I must say the conclusion I have come to is inescapable. Your wife never really ran away with Alex Christakos, did she?"

Sofie fell silent, waiting for a response from the elder Albert Cretingham. After an interminable twenty seconds, he finally shook his head, slowly and almost imperceptibly.

"Was that a no?" Sofie asked.

Cretingham nodded this time. The younger Albert spoke again.

"Dad, what are they talking about? You always told me Mum had run off with that Greek fella. Are you saying that didn't happen?"

"That is exactly what your father is saying, Mr. Cretingham," Sofie replied, not really knowing how else to refer to the man he's always believed to be his father.

"Come on, Albert, why not get it off your chest? You'll feel a lot better if you do," said Norwood.

"Sergeant Norwood is correct," said Sofie. "Why don't you tell us where your wife Patricia and Alex Christakos really went to, or more precisely, where they are now?"

Albert Cretingham took a deep breath, and then another one, and his hands, resting on the arms of his chair began to shake. Finally, he spoke, his voice so quiet they could hardly hear him.

"In the garden, under the greenhouse."

"Could you say that again please, a little louder this time."

"They're in the garden, under the greenhouse, where I buried the cheating mare and her slimy Greek bastard of a lover all them years ago."

"Why did you need to bury them, Albert?" said Norwood.

"Why? 'Cause I fucking killed the pair of 'em, didn't I?"

"How did you kill them, Mr.Cretingham? Sofie asked, keeping her voice as level and dispassionate as she could.

"I found 'em at it in me own bed, didn't I? Came home from work early one afternoon 'cause I weren't feelin' well and there they were, large as fucking life, stark naked, him lying on top of her, between her legs, doing it to her. I stood in the doorway, looking at 'em and so you know what they did when they realised I were there? They fuckin' laughed at me. I turned on me heels and went downstairs. They must have thought I was thick or that I didn't care 'cause I heard 'em still laughing as I picked up the carving knife from the kitchen. They stopped laughing when I went back upstairs and walked in the bedroom. He were still on top of her so I stabbed him right where he lay, in the back, just like they'd been stabbing me in the back with their filthy carrying on. Pat didn't even scream. She looked at me from underneath him, and said, *"What the fuck did you do that for you soddin' retard?"* I just stared at her and walked round the bed, pulled the Greek off her and sort of smiled at her, and never said a word. She looked as if she was going to try and get up but before she could move I just plunged the knife into her chest, right between her tits. She sort of gasped, and her mouth opened and closed like a fish, so I stabbed her again and again, first in her tits, then in her guts, and finally in between her legs. She bled like a stuck pig and must have been dead before I finished stabbing the cheating bitch. I didn't care. I was just happy to see the back of 'er, the cheating cow."

Cretingham fell silent, his incredible memory having allowed him to provide the two shocked officers with a graphic and bloody recollection of the murders of his wife and lover. Sofie asked him a question that had been burning in her mind since he'd begun describing the killings.

"Where was young Albert while all this was going on, Mr. Cretingham?"

"He were asleep in bed. He were only a toddler, and had a good sleep every afternoon, so he never 'eard a thing. See, I knew he couldn't be mine, 'cause when she were expectin' she 'adn't let me touch 'er in bed for ages. I knew how long it took for babies to come, so I figured the baby had to be the Greek's. I still loved him when he were born though and always treated 'im as me own. I still love him now, but that day, I couldn't take it any longer. I had to do what I did. They were making a right bloody fool of me, and in me own bed too."

Tears were beginning to show in the eyes of the younger Albert, still standing like a statue, though his body seemed to be shaking from head to foot. Sofie had to ignore him for now, and continued her questioning of Albert senior.

"How did you clear up the mess and get the bodies out of the house?" she asked next.

"I wrapped the two of 'em in a blanket off the bed and tied it up with some rope from the shed in the garden. Then I cleaned the blood up as best as I could using a scrubbing brush and bleach. When it got dark I carried both of 'em out to the back garden and dug a nice big hole and rolled them into it. I covered 'em up well, and went back indoors, and took all the sheets off the bed. Next day I emptied the wardrobe of her clothes and got rid of 'em on the council tip. I 'ad a nice bonfire and burned the sheets. There were some stains on the carpet that didn't come out, so I waited a couple of weeks and then got rid of it and bought a new one. It's not like we ever 'ad visitors so nobody really noticed she'd gone. Then I bought the greenhouse and put it up right over where the pair of 'em were buried. They've never been disturbed since that day."

"I think you've said enough for now," Sofie said. "You can make a full statement at the station, under caution, but I do have another question I would like to ask."

"Go on the lass, I think I know what you want to know. You're going to ask about Edwin. You want to know who is mother was, am I right?"

"That is correct," Sofie admitted. "If you murdered your wife, then who gave birth to Edwin, and why has she never been mentioned?"

"I paid a prossie for sex, see, 'cos I were desperate for a bit of the other, like, you know?"

When Sofie said nothing, he went on.

"A while later, she comes knocking on me door, sayin' she's up the duff"

Sofie Meyer looked mystified, until Cretingham, realising she didn't know the phrase, added, "Pregnant, lass. She were having a nipper and said it were mine. I asked her why she didn't just get rid of it and she said she didn't believe in aborting babies. A whore with a bloody conscience, can you believe it? So, I told her I'd take care of it right? Then when she 'ad it, she looked after it for a few months and then one day, she just dropped the nipper off, with all 'is stuff and told me she were leavin' town. When she'd gone I looked at what she'd put in the bag of stuff. There were nappies, baby milk, all that kind of stuff and then I found an envelope, and it were 'is birth certificate. That fuckin' bitch had put *father unknown* on it. His dad could 'ave been any of a thousand bloody punters, but she conned me in to thinkin' he were mine. That were the last time I saw her. She just left the kid with me and I had no choice but to bring him up. I weren't surprised when 'e turned out a bit of a wrong 'un. I can't remember the last time I saw 'im but someone at the pub told me as he'd turned all weird and they'd seen 'im walking round in a bloody skirt. I don't want no fuckin' drag queen as a son of mine, I can tell you that."

"But, when he was a baby, what did you tell people about where Edwin had appeared from?"

"I told them the truth, lass, and made 'em swear they'd never tell the kid about his mother as he grew up. Better he thought of Pat as his mum, what'd run off with another bloke, than know he were the son of a prossie who ran away and dumped him."

Sofie couldn't see much difference between the two scenarios but decided not to say any more on the subject.

"Raised two lads on me own, I did, Sergeant. Not bad for someone who they always accused of bein' slow and dim-witted eh?" Cretingham said, and Sofie Meyer, while having a grudging admiration for the man's efforts, despite his autism, couldn't help feeling that Albert hadn't exactly been the perfect father to either of the two young boys he'd brought up.

With that, she placed Albert Cretingham senior under arrest after reading him his rights. As she clicked the handcuffs in place the younger Albert suddenly sprang into action. A sudden lunge took the younger Albert three steps closer to the man who he'd always thought of as his father. Brian Norwood, who'd been poised, expecting a reaction from the younger Cretingham, instantly reached out his right arm and with an almost practised elegance, swept the man off his feet with one powerful swipe, sending young Albert Cretingham sprawling on his back in his own living room.

"Now then, we'll have none of that," the burly sergeant snarled at the man lying prone on the floor.

"Let me get to him, please," Cretingham whined from his place on the floor. "All these years he's lied to me. I believed every word he said about my Mum and all this time her bones have been lying rotting in our back yard, for fuck's sake. He killed her. He murdered my Mum, the evil, lying bastard. I've done everything for him since he became ill, and now I find out he killed my own Mother. Just give me five minutes with him, please," he begged.

"That's not going to happen," Norwood responded, holding a hand out to help Cretingham to his feet. "Come on now, up you get, and forget any more stupid attempts to attack your father, there's a good lad."

"He's not my bloody father though is he? You've found that out from your damn DNA tests. I bet my Dad was the man who's lying in that grave in the garden with my Mum, don't you think?"

"It looks like it, Albert," this came from Sofie Meyer. "Are you sure you never knew any of this information about your paternity?"

"Eh?"

"You have never been tempted to take a test to find out if Albert here really is your father?"

"Of course not. Why would I? I've always believed, up until a couple of minutes ago, that he was my Dad. Why would I need a piggin' DNA test to prove what I thought I already knew?"

Sofie admitted he had a point. The thought that he could have gone on a killing spree after finding out his Dad was not his Dad after all simply didn't hold any merit. She instructed Young Albert to sit down, and he more collapsed than sat onto the sofa, his face a mask of tears of anguish mixed with tears of pure anger. His body shook, and his hands trembled, but the fight had all gone from him after Brian Norwood's timely intervention. While Norwood stood guard on the handcuffed man, Sofie called headquarters, informing a surprised but delighted Paul Ferris of the results of her visit to the Cretingham home. Ferris would organise the deployment of SOCOs and a full forensic gathering team. Sofie didn't envy those whose job it would be to dismantle the greenhouse and uncover the buried remains that lay beneath. It didn't take long for the first of the requested personnel to arrive, led by Doctor William Nugent, who, as duty pathologist was also the medical examiner, and his assistant Francis Lees. Also, as Sofie had requested from Paul Ferris, two uniformed constables arrived to secure the crime scene, while Sofie and Norwood delivered their prisoner to headquarters for further questioning.

"No D.I. Ross today?" Nugent asked, looking around the sitting room and seeing only Sofie Meyer, Brian Norwood and the two Cretingham men. He'd received a quick briefing over the phone when Paul Ferris called to request his presence at the crime scene, so he was in a hurry to get things moving at the burial site.

"No Doctor Nugent. We didn't expect quite the outcome we have discovered when we came to interview Mr. Cretingham, today."

"I bet you didn't Sergeant Meyer. Aye, for sure, I bet you didn't. Well, I'll be leaving you to do whatever you have to do while I organise things out in the garden. It may take a while before we unearth the remains, you understand?"

"Of course. Thank you Doctor. I'm sure D.I. Ross will be along to view the scene before long," Sofie replied. "I will leave you to your work while Sergeant Norwood and I deliver this man into custody."

A few minutes later, Sofie left the scene with Norwood and Albert the elder, bound for police headquarters. Sofie had been pleasantly surprised by the arrival at the house of D.C. Ginger Devenish, who explained that he was about to head out to Hale when Sergeant Ferris had redirected him to come out and hold the fort until D.I. Ross and Sergeant Drake could get away from the office to come and see the newly unearthed murder scene's burial site.

Sofie very much wanted to come back herself. She'd broken a years old murder case which until now, had remained unknown and had now brought to justice a killer who had lived for years feeling safe in the knowledge he'd literally got away with murder. She felt a need to be there when the bodies of Patricia Cretingham and Alex Christakos were raised from the ground after so many cold and lonely years in the unhallowed ground of Albert Cretingham's garden.

Chapter 23

Excavate, Evaluate

Ross and Drake walked into the squadroom to be greeted by Meyer's news, related to them by Paul Ferris.

"You knew it, didn't you?" Drake instantly said to Ross. She knew he had some suspicions in the back of his mind where Albert Cretingham was concerned, but he'd kept his thoughts very much to himself so far.

"Let's just say I had certain misgivings about the story Albert gave us about the way his wife and her lover suddenly upped sticks and left Liverpool, never to be heard of again. I asked Paul to quietly do some digging for me and though we had no proof of foul play, I thought Sofie's rather unique style might just break the older man down and get him to admit the truth."

"It's her German directness," Izzie agreed. "She comes straight to the point and goes right for the jugular."

Ross smiled. "Yes, and I had a feeling that style would work with Albert Cretingham. One of the things that was mentioned in the report we received when she joined us was her intuitive thinking. She's a lot like you in that respect. I had a feeling that once she got talking with Cretingham, she'd quickly realise what I'd been suspecting and would push for some answers. Even I didn't think she'd be quite so successful so quickly."

"Thanks for the compliment. I'm not sure I would have instinctively worked out that he'd killed his wife and her boyfriend, though."

"I think, if you'd had the time to think it through, you'd have arrived at the same conclusion, Izzie. Especially once you knew what Paul had dug up, or rather not dug up about the wife and boyfriend."

Izzie smiled. Ross hadn't realised the words he'd just spoken were rather ironic in the circumstances, but then he smiled too as he caught on.

"Ah, right, not the best choice of words, I agree, but my point stands, anyway."

"What now, with regards to Albert?"

"He can stew for a while. It's an old case and there's no mad rush to push things. He isn't going anywhere and I'm sure Sofie will want to get back to the house to see how the retrieval of the bodies is going."

"And Hale, sir? Won't we need her intuitive skills out there too?"

"Yes, but we owe her the chance to see this one through. If Cretingham was telling the truth about where the bodies are, it shouldn't take long for Miles Booker and his Crime Scenes people to bring them up from under the greenhouse. As soon as the Doc makes his determination of death Sofie can see them off to the morgue and her job there will be done. She and young Devenish can then join the rest of the team in Hale and follow up on the Cretingham case after Fat Willy's done his thing with the remains."

Miles Booker led what Ross believed one of the finest Crime Scene Investigation units in the country. If there was anything to find, any clue to discover, they were the people to deliver the goods.

"Bloody gruesome isn't it though?" Drake went on. "That poor woman and her lover lying there in the back garden for all this time, and him knowing they're there all the time his son was growing up, playing in the garden, right where his mother was buried."

"Yeah, but he wouldn't have thought like that, would he? As far as he was concerned, he probably suspected young Albert wasn't his own son, so he'd have been ambivalent about having the kid's mother buried in the garden."

"He's got to be a cold-hearted bastard, that's for sure," Izzie concluded.

"Can't argue with you on that one," Ross agreed, as a knock came on his door, which opened slowly as Sofie Meyer poked her head around the door and walked in as Ross beckoned her into the office.

"Good work, Sofie, I take it you have Albert Cretingham safely in custody?"

"We do, sir. Thank you for trusting me with the task of going out to see him, to ascertain if I could agree with your feelings about the man."

"No thanks needed," Ross smiled. "I had a feeling you'd be able to work out what I was feeling, and that you'd have the confidence to act on your findings."

"I was very ably assisted by Sergeant Norwood, sir, one of the uniformed officers under Inspector Brough. He was very good at his job. The younger of the two Alberts might have made things difficult but Sergeant Norwood handled things very efficiently."

"Glad to hear it. Sounds as if Inspector Brough picked the right man for the job of accompanying you."

"I am pleased to agree with you, sir," Sofie Meyer concurred. "May I ask if I will be able to return to the house in order to see how Mr. Booker and his team are progressing?"

"Of course you can. I spoke with Miles a short time ago and if you set off now, you should be just in time to see the bodies being recovered. Oh yes, take young Devenish with you. The experience will do him good."

"I agree sir. He is becoming a very able detective, is he not?"

"He certainly is," Ross agreed, just as the phone on his desk began to ring.

"Miles, hello," he said as he heard the voice of the Crime Scene Supervisor. After listening for a minute, he spoke again. "Okay, understood. Sergeant Meyer and D.C. Devenish will be with you shortly, so I would appreciate it you can hold off on the final body removal until they get there."

Sofie actually heard Booker reply to Ross, "No problem, Andy. The lads and lasses will appreciate a short coffee break while we wait for them."

"How has the younger Albert Cretingham reacted to what you're doing, by the way?"

"Hardly seen him," Booker replied. "The two constables who were sent to oversee the site until your people returned have kept him away from where we've been dismantling the greenhouse and digging up the garden where it stood. I've seen him looking out through the kitchen window a few times. If I had to describe the man's face, I'd say it bore the look of a broken man, Andy."

"Well, I suppose he's entitled," Ross replied. "It's not every day you find out your father is not your father and he also murdered your mother and planted her in the garden, is it? Right, Sofie and young Devenish are leaving now," he signalled to Meyer who nodded and made her exit from his office, stopping only to pick up the young acting detective constable as she made for the crime scene once more. "Keep me posted on what you find, Miles. You never know what else you might unearth there."

"I hope you're not going to tell me there could be more bodies?" Booker asked.

"I doubt it, Miles, but, well, you just never know, do you?"

"Bugger off, Ross, and stop delaying me from getting me hands on a nice cup of coffee. I'll be waiting for Sergeant Meyer, and then we'll see what we finally have to raise from the earth."

"Good man, Miles, talk again soon," said Ross as he hung up, replacing the phone on its cradle and smiling at Drake.

"Never hurts to keep old Miles on his toes, Izzie, does it?"

"You don't really expect to find any more bodies there, do you?" Izzie looked at him intently as she waited for his reply.

"No Izzie, I don't. I don't think Albert Cretingham is serial killer material somehow. I think he committed a crime of passion and has probably lived in fear of being found ever since. Anyway, come on, let's go and jolly the others along. We're still racing against the clock, and up to now, we're coming a bloody poor second, I hate to admit."

* * *

Sofie Meyer and Ginger Devenish soon arrived once more at the Cretingham home, where they found Miles Booker waiting for them in the small, neatly tended front garden, smoking his pipe, loaded with an aromatic tobacco that the German officer recognised as soon as she reached the garden gate, and caught the aroma immediately.

"Holland House is it, Mr. Booker?"

"You're quite right, Detective Sergeant Meyer. Well done. Not many ladies are able to identify a tobacco by its aroma nowadays, that's for sure. You're a veritable Sherlock Holmes."

"Ha, I am not quite so clever as you may think, Mr. Booker. My father, he too smokes that blend of tobacco in his pipe. It is very distinctive. So you see, I cheated," she laughed.

"Ah, I see. Elementary, my dear Sofie," he joked and Sofie grinned in return.

"Very good, Mr. Booker. I too have read the Sherlock Holmes stories. Your Sir Arthur Conan Doyle was a superb writer of crime fiction, I think."

Sofie introduced the new acting Detective Constable to Booker, who led them through the house to the back garden after first extinguishing his pipe. The aroma of the aromatic tobacco followed him as he led the way, giving Sofie a few seconds of nostalgic memory of her home in Hamburg, where her father would doubtless be smoking a pipe or two before the day was over. Booker had the two detectives suit up in white forensic suits and boots and proceeded to lead on into the garden. Sofie was amazed at the progress Booker and his team had achieved in the short space of time she'd been away. Where the greenhouse had previously stood, there was now an area of bare earth, with a large hole having been excavated in double quick team by the Crime Scene Technicians. The glass panels and aluminium frame of the structure now stood to one side, leaning against the wooden panels of the garden fence. Two of Booker's people stood at the edge of the hole in the ground, and as they drew closer, Sofie saw two more, already in the hole, beside what appeared to be two old grey army blankets, rolled up and tied with lengths of rope of indeterminate manufacture. Booker's Crime Scene technicians had already brushed away any residual soil and mud that had adhered to the two makeshift burial shrouds. The two technicians standing at the top of the hole passed thick lengths of webbing down to the two men in the hole and gradually these were gently wrapped around each body in turn and the remains were gradually hauled to the surface, and laid upon the grass of Albert Cretingham's neatly tended lawn, now well- trodden and bruised by the steady trampling by numerous boots, and the placing of various pieces of equipment.

Miles Booker himself took on the task of cutting through the bindings that held the old, grey blankets that were the couple's burial shrouds in place. As they fell away, what remained of Patricia Cretingham and Alex Christakos was revealed to the watching officers. During her career, Sofie Meyer had seen her fair share of corpses, Ginger Devenish less so, but both were unprepared for the sight that now assaulted their eyes.

The quality of those old army blankets had probably played some part in maintaining the bodies in the condition in which they were found in the damp, clinging Liverpool earth. Patricia lay on her back, the remains of a yellow dressing gown clinging to parts of the body which surprisingly retained a few remnants of wet, grizzled flesh, hanging loosely from the now grey and degraded bone structure of the skeleton. What appalled Meyer most of all and what would give young Devenish nightmares for weeks to come was the fact that Patricia's skull revealed that she must have died quickly, as her mouth lay wide open as if she'd died in the midst of last, awful, tortured scream, as the reality of her impending doom hit home as Cretingham must have plunged his knife deep into her body. It was easy for Meyer to make out certain marks where the knife had scraped her breastbone as old Albert used his full strength to force the killing blade deep into the young woman's chest cavity. Cretingham must have wrapped her in the dressing gown, in an attempt to afford her some kind of twisted modesty in death, but not so with Alex Christakos, whose skeleton was clearly devoid of any remnants of clothing. Sofie guessed that Cretingham must have simply wrapped the naked lover in the blanket and buried him as nude as the day he was born. Alex had been a tall man, and Albert hadn't quite made the grave long enough, as Sofie noticed that he'd broken both of the man's ankles and twisted the feet upwards in line with the legs, rather than dig an extra few inches of soil to extend the grave. Even though the man had been dead when this last action had taken place, it only served to reinforce in Sofie's mind, just what a cold-blooded and ruthless killer the seemingly nice old Albert Cretingham had been when he'd killed his wife and her lover.

You alright young man?" Miles Booker asked Ginger Devenish who looked a little green around the gills. "First time you've seen a body excavation is it?"

Devenish nodded, saying nothing. He couldn't think of words to describe how he felt at that moment.

"Don't worry about it, Ginger," Meyer said, placing a hand on his shoulder. "We all go through these events as we begin our careers. It is not easy to see these things. Believe me, I went through something very similar in my early days as a detective. We found four bodies that had been buried in the foundations of a house as a result of a gangland vendetta. If you wish, go in the house and have a drink of water or maybe a cup of tea."

"I'll be fine, Sarge, honest I will," Devenish replied, feeling more than a little embarrassed. "It was a bit of a shock, that's all, seeing them like that. I think I was expecting skeletons, you know, just bones, not bits of rotted flesh and bits of clothing."

As well as the remains of her dressing gown, the CSI's had also found the poor woman's carpet slippers, close to the skeletal feet. Albert Cretingham, in his twisted state of mind after the killings, had clearly tried to dress his dead wife to cover her nudity. Sofie wondered if they would ever find out why.

"Well, well, ma friends, and just what do ye have for me today?" came the booming voice of the Glaswegian pathologist and medical examiner. Doctor William Nugent, (Known behind his back as Fat Willy), was accompanied as always by his assistant, the cadaverous-looking Francis Lees, armed as usual with his large black bag of forensic tools and with his high-powered camera hanging round his neck.

"Two bodies, one male, one female, probably been under the ground for about thirty-five years, Doc," Booker spoke to the pathologist. "The woman's husband has already confessed to the killing of both of them, so we just need you to certify them as being deceased and we can have them removed and sent to the morgue for autopsy."

"And why, pray tell me, were they removed from the ground before I'd had an opportunity to examine them in situ?"

"Because, Doc, there was very little room down there and as D.I Ross needs his people back as soon as possible to pursue a serial killer, who is likely to strike at any time, we needed to work fast. It's not as if they needed you to examine them in the grave in order to certify death."

Booker was firm with Nugent, one of the few people who could act in such a bluff manner towards the man. Nugent knew Booker was the ultimate professional and even more, he knew and understand exactly what Booker was saying.

"Aye, ye're correct of course Mr. Booker. I'm aware of what D.I. Ross and his people are up against. Now, let me at yon bodies of yours, get the deaths certified and then we'll let you and your people get on with your site examination while the ambulance ferries these two to my lab for examination."

Nugent and Francis Lees set to work, with Lees taking photographs of the remains from all angles and of the grave interior. Nugent bent to examine what was left of the couple and had no hesitation in announcing them as being deceased, the formalities concluded.

Before they could be taken away however, Sofie Meyer insisted on carrying out her own examination of the site and the remains. Together with one of Booker's CSIs she first entered the grave itself, not sure what, if anything, she was looking for. Finding nothing of interest she knelt on the ground next to the tarpaulin on which Booker's team had laid the remains, and carried out a brief examination of her own, again finding nothing of significance. She was fairly sure that this would be a straight forward prosecution of Albert Cretingham, based on his own confession to the murders. There was certainly nothing here to suggest anything to contradict his version of events.

As soon as the remains were removed and were followed to the morgue by Nugent and Lees, where they would undergo further examination, Meyer and Devenish departed, leaving Miles Booker and his team to complete their forensic examination of the site. Open and shut case it may be, but Booker wanted to be certain there was nothing that had been missed or that could interfere with the successful prosecution of Albert Cretingham.

"Feeling better?" Sofie asked young Ginger Devenish as they motored back to headquarters.

"I'm fine, thanks Sarge. Sorry about back there. I feel a right bloody wimp for behaving like that."

"Do not feel like that, it was nothing for you to be ashamed of. As I told you. I also had a moment like that in my early days as a detective. Just put it aside now and move on."

"Thanks," said Devenish. "Er…I don't suppose I could ask you not to say…"

"Do not worry. I will not be saying anything to anyone about your reaction. Why should I? You are only human, after all, are you not?"

"Yes, of course. Thanks Sarge, really, I mean it." Meyer wouldn't have realised it, but at that moment she had made a friend for life. Devenish's respect and admiration for the German detective was such that he would follow her through the jaws of hell if she asked, and it certainly helped that she was, in Devenish's thoughts, a 'real looker' too.

Sofie said no more but smiled as she accelerated and motored the last mile to headquarters at just over the speed limit. They still had work to do, and another killer to find, without delay!

Chapter 24

Breakthrough?

"It's not looking good Andy, is it?" D.C.I. Oscar Agostini said, peering at Ross over a copy of the latest case report as the pair sat in Agostini's office, together with sergeants, Izzie Drake and Paul Ferris, and profiler Christine Bland.

"Give me a bloody complex international conspiracy with multiple murders thrown in, any day," Ross said, ruefully. "I mean, come on, we're looking at another potential murder taking place within twenty-four hours and we're reduced to trying to get the people of Hale to voluntarily give us DNA samples, most of which we have no chance of checking by tomorrow."

"How are you getting on with your search for locals who might have suffered some recent trauma, Paul? Anything that might be a trigger that could have set the killer on his course of action?" the D.C.I. asked Ferris.

Christine Bland had suggested some recent setback or upheaval in the killer's life was the catalyst for the current murders. If they could link such an event to anyone who was connected, no matter how loosely, with the original Lighthouse killer, she felt they might yet be able to identify whoever was behind the recent killing spree.

"Still working on it sir." Ferris replied. "It's not like there's a special internet section devoted to traumatic events in the lives of the families of Hale, you know."

"I know, Paul. We're clutching at straws."

"All the teams on the streets in Hale have instructions to ask if any of their friends or neighbours have suffered any great loss or trauma lately," Ferris added. "That might be our best source of intel."

"I agree with Paul," Bland interrupted. "Never underestimate the power of local gossip."

"We know that only too well," Drake agreed. "We might be playing catch-up with this bastard, but we can't be that far behind him, really. We just need a little bit of luck."

"And, if we can associate a traumatic experience suffered by one of the current residents of the village with anyone who spent time living in the home of Mrs. Biggs in their younger days, we will have a substantial link to a viable suspect," Bland added.

"Every officer involved in this case has instructions to report in immediately if they uncover anything that could prove to be our killer's trigger," Ross said, knowing he was placing a heck of a lot of faith in just such a discovery.

Everyone fell silent, and Oscar Agostini looked from one face to the other of those seated opposite him, and standing against the wall beside the door in Bland's case. The D.C.I. had his hands steepled together, a sure sign to Ross that his old friend was deep in thought. Finally, Agostini broke the silence.

"Okay, listen up. The odds on us finding this bastard before he strikes again are growing longer with each passing minute. I know it, you know it, and the entire team knows it. Even the bloody killer must be rubbing his hands with glee knowing we're nowhere near apprehending him. But we do only need one break, a tiny slice of luck, one minor slip up by this evil piece of shit. Then, he's ours."

As luck would have it, right at that moment, there was a knock on Agostini's office door and it began to open, just enough for Kat

Bellamy to squeeze her head and shoulders around the door, enough to address the boss.

"Sorry to interrupt, Mr. Agostini, but D.C. McLennan just phoned in, wanting to speak to D.I. Ross," Kat looked directly at Ross as she spoke. "Derek thinks he may be on to something."

Instantly on his feet, Ross was almost out of the door when he turned and said, "Excuse me sir," and grabbed Kat, gave her a perfunctory hug and was pulling his mobile phone from his pocket, all in the space of a millisecond, or so it seemed.

"Carry on Andy, don't mind us," Agostini smiled, inwardly hoping this might be what they'd all been waiting and hoping for.

Drake, Ferris and Bland remained in the seats in Agostini's office. Everybody present knew without doubt that Ross would be back just as soon as he'd spoken to Derek McLennan.

"Okay, Derek. What've you got for me?" Ross said, leaning against the wall in the corridor outside Agostini's office. He'd exited the office because he wanted to hear Derek's news in private to assess its value before sharing it with the boss and his colleagues.

"Sir, it may be what we're looking for. Doctor Bland said to look for potential triggers, anything that might have sent the original Lighthouse killer over the edge and brought him out of retirement, so to speak."

"I know that Derek. Stop bloody prevaricating and tell me what you have."

"Okay, sorry sir. Did you know they have a free newspaper in Hale?"

"No, but you're going to tell me about it, aren't you?"

"Yes, sir. It's called The Chronicle of Hale but despite the grand literary-sounding title it's basically one of those free, through the letterbox advertising rags. You know the formula, a couple of pages of local news followed by about twenty pages of nothing but adverts. But about three weeks before the recent murders began they ran a piece on their front page about the Lighthouse murders in 1966. They devoted a page and a half to the case, and closed by saying, and I quote, *'The evil and perverted monster who perpetrated these heinous crimes against the innocents has never been brought to justice. Is there hope that after all these years, those three young women can still find justice in this world?'* That would have given our killer a jolt don't you think?"

"I do indeed, Derek. That last sentence could have been like a red rag to a bull in his twisted mind. You might just have hit on the trigger we've been looking for."

"If that's true sir, it also means our killer is still in Hale, surely? The Chronicle has a very small circulation, and is only delivered to homes in Hale by a small team of volunteers who post it by hand through people's letterboxes."

"It could have been sent by a Hale resident to our killer who could live elsewhere, Derek." Ross said, playing Devil's Advocate.

"I know, sir, but do you honestly see that as a possibility in this case?"

"No Derek, I don't. I think you're right. We're looking for someone who lives in or around Hale, I'm sure of it."

"So we just have to find someone who could have been sufficiently affected by the printing of the story to start the latest killing spree. By the way, the Echo covered the story, just in a single column buried away on page four on the actual anniversary of the first murder."

"That's right, Derek, cheer me up why don't you, but yes, I agree with you, and I still feel sure the key lies somewhere in the life of Carol Biggs. Don't forget, Alex Sefton found the diary in Mrs. Biggs's old house, so it's likely our killer either stayed there under foster care, or later in life, lived with Carol Biggs as a lodger."

"Or as a lover, sir," McLennan replied, and Ross instantly felt a fool for not having thought of that scenario.

"Bloody hell, Derek, you're right. I wonder if Alex Sefton knows if Carol Biggs shared her life with anyone who previously lived or was brought up in Hale."

"Do you want me to call her and ask the question, sir?"

"No, leave it with me, Derek. I've an idea she'll talk more readily with me or Izzie than with someone she hasn't met or spoken with before."

"Okay, sir. I'll get back to tramping the streets and knocking on doors."

"Good lad, what's it looking like out there"

"Really warm, lots of tourists about, and of course, just about every other one wants to know why there are so many police officers on the streets."

"What are you telling them?"

"Just what we were told to tell 'em, that we're investigating a recent series of crimes in the area, nothing for them to be worried about."

"Okay, off you go, Derek. Time to talk to Alex Sefton again."

It was Izzie Drake who did the talking when Ross filled her in on McLennan's theory.

"Always thinks that little bit outside the box, our Derek," she'd smiled when Ross mentioned his lover idea. Apart from a few seconds of berating himself for not thinking of it himself, Ross was simply grateful to have Derek McLennan on his team. His quick thinking and incisiveness of thought was a very long way from the rather shy and gauche young detective who'd first joined his team in the beginning of the specialist squad, assigned by virtue of being deemed to have 'exceptional promise,' a promise that had definitely matured during his years working with Ross and Drake. Now, Izzie was hoping, like Ross, that Derek's latest idea might just bear fruit.

"Alex, it's Izzie Drake. We were wondering if you could help us out with something."

Alex Sefton liked the detective who had given her some sound advice after her interview at police headquarters. She'd advised Alex to be open and truthful with her new girlfriend if she held out any hopes of a future relationship with her. Alex knew it made sense and was ready to have a serious heart-to-heart with Lisa later that day. If it worked, great, if not, then as Drake had said, it wasn't meant to be.

"What can I do to help you now?" Alex asked. Izzie could feel her tensing up even over the phone.

"I'd like you to think back to when Carol Biggs lived in the house. Do you remember the names of anyone else who lived with her? I don't just mean foster kids, I'm wondering more specifically if she had any live-in boyfriends over the years."

"Bloody hell, Sergeant Drake, that's a tall order. I can remember a couple of chaps who lived with her, but there were probably more over the years."

"The ones you can remember would be helpful Alex, please try to remember their names."

Alex was silent for a few seconds. Drake correctly assumed she was having to think about her answer, dredging up memories from the past. Alex came back on the line at last.

"Okay, I remember a guy who lived there as a lodger called Sammy. I only met him a couple of times, but I do remember he was a Geordie, you know, from up Newcastle way. Then there was a local lad, a fair bit younger than Mrs. Biggs. I often wondered if he was just a lodger or maybe a toyboy. I was scared to ask her, even though we got on well. It wasn't my business after all. She did tell me he'd had to leave home in a hurry after a fall out with his father though."

"His name, Alex, do you remember his name? It could be very important."

"Yes, his first name was Terry, I think, or maybe it was Trevor. No, it was definitely Trevor."

"What about his surname Alex? Did you ever hear it?"

"I don't know, maybe. I think so, not from him though. I never spoke to him. He looked a bit rough, like, you know?"

"Think Alex, please. It really is important."

"I'm trying, honest I am."

"Okay, take your time. Try and think where you might have heard his name."

A few seconds of silence emanated from the phone in Izzie's hand as she waited for Alex to respond.

"I'm sorry, I just can't remember hearing a name, and if I did it's long gone from my memory. You have to remember I was going through a lot of personal trauma at the time with my operations and having to adjust to life as a woman and putting up with my fair share of hostile comments and snide remarks from a lot of people who should have known better."

Izzie released an audible sigh, thinking their chance of identifying another potential suspect might have eluded them. Alex however, wasn't finished.

"You were really helpful to me, Sergeant Drake. You didn't have to sit and talk to me as you did after my interview with you at police headquarters. I think I might be able to find out what you need to know. One of Mrs. Biggs's best friends still lives a few doors down the street. She might know the names of any of her lodgers or boyfriends. I could go and ask her, if she's at home, and call you back in a couple of minutes. Is that okay?"

"That would be great, Alex," Izzie replied. "Please go, and I'll be waiting for your call."

The line went dead as Alex Sefton hung up and Izzie turned to Ross and explained what was happening.

"Let's hope she gets back to you soon, Izzie. Ms. Alex Sefton seems to be playing more than a bit part in this case, though I doubt it was ever by choice."

"I know. Going through her sex change, sorry, her gender reassignment must have placed a great deal of stress on her as she underwent all the various procedures. It's a wonder she's as well adjusted as she is."

"Yes, well, after the way she reacted to the diary when she found it, I'm not so sure she's quite as well adjusted as you might think."

Izzie's phone rang. She answered it right away.

"Alex?"

"Yes, Sergeant, it's me. Mrs. Grant was at home and she does remember one *special friend* as she put it, of Mrs. Biggs's who stayed with her for quite a long time. He was a lot younger than Carol Biggs, but Mrs. Grant is sure they were together as a couple for a while. She isn't certain, but she thinks the man had an Irish sounding name, perhaps, Donnelly or Donovan. If she had to put money on it she'd go for Donovan. She used to see him at the post office regularly she says, when he collected his benefit payments. She's a bit of a busybody and if you ask me she probably peered over his shoulder to read the name on is payment book if she was behind him in the queue. She said she heard someone call him Tel once."

Izzie knew that Tel was often used as a shortened version of the name Trevor, so Alex's recall was probably accurate.

"Thanks Alex. We really appreciate your help, and Mrs. Grant's."

"I hope it helps you catch the killer," Alex replied, and Drake brought the call to a close, hung up and turned to relay Alex's information to Ross.

"Trevor Donovan," Ross mused and repeated the name a couple of times. "There's something familiar about that name, Izzie."

"I thought so too, as soon as Alex mentioned it. Where the hell have we heard it before?"

Ross reached into the top right-hand drawer of his desk, from where he removed the copy of the original murder files from 1966. Within a minute of beginning to speed read the first few pages, he found what he was looking for.

"Got it," he exclaimed. "Back in 1966 one of the bar staff at the Traveller's Rest was a Peter Donovan, known as Pete to his friends."

"But I thought all the staff at the pub had cast iron alibis," Drake commented.

"So it appeared at the time, Izzie, but maybe they missed something. If Pete Donovan was the Lighthouse killer, and he or his family have recently suffered some kind of severe trauma, as Christine suggests, then either he, or his son Trevor, might be involved in the current murders."

"So, if we can get a DNA sample from Pete Donovan, it could implicate him in the murder of Stella Cox and the other girls and lead us to the killer of our latest victims," Drake said, excitedly.

"Precisely," said Ross, rising from behind his desk. "I want Derek McLennan on this one."

Ross called McLennan as he walked out of his office with Drake in his wake. She didn't need telling where they were headed.

"Derek," Ross said as soon as McLennan replied. "Are any of the others nearby?"

"Tony Curtis is just up the road from me at the moment, sir."

"Okay, listen carefully. Grab Tony and his uniform shadow, and yours too. I'm going to get Paul Ferris to send you the latest address we have in Hale for the Donovan family. There's a chance that Pete Donovan, who was a barman at the Traveller's Rest in 1966, could be the Lighthouse Killer. He has a son called Terry who lived with Carol Biggs in Canning for a time, and who could be responsible for hiding the diary behind the false wall in the Biggs house, and who also could be our current killer. I want a DNA sample from Pete Donovan. If he refuses to give one, arrest him immediately on suspicion of murder. Got that?"

"Got it, sir," McLennan replied.

"Izzie and I are on our way, as soon as I've asked Paul to send you that address. We'll meet you there. And Derek?"

"Sir?"

"Be careful, okay?"

"Okay, sir. No problem."

Five minutes later, Ross and Drake were in a pool car, heading for Hale. Paul Ferris had found the last known address for the Donovan family and called Derek McLennan, as well as notifying the rest of the team on the streets of Hale of current developments. They would all be on standby to provide assistance if required.

"Do you think we have our man, this time?" Izzie asked as she drove south towards Hale."

"I bloody hope so, Izzie," Ross replied. "We don't have much time before this bastard is due to strike again if he's following the original timetable of the '66 murders."

"Surely this Pete Donovan must be a bit long in the tooth to have come out of retirement to start killing again?"

"Maybe," Ross was thoughtful. "But what about his bloody son?"

Chapter 25

Moment of Truth

Alex heard the familiar sound of Lisa's car pull up outside. Funny, she thought, how Lisa never seemed to have a problem finding a parking space within yards of her house. A now familiar frisson of excitement made Alex's skin tingle, though this time it was tinged with a hint of trepidation. She'd asked Lisa to come over deliberately in order to tell her the truth about her past, as the detective sergeant had advised her to. Now that the moment was drawing close, though, Alex was having second thoughts.

"Hi," Lisa greeted her cheerfully, and Alex responded by putting both hands on Lisa's shoulders and drawing her close, before giving her a meaningful hug.

"Hey, to what do I owe this honour?" Lisa asked, a little surprised at Alex's expansive greeting.

"Lisa, I'm so pleased you're here. I daren't beat about the bush. I have something very important to tell you."

"Oh, okay," Lisa sounded worried. Her first thought was that maybe there was someone else in Alex's life.

Alex led her friend through to the lounge where Alex sat on sofa and patted the seat next to her, where Lisa promptly sat beside her.

"Alex, what's wrong? This all seems as if you're building up to telling me something awful."

"No, not really, well, I mean, it might be, for you, anyway. What I mean is that after I tell you what I have to say, you might not want to be my friend anymore."

"Good God, Alex, what are you trying to tell me? Are you a closet serial killer or something? Are the police after you? Is there someone else?"

Alex twisted in her seat so she was facing Lisa and leant across and kissed her. Lisa kissed her back. Alex knew then that her feelings were real, and that the detective was right. If she wanted her relationship with Lisa to continue and to really mean something, it had to be based on the whole truth. She took hold of both Lisa's hand in her own.

"Alex, you're trembling. Please, just tell me whatever it is that's got you so worked up."

"Well, Lisa, you see, the thing is, when we made love the first time, I knew then that I had real feelings for you."

"I feel the same way about you, Alex. I told you that, didn't I?"

"Yes, I know, but, well, you see, if I want to have any kind of long-term relationship with you, I must be totally honest with you, from the beginning, else I'd always be afraid of you finding out the truth about me from someone else."

"What truth are you talking about Alex? What could be so terrible that me finding out would make me not want to be with you?"

Alex knew this was it, the moment she was dreading. How would Lisa react? She had no more options, it was time. Alex drew in a long, deep breath and prepared herself for either elation or rejection. Either way, she knew she couldn't put it off any longer.

"Lisa, I wasn't always the person you see before you today. Up until a few years ago…"

"You lived as a man." Lisa said, taking the wind right out of Alex's sails.

"What? Well, yes, but how did you know?"

"I just knew Alex. Women can sense these things. You were always so evasive about your past, and there was always a sense of something being hidden from the world about you. You mentioned having had several operations in the past and I could tell you weren't talking about simple cosmetic surgery. Then, when we were in bed together, and I saw and felt the merest hint of your operation scars, and where they were, it sort of became obvious."

All the while Lisa was speaking, Alex had been sitting with her mouth hanging open in shock.

"So you knew, and it hasn't repelled you or put you off me?"

"No, you dozy mare, it hasn't," Lisa laughed and grasped Alex's hands tightly in her own. "You're a lovely person, Alex, from the inside out, and it doesn't matter a flying fuck to me that you were born in the wrong body. You knew it from a young age obviously and then you must have been very brave to go through all you had to do to become the real you. It's that person, the real you that I've fallen for you silly bugger. If you think I'm bothered about the past, then you don't know me well enough yet."

"But, why didn't you say something?"

"Why should I? I thought that when the time was right, you'd tell me yourself if you really cared about me, and I was right wasn't I?"

Alex was so taken aback by Lisa's words, she was literally speechless for a few seconds.

"Lisa, I..."

Lisa placed a finger on Alex's lips to silence her. Instead of speaking, she leaned across, pulled Alex in close, and kissed her, and in that kiss, Alex suddenly felt something she'd never felt before in her life, a deep sense of contentment!

"Listen to me Alex. As far as I'm concerned, you're all woman, and like I said, the most important thing to me is the person inside, and that's where I know you are a good person, and that as long as you want to be with me, I'll be here for you."

"I just don't know what to say," Alex replied, with a tear in her eye.

"Then don't say anything," Lisa said, quietly, holding Alex closely and the pair stayed like that, saying nothing for the next five minutes. It was Alex who finally broke the silence.

"There's something I should tell you about what's happening at present, just in case the police call round while you're here."

"Okay, tell me."

Alex spent the next ten minutes explaining her unexpected involvement in the ongoing police inquiry into the current murders of young women in Hale. Lisa never once interrupted, she simply sat holding Alex's hand as she told Lisa everything, including her finding of the diary and how she'd held on to it, using it as a form of almost masochistic-like pornography until she'd realised its importance when the police visited, looking for Carol Biggs. If Alex expected some form of recrimination from Lisa, she was quickly proved wrong, yet again.

"You poor thing," Lisa said as Alex came to the end of her narrative. "You must have been so lonely, so mixed up, if you thought the only way you could achieve any kind of sexual gratification was by reading that awful diary."

"You don't think I was being weird or perverted then?" Alex asked.

"Of course not, you silly bugger. You found something that provided you with an outlet for your sexual frustrations. If you don't watch the news or read the papers, how were you supposed to know it might have some significance to the murders?"

"I can't believe how supportive you are, Lisa. You're a real star."

"Look, kid, it's just how people who care about each other carry on, nothing unusual in it. Do you think the police will need you again?"

"I hope not, unless it's that detective sergeant. She was totally different after we'd finished talking about the case. It was her who really convinced me to be open and honest with you."

"Well, whatever she said to you, I'm glad you listened."

Alex laughed, at long last as she felt her own tension disappear, to be replaced by the feeling that here, at last, was someone she could trust, could rely upon to support her when the chips were down. Maybe that damned diary had served a useful purpose after all.

"So, is that all you wanted to tell me?" Lisa asked her friend, because if it is, I can think of something I'd much rather be doing than sitting here talking about dead people and serial killers, and without waiting for an answer, she rose from the sofa, leading Alex by the hand, and led her up the stairs, where talking could be forgotten about, at least for a while.

Chapter 26

One down, one to go

Ross and Drake arrived in Hale to find Derek McLennan, Tony Curtis and their uniformed shadows waiting for them outside the Donovan's home. Ross was perplexed by the fact they weren't inside the house, either questioning or arresting Pete Donovan. Exiting their car, the pair walked quickly to meet up with their colleagues.

"What's happening Derek?" Ross asked as soon as they were in earshot.

"You're not going to believe this, Boss," McLennan replied. He only referred to Ross as 'Boss' if things were bad.

"Go on, man, spit it out."

"Pete Donovan is dead, sir."

"What?"

"It's true sir. He died six weeks ago, in Walton of all places. I spoke to his widow. Seems our man was in and out of jail for the last few years, usually for handling stolen property or minor drugs offences. They thought he'd get a lesser sentence this time because he cooperated in putting a gang of house breakers behind bars, but someone got to him in the prison and he was found stabbed, but still alive in the showers one day. The guy who did it was found very quickly, he was even bragging about it. You know what cons are like. The reason he gave for killing Donovan was just that he'd disrespected him. Bloody pillock! They tried to save him but he'd lost too much blood."

"Fucking hell!" Ross exclaimed. Her Majesty's Prison, Liverpool, formerly known as Walton Jail, was a category B/C facility. Donovan, as a criminal who'd assisted the authorities should have been given some measure of protection from other inmates, who had a very effective grapevine of information, but it appeared he'd been badly let down. "So much for our DNA test."

"Not quite, sir. We might not have the man himself, but Mrs. Donovan gave us a couple of personal items that might be helpful. Show him, Ajit," McLennan spoke to the Asian officer standing slightly behind him, who now stepped forward, holding two plastic evidence bags in his right hand.

"Mrs. Donovan allowed us to have one of her husband's combs, sir. You will see there are several hairs attached. Also, we have a clothes brush which he used frequently and which should contain many hairs."

"Thanks, Constable…?"

"Kumar, sir. Ajit Kumar, been on the force for three years now."

"Right, thanks Constable Kumar. I suppose this means we might still be able to extract Donovan's DNA from these, but will we be able to do it in time? It's not like a direct sample is it?"

Drake agreed with him.

"Do you think we need to talk to the widow, sir?"

"Done already sir," Derek commented. "We all attended the briefing, so we knew what we needed to find out. Her son, Trevor, and his Dad fell out years ago, when Pete was put away the first time. Trevor hated the fact his dad's been in and out of prison for years, all for minor stuff. Trevor told his Dad he was a fool and a waster who didn't give a shit about Mary, Trevor's Mom. The two men almost came to blows and Trevor threatened his father."

"Did she say what he threatened him with, Derek?"

"Yes sir. Apparently old Pete had some sort of secret and Mary overheard her son say to him, just before he left, *"It's mine now, and it'll stay mine unless you start pulling your weight round here."*

"The diary!" Drake said excitedly.

"Just what we thought, Sarge," D.C. Curtis agreed.

"Does Mrs. Donovan know where her son is now?" Ross asked his detectives.

"She says not, sir, but Tony doesn't believe her, and to be honest, neither do I," said McLennan. "We thought it best to leave any further questioning until you and Sergeant Drake got here, in case you have specific questions to ask the lady."

"Good thinking Derek." Ross smiled and turned to Drake.

"A word with the grieving widow, Izzie?"

"After you, sir," Drake replied, waving her hand to give him the signal to precede her. A minute later, they were seated in the comfortable living room of the home of the late Pete Donovan and his wife, Winifred. Mrs. Donovan sat opposite the two detectives, in an old-fashioned fireside chair, covered in an equally old-fashioned red chintz fabric. The entire room was like a throw-back to the nineteen sixties, from her chair to the flock wallpaper that decorated the walls and the trio of ducks in flight that adorned the wall over the fireplace. Winifred wore a flower-patterned dress in multiple hues, with flesh coloured stocking or tights, and a pair of well-worn brown fluffy slippers. Her permed grey hair made her look more like eighty-something than seventy-something, and Ross thought her troubled marriage was probably responsible for adding years to her appearance.

"I don't know what else I can tell you that I didn't tell the other young men who called a while ago," she told them.

"Mrs. Donovan…"

"Call me Winnie, please. Everybody does," she said, interrupting Ross.

"Okay, Winnie, we know your son Trevor and his father fell out some years ago, but you don't know what it was Trevor threatened his father with before he left, is that right?"

"Yes, I told the other officer that. I heard our Trevor say he'd got something of his Dad's and he was going to keep it until Pete went straight and started looking after me properly. He always cared about me, did our Trevor."

"You see, Winnie," Ross countered. "That's why I find it hard to believe that a son who cares so deeply about his Mum wouldn't have kept in touch with you over the years, and not let you know where he was living."

"Oh, but he did, Inspector, for a while, anyway. He lived over in Canning for a long time with a woman called Biggs."

"We know about that, Winnie. Carol Biggs died a couple of years ago and we've spoken to the lady who lives there now. She can remember seeing your son during the time he lived there. It appears he moved on after a while, and like I said, I can't believe he didn't let you, his Mum, know where he was, like I can't believe you have no idea where he is now."

Winnie Donovan was in her late seventies, and as much as Ross hated using bullying tactics, he knew time was running out. If Trevor Donovan was the killer they were seeking, he had to ramp up the pressure on the old woman.

"I know he stayed in a few places after he left the Biggs woman, mostly with friends he used to tell me, but he lost touch with me about a year ago, and that's the truth."

"And he never even phoned you to see how you were?"

"Well, yes, sometimes."

"And you never asked him where he was living?"

"*Around.* That's what he'd say to me, just, *around.*"

"What about his father's funeral, Winnie?" Izzie Drake suddenly interrupted. "Didn't Trevor attend to pay his respects, or at least to support you through the service?

Ross winked his approval at Izzie. These were the kind of tactics; the pair had used for years. Izzie would patiently wait, silent in the background as Ross began the questioning of a subject or interview subject such as Winnie, and then, when the person had all but forgotten that Izzie was in the room, she would seemingly come to life, like a Praying Mantis, with her own well thought out questions which often took the subject by surprise. Such a tactic had proved effective in extracting important information so often in the past. Her sudden mention of Pete Donovan's funeral certainly caught Winnie off guard.

"Er, well, yes, he did come to his Dad's funeral. They might not have got on, but Pete was his Dad, after all," Winnie replied, defensively, Izzie thought.

"And how did you manage to contact Trevor to let him know his father had died, and to give him the funeral arrangements? You said you didn't know where he was living, or how to get in touch with him," she pressed on.

"*Check mate. Nicely done, Izzie. Try and get out of that one Winnie.*" He thought to himself, as he waited for Winnie to try and extricate herself from Izzie's well laid trap.

Winnie looked at Drake, with a guilt-ridden look on her face. She had clearly been doing her best to cover up something to try and protect her son, understandable perhaps but she could never have hoped to outwit two experienced detectives, working in tandem to obtain the truth.

"Well, I..."

"Yes, Winnie? We're waiting," Ross spoke firmly.

"Look, why are you asking all these questions about my Trevor? What has he done wrong? You people are scaring me."

"We're sorry if we're scaring you, Winnie," Drake spoke once again, "but it's very important that we speak to Trevor. He might hold important information about several serious crimes committed in the area. If you know where he is or how we can get in touch with him, please don't think you're helping him by withholding his whereabouts from us, because you're not."

"Crimes, what crimes? You don't think my lad is a criminal surely, and what serious crimes are you taking about? This is Hale, and we don't get serious..."

Winnie Donovan stopped speaking as sudden realisation dawned on her. There was only one serious crime, or crimes that had occurred in Hale in recent times. When she spoke again her voice had risen by at least half an octave and there was an element of panic in her voice.

"No, you're not serious. My Trevor and those women. That's what you're talking about isn't it? You think he had something to do with those murders and the bodies at the lighthouse, don't you?"

"We just want to talk to him, Winnie."

"You think he's a killer, don't you?"

Ross took over once again. It was cards on the table time. What he was about to say would possibly shatter this poor woman's life completely, but if he was to prevent another murder, he felt he had no choice.

"Listen to me carefully Winnie. We have evidence which points to the possibility of your husband having been involved in the series of murders that took place in and around Hale in nineteen sixty-six, and there is also a strong possibility that your son may be implicated in the current series of copycat murders."

Winnie Donovan looked as if she'd just been struck by a double-decker bus. Her face became a mask of horror and her body began to shake and tremble as she sat in her fireside chair, in total shock at Ross's accusations. Her mouth opened and closed reminiscent of a fish out of water, gasping for air.

"I know it's hard for you to take all this in," Drake attempted to sound comforting and sympathetic, "but nobody's blaming you for any of this, Winnie."

"But, Pete, my husband. You're saying he was a murderer, that he raped and murdered those girls all those years ago, and now you think my son is doing the same thing. Why? Why would my husband and then my son do such a thing?"

"We think it may be linked to his relationship with his father," Ross said. "When his father died it likely triggered something in Trevor's brain that set him on this course."

"Tell me something, please Winnie," Drake added. "When were you and Pete married?"

"Nineteen sixty-five," she replied.

"And the murders that took place in July, a year later, how were you and Pete getting along? Was everything alright in the bedroom department?"

Winnie Donovan blushed, her face turned pure embarrassment vermillion.

"I don't know what that's got to do with you or anyone else," she protested.

"Please Winnie," Ross said, quietly but firmly.

"You might find the question embarrassing but if you were having problems as a couple it might throw some light on your husband's motive for the murders, surely you can understand that?"

Burying her face in her hands, Winnie began to sob, quietly at first, then the tears began to really flow. Izzie Drake rose from her seat and walked to the small table under the window, from where she picked up a box of tissues and placed them on Winnie's lap, first passing her one which the old woman quickly used to wipe her tears away. She finally managed to compose herself sufficiently to answer Drake's original question.

"We lost a baby. I was a couple of months pregnant when we got married, and I miscarried three months after that. I wouldn't take the risk of getting pregnant again so soon after losing the baby. I wouldn't let Pete... you know, do it for a long time. I knew he was frustrated, but I would never have dreamed he would do anything like what happened to those poor girls. I do remember the case you know. I'm not exactly senile, or going gaa gaa yet you know."

"I see," Drake nodded and tried her best to sound sympathetic. "But, couldn't you have used some form of contraception, Winnie? You didn't have to totally abstain from sexual contact with your husband, did you?"

"That's what Pete said at the time. He wanted to use those horrible condom things, them Durex thingies. I wouldn't let him, Sergeant

Drake. I was brought up strictly Catholic. Contraception is banned by the Pope you know."

"Yes, I know the rules about contraception laid down by your church," Drake replied, silently cursing the strict edict imposed by the Roman Catholic Church on all matters relating to birth control. She's witnessed too many teenage suicides, too many botched abortions, and too much heartbreak to have any sympathy for what she saw as an outdated and unnecessary restriction on the freedom of choice for millions of Catholics around the world.

"Pete didn't like it, it's true. He kept saying it was his right, you know, to have it, as he put it, but I told him he'd have to force me if he wanted me to do it when it could lead to another miscarriage. Oh God, you think that's what he did, don't you? He went out and did it to those other women because he couldn't get it at home."

"That's what it looks like," Drake nodded at Winnie.

Ross was sure now that they had the right man for the original Lighthouse murders, and it was pretty much certain they now knew who they were after for the current murders. The question was, could they find Trevor Donovan before he struck again?

"Do you have a recent photograph of Trevor, Winnie?" he asked the shocked widow, who without a word, rose slowly from her chair and walked across the room to the old-fashioned sideboard and opened a drawer. She lifted out a large photograph album and turned to the final pages. She pointed out a picture of a man in his thirties, tall and slim, but athletically built, standing with an arm around Winnie's shoulder. Trevor Donovan had short, dark hair cut in an old-style short back and sides, and was dressed in t-shirt and jeans, and was smiling a smile that looked decidedly false. Ross could see, even in that six by four colour print, that Trevor's eyes held the look of a predator. He'd seen that look too many times in the past not to recognise it when he saw it. Izzie Drake looked at the photograph and saw that look in Donovan's eyes. It was Ross who spoke next.

"When was this taken?" he asked Winnie.

"Two years ago," she replied. "Trevor came to see me on my birthday. He knew his father wasn't here. He was doing three months for petty theft. Trevor brought me a box of Black Magic and a card. They're my favourite chocolates, he brought me the biggest box I'd ever seen."

"Can we borrow this photograph please?" Ross asked.

"I suppose so," Winnie replied.

"We'll make sure it's returned," Drake told her as she took the photo from Winnie's hand, quickly placing it in a see through plastic evidence bag for safe keeping.

"I'm sorry this has been upsetting for you, Winnie," Ross said, "but I have to ask again, how did you get in touch with Trevor to tell him about his father's death and funeral arrangements?"

Winnie Donovan could take no more. Sitting down heavily in her fireside chair, she had the look of a beaten woman.

"Trevor's got one of those modern mobile phones, she replied. "He showed it to me once. I've got the number in the telephone book on the hall stand, next to the telephone."

Ross nodded and Drake stood up, and went to the hall, found the telephone book and made a note of Trevor's number in her notebook. Returning to the sitting room, she nodded to Ross, who had one more question to ask Winnie Donovan.

"Does Trevor have a job, Winnie? If so, where does he work? Tell us now please, because if you lie or mislead us, and another woman dies because of your failure to cooperate I will press charges of obstruction against you, and that's a promise."

"He's a plasterer, and does general decorating work, Inspector. He works for himself most of the time, but sometimes works for a man called Benny. That's all I know and that's the truth."

Ross felt he could find out little more from Winnie Donovan and after asking if she had a friend or relative who could call round to give her some company after the shock she'd received and being told she'd rather be alone, they thanked her and left her to her own thoughts and possible regrets.

Outside, back on the street Ross quickly organised his people. Tony Curtis was quickly dispatched to headquarters, armed with the photograph of Trevor Donovan. Within hours, copies would be distributed to police stations and officers all over Merseyside. If Trevor Donovan was sighted anywhere on the streets, officers were instructed to approach with caution after summoning back-up. Under no means were they to attempt to bring him down without help. Before recalling the rest of the officers from their house to house DNA gathering exercise, Ross turned to McLennan and the two uniformed officers who had been patiently waiting outside the Donovan home.

"Do any of you know anything about a man called Benny? Apparently, he's a home decorating contractor. I need to know where we can find him, and fast. He might be the only person who can tell us where to find Trevor Donovan."

"Are you satisfied he's our man, sir?" Derek McLennan asked.

"Oh yes, Derek, I'm sure of it," Ross replied.

"Sir," P.C. Kumar said.

"Yes, Constable," Ross acknowledged him.

"I think I know who you're looking for."

Chapter 27

Benny and Betty

The lock-up used as a base of operations by Benny Jarvis, was securely locked. The giant padlock attached to the heavy-duty hasp on the double doors looked as if nothing short of a set of industrial bolt cutters would be needed to effect an entry and that was exactly what Ross had sent Ginger Devenish in search of. Where he was supposed to find such an item amidst the various small businesses and industrial start-ups on the small industrial estate close to the docks in Seaforth, was anyone's guess.

P.C. Ajit Kumar, who Ross had learned was known in his off-duty hours as 'Rocky' due to his penchant for amateur boxing, had informed Ross that Benny Jarvis had been quite a well-known amateur welterweight up until a badly broken wrist put paid to his ring career. He was now well known among the local community as a general handyman who employed other tradesmen on an ad-hoc basis in order to complete his various 'contracts' as he always referred to whatever job he was employed to do, large or small, usually small, Kumar stressed to Ross.

"Let's just say he's never going to get rich, sir, and neither is anyone who works for him. We're talking Benny Jarvis here, not King

Construction, referring to one of Merseyside's largest civil engineering companies. If Benny constructed a garden wall for me, I'd be very sure not to walk or stand too close to it in a strong wind."

"That good eh?" Ross quipped and a grim-faced Kumar simply replied,

"Not even that good, sir. Benny gives the name cowboy builder a bad rep."

Despite the seriousness of the current situation, Ross allowed himself a small smile as he mentally pictured dozens of sub-standard brick walls causing small injuries to the unfortunate victims of the shoddy work of Benny Jarvis. A visit to his home address in Huyton had seen Ross and Drake faced with the cheerful, smiling face of Benny's wife, Betty, a large, rotund woman who looked as though she herself could have given Benny a run for his money in a straight fight between the two, even though he hadn't met her husband as yet.

"What yer wantin' my Benny for then?" she asked. "Not been up to no good 'as he?" she laughed as she spoke.

"Not that we know of, Mrs. Jarvis. We just need to speak to your husband about someone who might have done some work for him," Ross replied.

"Ooh, right. Who (she pronounced it 'oo') might that be, then?"

"Maybe you know him. His name is Trevor Donovan."

"Can't say as I've had the pleasure," the woman said, "though I don't know many of Benny's lads, as 'e calls 'em."

"Do you know where your husband is, Mrs. Jarvis?" Drake asked.

"No love, I don't, but it'll be tea time soon and he's never late when there's food to be had. You might find 'im at 'is lock up. That's where 'e leaves 'is tools at night. We used to get attempted break ins when they were kept in our garage. Even the alarm didn't put the thievin' little scallys off."

"And where can we find this lock up?" Ross asked.

Betty Jarvis happily provided them with the location of Benny's lock-up and now they patiently waited for the expected arrival of the man they hoped could be the key to them finding their new chief suspect. Before long, they saw an almost new, though dust covered, black Mercedes van turn into the gates that led into this corner of the industrial unit, which contained eight individual units. It drove straight towards Unit 4, that carried only a small sign announcing *Benny's*, with a mobile phone number below the name, where they were parked in the unmarked pool car.

Benny Jarvis stepped from his van, wearing the ubiquitous 'uniform' of his trade, navy blue overalls, paint and plaster splattered of course, and boots that were probably black under the multiple layers of various coloured paint and other nondescript materials that had deposited themselves there over time. His work ensemble was topped off by a woolly hat that made Ross instantly think of the character of the same first name who at one time appeared almost nightly on British TVs in the soap opera *Crossroads.*

"Afternoon folks," he greeted them with a broad smile, that both could see was genuine and warm. As he stepped closer, they could see that Benny Jarvis the boxer had long been replaced by Benny Jarvis, lover of too many pizzas and takeaway dinners. Together, he and Betty made a pretty good matching pair. "What can I be doing for you today?" he asked, holding out a paint-stained hand that he first wiped down the front of his overalls. Ross reluctantly shook it, and wished he had something he could wipe his hand on too.

"Benny Jarvis?" Ross inquired, knowing it was unlikely to be anyone else. He held out his warrant card so Jarvis could see he was a police officer. "I'm Detective Inspector Ross, and this is Detective Sergeant Drake. We hope you can help us find someone"

"Ah, right, and who might that be, Detective Inspector?"

"Trevor Donovan."

"Oh aye, and what's that little toe-rag been up to now, the thievin' little bastard."

"I take it you're acquainted with Mr. Donovan, then?" Drake added.

"You could put it that way, Sergeant. Comes to me bleating he's short of money. Asks if I can give him a bit of work, right? So me, soft lad that I am, I takes pity on 'im, seeing as how he's done work for me in the past. I sent him to do a job in Fazakerley. It's an old house on Bradstone Close, off Bridgehouse Lane. Standing empty it is and the owner hired me to do it up, top to bottom, see? Now, when he puts his mind to it, Tet, that's what I calls him, can be a fucking good plasterer, so I sent him to do the downstairs walls, saying if he did a good job I might let 'im do the whole house. Paid him two hundred up front and told 'im there'd be another two hundred when he finished. So I loads him up with the gear he needed and off he went. I've never seen him or me equipment since, the thievin' scally."

"When was this, Mr. Jarvis?" Ross asked him.

"Three weeks ago, today," Jarvis replied. "I went round to Bradstone Close a week after I hired him as I'd heard nothin' from 'im. No work done, not a thing, and no sign of that fucker or my gear either."

"Hang on," Drake interjected. "You said you loaded him up. What was he driving?"

"A battered old Peugeot van, must be about twenty years old. Got more rust and filler on it than paintwork. God knows 'ow it got through an MOT test. Knowin' Tet, he'll have bought a bent one in some pub somewhere down the docks. Bet he never paid more than thirty quid for it, bloody real old banger it were."

"I don't suppose you noticed the registration number?" Drake asked in a forlorn hope.

Benny simply shook his head.

"Have you reported the loss of your equipment, Mr. Jarvis?" Ross asked him. "If you believe he's stolen your property you should do you know?"

"Yeah, I suppose I should. I haven't done that so far 'cos I was hoping he'd turn up, but maybe I should stop hoping and do just that. It's just that he's never let me down in the past. He's done a few jobs in the past and never done nothin' like this before."

"I take it you don't know where Donovan lives?" was Ross's next question.

"Sorry, can't help you there. Either he comes to me lookin' for work, or if I need 'im I calls him on 'is mobile. I can give you 'is number."

Benny looked up Donovan's number on his own mobile and provided them with the number they'd already been given by his mother.

"Thanks," Drake said, disappointed. "I wonder, Benny, if you might have an idea of the area where he might be living, even if you don't know his address."

"Not really," said Benny, "but usually, when he's called asking for work, it only takes 'im about ten minutes to get 'ere if I want to see 'im to talk about a job, so it can't be far away, if he were at 'ome when he's been calling me, can it?"

"That's quite right, thank you, Benny," Ross said, thinking they'd got all they could from Benny Jarvis. He asked Drake to show the man the copy of the photograph Mrs. Donovan had given them. "Would you say that's a good enough likeness of how he looks at present?"

"Aye, near enough," Benny confirmed. "He looks a bit older, but apart from that, it's Tet, no doubt about it. That reminds me of somewhere you might find the little scrote."

"And where might that be?" Ross was on full alert. If Benny could lead them to Donovan...

"D'you know The Seven Seas, Inspector?"

"As a matter of fact, I do."

The pub Benny was referring to was well-known to most police officers in Liverpool, as a haven for small-time drug dealers, users, and petty criminal of various types, almost a kind of criminal employment bureau. Whatever type of ne'er-do-well you were seeking to carry out almost kind of felonious activity, the Seven Seas, just minutes from the city's thriving container port, was the place to be. Throw in the added attraction of a number of the city's less expensive prostitutes, and one could call the seedy, run down pub a one-stop shop for all things low and seedy, a veritable nadir for all those on the opposite side of the forces of law and order. Any lower, it was difficult to fall.

"Well, I do know it's one of Tet's favourite haunts. Benny hesitated for a few seconds and then added, "Seems one of the prossies that regularly hangs out there is one of 'is favourite fu...er, I mean..."

"It's alright, Benny, we get the picture," Drake almost laughed at his discomfiture.

"Do you know this prostitute's name, by any chance, Benny," Ross asked him.

"Yes, I do. Tet never stops talking about 'er. Says she's red hot in the sack, like. "If ever you wants a good shag, go and get in Dolores's knickers," he always says. "I tell him to fuck off. I'm a happily married man, I am. What would I be needin' a prossie for, eh?"

The thought crossed both Ross and Drake's minds, having met Betty Jarvis, that nobody would blame Benny for seeking a little solace elsewhere. With all due respect to Betty, neither of them could envisage Betty as a sexy femme fatale, but then again, maybe Benny liked things just the way they were. The thought of what Betty would potentially do to Benny if she ever found out he'd been 'playing away, was more than either of the detectives wished to contemplate. Ross affected clearing his throat before he spoke again.

"Of course, Benny. I fully understand. So, do you know what this Dolores looks like?"

"Sorry, Inspector, I've got no idea. You wouldn't find me dead in the Seven Seas. I do know she's a redhead though. Tet's always going on about her gorgeous red hair. Never been keen on redheads meself."

"Thanks Benny," Ross said, having re-evaluated his first of impression of Benny Jarvis. The man might be rough, and perhaps he sailed a little close to the wind, business-wise, but he seemed a genuine enough kind of man, and Ross held his hand out and shook Benny's hand enthusiastically. "It's vital we find Trevor, so please, if you hear from him or hear anything about is whereabouts in the next twenty-four hours, please, call me, or anyone on my team. The numbers are on my card," he said, passing his business card to Benny, who quickly secreted it in one of the pockets of his stained overalls.

"Sure thing, Inspector. I want my stuff back, so don't you worry. If I find out where he is, you'll be the first to know about it."

The pair took their leave of Benny Jarvis. For some reason, both felt a hint of optimism after meeting Benny Jarvis. They had a couple of leads, two fragile links to Trevor Donovan. Now, all they needed was a lucky break.

Chapter 28

The Seven Seas

"Everyone ready?" Ross spoke in a quiet, determined voice as he, Izzie Drake, Sergeant Sofie Meyer, together with Detective Constables Derek McLennan, Tony Curtis and Sam Gable, exited the two unmarked police cars about a hundred yards distance from The Seven Seas, public house. It wouldn't help their cause to be seen pulling up right outside the notorious drinking den. Nothing would be guaranteed to empty the place in a hurry than the arrival of two car loads of police officers, and Ross had no doubt that unmarked cars and plain clothes would in no way prevent the denizens of such an establishment from instantly 'making' Ross and his people as police officers.

A round of acknowledgements followed his question and together, they made their way along the footpath, strode across the small car park which was the temporary home to about a dozen vehicles, none of which resembled the van owned by Trevor Donavan as described by Benny Jarvis. With a last nod to the team and with their senses on full alert, led by Ross, the detectives entered the den of iniquity that was The Seven Seas. As about twenty pairs of eyes turned to gaze at the newcomers, it was clear that Ross's assumption had been correct. With furtive nods and whispered comments being immediately bandied around the surprisingly spacious bar, a number of those present wasted no time in draining their glasses and making a hasty exit. Ross had no doubt that some of those who seemed so keen to leave had something to hide, but his powers of detention didn't run to forcing a pub full of people to remain in the bar against their will, at least not without good cause. Sadly, the fact that a suspect may or may not be a regular at the pub didn't quite fall into the category of a 'good cause' so Ross was powerless to prevent the mini-exodus from taking place.

Sam Gable, who had worked in Vice for some time before being recruited for Ross's specialist squad, had no trouble recognising the woman who must be Dolores, as described by Benny Jarvis. The woman must have been in her late thirties though her make-up and dress made her look considerably younger, until one got closer. Dolores was sitting on a bar stool, wearing a flouncy white blouse and red pencil skirt, with a split on one side that went from the hem, right up to her thigh, giving potential punters a clear view of her still-shapely legs, which were crossed, ensuring the other leg was thus equally well displayed. Black patent high heels completed the woman's working ensemble, and her well-styled auburn hair cascaded over her shoulders and reached halfway down her back. In her hand she held a large gin and tonic, Sam guessed, as she wasted no time in walking directly up to her and standing right in front of her, virtually trapping Dolores in place on the stool. Ross and Drake manoeuvred their way to the bar, while the others waited close to the doors.

"You must be Dolores," Sam said to the woman on the bar stool.

"And who wants to know?" Dolores replied, her Irish accent clearly evident.

"D.C. Gable, Merseyside Police," Sam replied, holding up her warrant card for the woman and everyone else in the vicinity to see. "We need a word."

"And what might you be wantin' to talk to me about? Since when do Vice send detectives out to talk to the likes o' me?" Her words were spoken as if she knew Sam from her Vice Squad days. Sam wondered if their paths had crossed, however fleetingly in the past.

"I'm not with Vice, Dolores. I'm from the Specialist Murder Investigation Team."

"Murder you say? Now, I'll not be knowin' anything' about that kind of stuff."

"Maybe not Dolores. What's your surname by the way?"

"It's Lafontaine," Dolores replied. "Dolores Lafontaine."

"Very Irish, I don't think, Dolores. Cut the crap, darling, and give me your real name, unless you want me to drag you down to the station and have a nice wee chat there, instead?"

Sam had dealt with many women like Dolores in the past. She knew the woman would definitely not want to lose the chance of making money by being taken in by the police.

"My, aren't you a tough one?" Dolores replied. "Well now, just between you and me," she said, lowering her voice to barely it's a whisper, "It's O'Shaunessy, Claire O'Shaunessy, but be a darlin' and stick to Dolores okay? It's better for business."

"Sure," said Sam. "Now, you do me a favour, okay? Quid pro quo, Dolores."

"Aye, I know what that means. I've watched *Silence of the Lambs* you know," she smiled with self-satisfaction, referring to the phrase often used by the leading character in the well know movie. "Wait a mo, I do know you, and you are, or you were Vice once, weren't you?"

"Maybe," Sam was cautious.

"You helped me once, and some other girls when Mickey the Fish tried to put the frighteners on some of us who worked for Maggie Bull."

"Yes, you're right, Dolores. That was a few years ago. I don't recall your name from those days, though."

"Oh no, you wouldn't. I was Molly Raven then. I had jet black hair and the name suited me."

Sam Gable grinned. She should have known the red hair was a dye. She'd been away from Vice too long, she quickly concluded.

"Molly Raven, yes, I think I vaguely remember you. You were a lot younger in those days."

"I was, for sure," she sighed. "But I do know you and another copper tried to help us get out of the life, but the money was just too temptin' my lovely."

"That's a shame, Dolores, but now, we need to find a regular of yours, bloke by the name of Trevor Donovan."

"That fuckin' pervert? If I never see him again it'll be too soon, sure and it will be."

"Why do you call him a pervert, Dolores?"

"Likes a bit of the kinky stuff. Thinks he's a real tough guy. Likes to hurt women, Trevor fuckin' Donovan does."

Sam's antennae were on full alert now. Her eyes sought out Ross, who was talking to the man behind the bar, and she nodded imperceptibly as if to say, *"I'm on to something."*

"Look, I could tell you plenty, but let's just say the last time I went with him, the bastard gets me to go down on me knees so's he can do it from behind, like, and next thing I know, the shit-faced bugger has his hands round me neck, trying to throttle me, he was. I started choking fit to give the Pope a heart attack, God Bless him, and that fucker is shoutin' in me ear, *"You're mine, you bitch, you're mine."* Somehow, I managed to squirm away from the bastard when he released my throat a bit. He starts groveling then and sayin' he's sorry. Tells me he worships me and my beautiful hair. I told him to fuck off and never come near me again or I'll get my friend Buster to have him crippled. Just for good luck I gave him a good kick in the balls for his trouble, picked up the cash he'd put on the side table, and buggered off while he was rollin' on the floor in agony."

There was no doubt now. Sam knew for sure that Donovan was the killer.

"You didn't take him back to your place did you, Dolores?"

"Come on, constable, you don't think I was born yesterday do you? Let a punter know where I live? No way. It was raining that night so I let him take me back to his place."

"And can you tell me where he lives?" Sam was really getting excited now. All they needed was an address and they might just nab Donovan before it was too late.

Meanwhile, Ross and Drake were engaged in conversation with Graham White, the landlord of the Seven Seas. White was a portly man, in his fifties with a few wisps of grey hair combed over his otherwise bald head á la Bobby Charlton, for those who recall one of England's greatest footballers. His belly had encroached over his waistline, hanging over his belt, and his jeans bore numerous beer stains, giving him the appearance of a rather poorly dressed professional drinker, rather than the man who held the licence to sell alcohol from the Seven Seas. He knew the score however, and in his own way, he attempted to be cooperative with the Detectives. The last thing he, or his customers wanted was to be pestered by the police.

"He's trouble, that one," he replied, in response to Ross's questions about Trevor Donovan.

"So we've heard," said Ross.

"Why do you say that, though, Mr. White," Drake asked. "You must have a reason. With all due respect, most of your regulars in here might qualify for a similar description."

"Diplomatically put, Inspector. You know the way it is, I'm not going to deny we seem to attract a certain type of punter in here, but Trevor, well, he used to be okay, but he's changed."

"In what way?"

"Look, I know some dodgy stuff goes on in here, but I have to turn a blind eye if I want to stay in business, right?"

"Go on, Mr. White," Ross said, knowing just what the landlord meant. It took a certain kind of fortitude to face running a pub like the Seven Seas, day in and day out.

"I always knew he did a bit of trading, you know? Low level fencing of stolen gear, even a bit of drug dealing if the chance came his way, but a few months back, he showed a violent side to his nature."

"What happened Mr. Wright?"

"One of the lads in here owed him money, so I was told, and he was late paying up. Stupid bugger for borrowing from a scally like that in the first place if you ask me. Anyway, Trevor cornered him behind the pub one night, and beat seven shades of shit out of the poor bastard. The lad never even got any extra time to pay his debt. Bloody Donovan just went for him, and then told him if he didn't pay up by the weekend, he'd have his wife next. Poor kid, was only about twenty-two or three. He went and borrowed from a real loan shark to pay Donovan off, but that creep still started stalking the lad's wife, just to put the frighteners on him. Did it so she knew he was around, so I was told. She thought she was going to be raped or something every day until he got fed up with his bit of sport. Then he went too far with one of the girls who comes in here. He's besotted with her. That's her over there, talking with one of your lot now. She told me herself what he did and I had words with him myself. She's okay, is Dolores, for a tom, if you know what I mean. I told him to cool it round Dolores and around my customers, or I'd make sure some of them got to know what he was up to. We get real hard cases in here, Inspector. I could have someone like Trevor Donovan done over any time, if I really wanted to, but I do my best to stay out of my customers' affairs."

Ross knew what the landlord meant, though he found himself wishing that White had arranged a spot of drumhead justice for the man they were seeking.

"When was the last time he was in here?"

"Two nights ago, I think it was, yes that's right, it was. He kept himself to himself after Dolores refused to go with him and he sat in the corner over there, until she left with another punter, and then he buggered off soon afterwards."

"So, you wouldn't say he was a daily regular then?"

"Most days, yes, but not so much lately. It feels like he's got something on his mind when I speak to him. Sort of distracted, if you know what I mean?"

"I think I do," Ross said, knowing only too well just what Donovan had on his mind at present. "Do you know where he lives, Mr. White?"

"No, but Dolores does."

Ross left the landlord in peace and as he started to walk towards her, Sam moved away from Dolores Lafontaine and moved to join him. She had indeed obtained an address for Trevor Donovan, and held it up to show him as they met. Two minutes later, Ross and his team left the denizens of the Seven Seas to their drinking and whatever nefarious deeds they may be up to. For now, the police had bigger fish to fry.

Chapter 29

“Kiss me, Derek”

“Where we going Boss?” Tony Curtis asked, as Ross gathered the team around him in the car park of the Seven Seas, before taking the short walk to where they’d left the cars.

“I’d like to go back to the office and pick up a firearm or two, but the time constraints mean we need to get to Bootle as soon as possible.”

“We’ve actually got an address for the bastard?” Curtis was impressed.

“Yep! Sam got it from the prossie that Donovan was obsessed with,” Ross informed them all.

Izzie Drake interrupted him.

“Why don’t we get Paul down here? He’s firearms trained and we might need the extra pair of hands. There’s no point in him sitting at his computer screen when we know who we’re looking for now, is there?”

“True,” Ross agreed. “Call him and tell him to sign out two firearms, one for him and one for me. D.C.I. Agostini will sign the authorisation. And you can tell him to bring young Ginger along too. I want us all in on this. If Donovan decides to make a fight of it, or even tries to do a runner, I want all our bases covered and all his possible exit routes covered.

As Drake made the arrangements for Sergeant Paul Ferris and D.C. Ginger Devenish to join in the operation, Ross made a call to Oscar Agostini.

"Oscar, we know who the killer is, it's Trevor Donovan, ninety nine percent certain and we're closing in on his home address."

"Thank God, Andy. Where are you heading? What about back-up?"

"Beatrice Street in Bootle. Not far from here. I wouldn't mind if you could arrange for the uniform boys to throw a cordon round the area, cut off all exits from the area etc."

"Consider it done. I've got Inspector Brough and his lads champing at the bit downstairs. They're keen to help resolve this business after helping out in Hale."

"Thanks Oscar. Izzie is on the phone to Paul Ferris right now. We don't know what we might find there so I've told her to get Paul to arrange the issue of firearms with you. I want him and Devenish here asap with weapons for Paul and me. They can meet us at the end of Beatrice Street. Silent approach so make sure they get a decent looking pool car, okay?"

"No problem, and Andy?" The serious note in Agostinis's voice made Ross turn deadly serious.

"Sir?"

"Be careful, understand?"

"Got it, Boss. You know me."

"Too bloody right I do," Agostini smiled as he spoke. "Why d'you think I told you to be careful?"

"Don't worry about us, Oscar. I won't be taking any unnecessary chances. I've got virtually the whole team behind me on this one. We want this bastard badly, and we're going to bring him down, don't you worry."

"Good, and let's hope we can do it without anyone getting hurt."

"I agree Oscar. I told you, we're going softly, softly on this one, but if Donovan doesn't play by the rules…"

"I know, Andy. Like I said…"

"I know, be bloody careful. You've made it abundantly clear."

* * *

Oblivious to the police activity taking place only a hundred yards from his home, Trevor Donovan was busily making preparations for the coming evening. He'd followed his target regularly since he'd seen her, soon after the murder of Cathy Billings. He'd become instantly attracted to her and as she was involved in the investigation of his second murder, that of the unfortunate Hanna Lucas, he'd had plenty of time to become acquainted with her daily routines, both on and off duty. He knew where she lived, and had made more than a few visits to view her home from the outside, especially since Hannah's death. He was virtually devoting all his free time to preparing for his third murder. After that, he would have recreated his father's crimes perfectly, so he believed, and as his father had got away with the Lighthouse murders in 1966, he saw no reason why he would be detected by the law.

Now, as he dressed for his next murder, he allowed his thoughts to wander back to his father. He and his Dad had never seen eye to eye, and Trevor had been first horrified, and later intrigued, by his discovery of the old diary he'd discovered one day in the bottom of an old tool box in his father's shed.

Pete Donovan had hidden it in what he thought was a safe place, the tool box secreted away under the shed's work surface, which ran the length of one wall of the shed. Unfortunately, probably during one of his drunken binges, Pete must have taken the diary out to relive his crimes, and had failed to secure the padlock which should have protected it from prying eyes. Although it appeared to be locked he'd failed to secure the auto-locking hasp in place and it was accessible to anyone who looked closely enough at it. Trevor was hunting for a wallpaper scraper one day when he saw the tool box, and found it devoid of any tools whatsoever. Intrigued, he'd searched the interior and found the diary wrapped in a piece of old hessian sacking. Realising what he'd found, he took advantage of his new-found knowledge to effectively blackmail his own father. One of the reasons for his father's return to a life of crime, which he'd given up after his one taste of prison, he now found himself on the wrong side of the law in his attempts to keep his son supplied with regular sums of cash, and Trevor had no intention of letting go. It had all blown up one day however, when Pete discovered Trevor sexually molesting a schoolgirl in his own shed, and the ensuing row led to Trevor leaving home, though he took Pete's old diary with him for safe-keeping and as potential future leverage. With both men knowing the other's darkest secrets, an impasse was reached and an uneasy truce grew between them, until their final fall out over Pete's inability to support his wife, Trevor's mother.

Now, with his head and body shaved, to eliminate the chances of his hair being lost and used for DNA tracing, he checked his 'murder kit' comprising his knife, rope, duct tape, condoms, sexual lubricant, gloves, both surgical and leather varieties, an old pillowcase to cover his victim's head and just in case, a hammer. He felt empowered as he dressed in his black track suit, black hoodie and t-shirt, and plain nondescript black trainers. Nothing could stop him as he prepared to finally emulate his father. Maybe, he thought, he might not stop at three, as his father did. There were plenty of tarts out there, he often bemoaned to himself. Why shouldn't he begin his own crusade to rid the world of as many as he could, and write his own name in the annals of crime?,

Unbeknown to Donovan, D.I. Andy Ross and his team had other ideas about that.

"Everybody clear on what we're doing here?" Ross spoke with quiet determination as his team gathered around him, together with Inspector Brough and his sergeants. Brough's uniformed constables were already strategically positioned to ensure Donovan would have nowhere to run if he managed to outwit the detectives and made a bid for freedom on foot.

Beatrice Street was blocked off from all traffic with police barricades in place at both ends, where the road joined Stanley Road and Hawthorne Road, and at it halfway intersection with Miranda Road, police cars formed an impenetrable road block.

"Don't worry, Boss. We're not going to let this slimy bastard slip through our fingers," Tony Curtis spoke for the whole team as they waited for last minute instructions from Ross. He'd already laid out his plan for the apprehension of Trevor Donovan, now it was time for last minute instructions before the operation commenced.

"Remember, this man is a ruthless rapist and murderer. If he somehow evades us now, there's a strong possibility that he will kill a woman police officer at some time tonight. We cannot let that happen."

Izzie Drake backed up Ross's words.

"We're confident that Donovan has no idea we're on to him. From what we've learned, it appears he's not been seen in his regular haunts and he's virtually isolated himself from his known contacts, not surprising given what he's been up to for the last few weeks so we should have the element of surprise on our side."

Ross carried on, "Taking all that into consideration, I repeat, we cannot afford to fail, and I want everyone on their toes when we go in. Take no chances. We have no reports of Donovan being in possession of firearms, but nothing is guaranteed. Sergeant Ferris will be here any minute with firearms for himself and me. As such, we will lead when we make our approach, me from the front and Paul from the rear. Let me stress, if Donovan makes it out of the house, and worse still out of the street, we could have major problems containing him. If he gets through our cordon and heads south, it's not far to Kirkdale station where he might get lucky and hop on a train. North, and he could make it to Bootle South Recreation Ground. There's a good chance he could lose us if he gets that far, so let's make sure it doesn't happen. With luck, we'll get him without a fight, in his home, so let's be professional and get this bloody bastard in custody asap."

As Ross finished speaking, he received a whole series of comments confirming everyone's determination to achieve the arrest of Trevor Donovan. Right on cue, the car bearing Paul Ferris and Ginger Devenish pulled up behind the other police vehicles and the two detectives made their way to join their colleagues.

"I've got what you asked for, sir," Ferris announced, as he indicated the case he was carrying. Ross pulled him to one side and Ferris unlocked the weapons carrying case, to reveal two Glock 17 semi-automatic pistols.

"Full magazines in both, sir," he reported.

"Excellent, Paul, but let's hope we don't need them."

"Agreed, sir."

Beatrice Street comprised a mixture of two and three bedroomed terraced houses dating from the turn of the 19th/20th centuries. As such most possessed small front and rear gardens, and some residents had worked hard to increase their privacy levels by fencing in the rear gardens with tall fences that would probably help the police more than Donovan. If he tried to escape from his pursuers, he'd find it virtually impossible to do so by hopping from garden to garden thanks to the height of those fences. Ross didn't know at that point what the set up was at the rear of the house Donovan was occupying so he sent Sofie Meyer and Derek McLennan, posing as a courting couple, to slowly meander down the alleyway that ran behind the houses to check it out.

The pair walked arm in arm along the narrow alley behind the houses, to all who saw them, just another couple in love, counting as they went, as there were no numbers on the backs of the houses. A few had gates in the fences that most had erected, and a couple who had built 5 or six foot walls had installed wooden doors in their walls, but when they reached the house of the man they sought, they saw nothing more secure than a three foot fence with an everyday latch type gate, easy for their man to make his escape if allowed to get that far.

"We will need to have men out here for sure," Meyer said quietly.

"Stand still a moment," Meyer ordered, "and hug me as if you are about to kiss me."

"Eh?"

"Just do it, Derek. I wish to see if I can detect any movement in the house."

"Right, ok," McLennan said as he followed her instructions.

He took Sofie in his arms and pulled her close as she turned slightly in the clinch so that she was looking directly into the small garden of Donovan's home.

"See anything?" Derek whispered.

"Shut up and kiss me," she whispered in return. "And make it look real."

Derek may have felt awkward, kissing a woman other than his fiancée, Debbie, but he thought, *Orders are orders,* and gently kissed Sofie Meyer, whose eyes never stopped scanning the house throughout the few seconds the kiss lasted. He couldn't help but feel a sense of heady intoxication at the feel of her lips against his, and the scent of whatever body spray or perfume Sofie wore. He felt almost as if he was betraying his fiancée, Debbie in those few seconds even though he knew it was only a ploy to give Sofie a view of their target. As they pulled apart, and turned to carry on walking along the alley, a slightly breathless, red-faced Derek turned to Sofie.

"Did you see anything, Sarge?"

"Unfortunately not. The windows are quite small and have lace curtains hung to obscure a direct view into the house, with the exception of one, which I presume to be the kitchen window."

"So our little romantic couple subterfuge was a waste of time?"

"Oh, I don't know Derek. What is it you English say, "*How was it for you*?" and Sofie laughed as Derek McLennan's face turned an even darker shade of red.

"Eh, er, well…"

"I am joking with you," she grinned at the embarrassed detective constable. Kissing the pretty German had been the furthest thing from his mind as they'd meandered down the alley and her order to kiss her had been a total surprise. The trouble was, Derek had found it a pleasurable experience, one he knew he must rapidly get over and put down to experience. "Sometimes the job calls for us to do the most unexpected things, do you not agree?"

"Yes, of course, Sarge. I agree, totally," he almost stammered in response.

Meyer couldn't help but grin all the way to the end of the alley, where they turned left and made their back to the main street again, where the rest of the team awaited their return.

"Nothing to see sir," Sofie reported their findings to Ross. "Lace curtains everywhere except the kitchen window and there was no movement to be seen there while we were watching."

"I hope you weren't too obvious about your surveillance," Ross queried.

"Oh no, we were very discreet, weren't we Derek?"

"What? Oh yes, very discreet, sir."

Sam Gable saw Derek's face turn bright red as he spoke and couldn't resist making a comment.

"You alright, Derek? You've turned a funny colour."

"Yes, of course I am."

When he said no more, Meyer stepped in to rescue him.

"We had to do a little improvisation to maintain our ruse as a loving couple. We held each other for a seconds, and then I told him to kiss me."

"You what?" Sam Gable gasped.

"You're kiddin' us," Tony Curtis said, with a hint of jealousy. After all, kissing the gorgeous Sofie Meyer wouldn't be too hard an instruction for him to obey.

"I told him to kiss me," Meyer reiterated. "It was the only thing I could think of that would allow us to linger outside the garden gate so I could get a good look in the direction of the house without us looking too suspicious. I was able to look over Derek's shoulder as we kissed," she said. Being around the same height as Derek, he had proved the ideal partner for her improvised subterfuge.

"That was a great piece of improvisation, Sofie," Izzie Drake, smiled as she spoke.

"And how was it for you, Derek?" added Nick Dodds.

McLennan groaned, "Oh no, not you too, Nick?"

"What?" said Dodds, innocently.

"I asked him that too," Sofie grinned.

"Well, at least you didn't ask him to do anything more than that," Ross said, allowing the moment of humour to take some of the building tension to dissipate for a few seconds. He needed his team focussed but it wouldn't do to have them too 'wired' before they went in. Focussed but relaxed, that was Ross's way. Too tense and mistakes could be made from over-zealousness or by allowing nervous energy to lead to mistakes.

"Will you lot give over?" poor Derek pleaded with his fellow detectives.

"Don't worry, Derek, we won't tell Debbie," Sam Gable joked, and Derek blushed again.

"It was work, you teasing bastards."

"Please, everyone, enough is enough. Derek was a very good partner and an excellent kisser too," Meyer spoke with such conviction that the teasing instantly ended.

"Good, I'm glad we've got that sorted," Ross added. "Now, people, can we get back to work please? We do have a murderer to apprehend, in case anyone's forgotten why we're here."

"Perimeter's in place, Andy, and all my lads have their instructions and know what to do," the uniformed Inspector Brough brought them all back to reality.

"Thanks," Ross acknowledged. "Okay everyone, let's go catch ourselves a killer."

Chapter 30

Gallery of Horrors

As they prepared to move in on their target, Andy Ross, who would lead the assault on Donovan's house quickly changed into the uniform of a Royal Mail postal delivery worker. With a package, supposedly for the occupant of the house in his hand, he walked slowly towards Donovan's house. The rest of the team were strategically positioned to provide him with back-up as required. Sofie Meyer walked with him, ostensibly an ordinary citizen, just chatting to the postman. As Ross walked up to the front door of the house on Beatrice street, she walked a few yards past the house and stood, waiting to leap into action if needs be, in support of her boss. Meanwhile, Paul Ferris and Derek McLennan took up position directly behind the house in the back alley, which was effectively sealed off by the presence of Nick Dodds and Sam Gable, plus two uniformed constables at one end, and Tony Curtis, Ginger Devenish plus two uniforms at the other end. Beatrice Street itself was secured by the uniformed officers led by Inspector Brough with police cars still positioned to prevent any entry or egress from the street by foot or by vehicle. Ross had made sure of that final added security in case Donovan had access to alternative transport, outside their knowledge. There were plenty of cars on the street that, if Donovan accessed them, could lead the police on a potentially dangerous chase through the streets of Liverpool, placing not only his officers, but members of the public at risk. Izzie Drake, meanwhile was tasked with the job of overall co-ordinator, in charge of on the spot decision making if anything went 'pear-shaped' once Ross effectively set the operation in motion by knocking on the door. With her police radio in hand she was in touch with everyone involved in the operation and was now joined when none other than Oscar Agostini appeared at her shoulder, just as Ross was about to knock on Donovan's door.

"Hello, sir," Izzie said in surprise as the Detective Chief Inspector gently laid a hand on her shoulder to quietly announce his presence.

"Don't panic Izzie. I'm not here to interfere. Just wanted to add my support and be here when Andy brings this murdering bastard in. Please, carry on."

"Okay, sir, you're the boss."

Ross knocked three times on the door and waited, his faux package held in a clearly visible position in case Donovan peered through the downstairs bay window to see who was at his door. Izzie could see him from her vantage point on the corner of the street and she sent two quick squawks on her police radio, the signal to the rest of the team that Ross had made his move.

For a few seconds, time seemed to pass in slow motion for those watching from their vantage positions and even more so for those out of view of the house, who were reliant on Drake for updates and instructions.

True to human nature, Ross felt rather than saw a twitching of the curtains in the window and knew that Donovan was checking to see who was at the door.

"Who the fuck is this?" Donovan said aloud to himself. "Bloody post. Better get rid of him quick."

He didn't even realise he was talking to himself, as he padded quietly from the living room to the front door. He opened it as far as the security chain he'd fitted would allow.

"Yeah, what d'you want?" he said to Ross through the crack.

"Got a package to be signed for," Ross said nonchalantly.

"Can't you leave it on the step?"

"No can-do mate, like I said, it needs signing for."

"Fucking hell, alright, hang on a sec," Donovan replied, impatience evident in his voice.

The door closed for a few seconds and Ross heard the sound of the security chain being slid back and released from its fastening, and then the door opened slowly and Ross found himself standing face to face with Trevor Donovan. Before giving Donovan a chance to say anything, Ross immediately went into action.

"Trevor Donovan, you are under arrest on suspicion of…"

He got no further, as Donovan reacted instantly by attempting to slam the door in Ross's face. Ross was too quick for him and shoved his foot into the gap and it took the full force of Donovan's weight as it prevented the door from shutting. Ross shouted out in pain and seeing what had happened, Sofie Meyer was by his side in a couple of seconds, and the pair went into the house after Donovan.

Izzie sent three squawks on her radio to indicate that contact had been made and then spoke so that the team knew what was happening.

"Subject has run back into house. D.I Ross and Sergeant Meyer in pursuit, No further details. Cover all exits."

"Armed police," Ross shouted as he and Meyer began the search for Donovan, who'd moved quickly after shutting the door and could now be anywhere in the house. "Give yourself up, Donovan. There's nowhere for you to go."

Tentatively, he and Meyer checked the sitting room. No sign of Donovan.

"Sitting room clear," he shouted, for Drake's benefit. His radio was switched to send so she could hear whatever he said inside the property.

As they moved toward the kitchen they heard the sound of a door being opened.

"He's trying to make a run for it through the back door," he shouted.

Sure enough, Trevor Donovan was going to try to bolt through the back door and into the rear alleyway.

"Paul and Derek, he's yours," Drake shouted into her radio, her voice calm as she passed on Ross's information. "Take him."

As Donovan burst through the back door and began making his attempt for freedom by running towards the back-garden gate, Paul Ferris, Glock in hand, stepped into view, Derek McLennan at his side. Donovan halted in mid-stride, looked at the evil-looking weapon in Ferris's hands and then he started towards the two officers again, shouting as he ran,

"You're British coppers. You won't shoot an unarmed man. Stuff you, filth!"

"Maybe not," McLennan shouted back at him, "but we can do this," and he launched himself forward in a flying rugby tackle that took the legs right out from under Trevor Donavan, who fell to the ground with a heavy "oomph" escaping from his lungs as he hit the paved garden path, winding him and McLennan in the process. Paul Ferris moved like the wind and virtually threw himself onto Donovan, pinning him to the ground where he'd fallen face down. With his knees in Donovan's back, Ferris quickly stuffed the Glock into his trouser pocket and at lightning speed, withdrew his handcuffs and pulled the man's hands behind his back and had him cuffed and immobile in a few seconds.

"You okay, Derek?" he asked his colleague.

"Fine, call it in Sarge," Derek, still winded, gasped his reply.

"Subject down and in custody," Ferris shouted into his radio mic, and then, rising to his feet, he proceeded to pull McLennan to his feet, and the two of them looked down with sense of satisfaction at their prisoner, who lay cursing and struggling on the garden path at their feet.

Ross and Meyer burst through the back door in time to see Derek McLennan's flying tackle and Ferris cuffing their man. The two quickly joined them in a small group around Trevor Donovan.

"Get him up," Ross ordered, and Ferris and McLennan hauled him, non-too gently to his feet. As soon as he had the man standing directly in front of him, Andy Ross felt an immense sense of satisfaction as he delivered his next words.

"Trevor Donovan. I'm placing you under arrest on suspicion of the rape and murders of Catherine Billings and Hannah Lucas. You do not have to say anything, but it may harm your defence if you do not mention when questioned something which you may later rely on in court. Anything you do say may be given in evidence."

"Fuck you, copper," Donovan responded, and then fell silent.

"Take him away," Ross instructed Ferris and McLennan, just as D.C.I. Oscar Agostini and Sergeant Izzie Drake appeared, having come through the house and out into the garden.

"Well, well, not such a big man now are you?" Drake couldn't help herself a she taunted the prisoner, who looked less like a murderer and more like a rabbit caught in car headlights as he stood, surrounded by officers of the law. He knew his murderous spree was over and that he faced a long jail sentence. He remained silent.

"So this is the scumbag who thought he'd outwit us, is it?" Oscar Agostini's question was no more than a rhetorical statement. "Well done Andy."

"I think we have Sergeant Ferris and D.C. McLennan to thank for finally nailing him," Ross said, always willing to give credit to his team when due.

"Derek was the one who brought him down," Ferris admitted. "You should have seen him. A real flying rugby tackle and Donovan didn't know what had hit him. Derek could easily get a game for Wigan with tackles like that."

"So our Derek's the hero again," Sam Gable added, referring to a previous case when McLennan had taken a bullet while trying to prevent a robbery during his off-duty hours.

"Gonna have to watch you Derek," Izzie laughed. "The bloody SAS will be after you before long."

Everyone enjoyed the light-hearted moment as the tension of the arrest of Donovan eased a little. There was still work to do however. Ross had Ferris and McLennan remove Donovan from the scene and they quickly left with their prisoner, who'd be processed and placed in a cell awaiting further interview when Ross returned to headquarters. Meanwhile, there remained the job of searching Donovan's home.

After searching the downstairs rooms, which produced no incriminating evidence, Ross led the way upstairs, joined by Izzie Drake and Senior Crime Scenes Investigator, Miles Booker, who had recently arrived on the scene with his team. The first room they entered was clearly the master bedroom. In the centre of the room stood a double bed, covered by a black satin duvet cover, with matching pillowcases. A pine wardrobe stood to one side of the room, next to a chest of drawers, also in pine. There was more to see, however.

"Bloody hell!" Drake exclaimed as she took in the sight of the wall opposite the wardrobe. The wall was decorated with photographs. It was clear to see that Donovan had been stalking his victims before committing his rapes and murders.

"I know that face," said Miles Booker, as she stood at Drake's shoulder.

"Fuck, so do I," Ross confirmed Booker's recognition.

From the left, the wall was covered first in a series of photographs of Cathy Billings, taken at work in the pub, and outside, as she entered and left before and after work. Worse, there were photos of the young woman doing ordinary humdrum activities, hanging out washing wearing only a nightie, exercising in a gym, and swimming at what had to have been Crosby Leisure Centre on Mariners Road. It was likely the gym she'd been photographed at was the one at the leisure centre too. Before looking closely at the third set of photos however, they examined the others, in chronological order.

"He got his kicks by taking these. All of them show the girl wearing very little clothing," Booker commented.

"And look here," Ross pointed to the last pictures of Cathy.

"Bastard," Drake shouted as her mind processed the photographs that showed the sheer sadism and depravity of Trevor Donovan. "He took pictures of her before and after raping her and again after killing her."

"You're right," Booker said. "The poor girl has obviously been posed in the last one, with her knees drawn up and her legs apart. Andy, this is one sick individual."

"Possibly one of the worst I've ever come across, Miles. And look at number two, Hannah Lucas."

Sure enough, Donovan had photographed Hannah Lucas in the midst of her taking part in various routine daily activities. Again, he'd photographed the poor young woman as he'd abused, raped and murdered her, posing her body as he had with Cathy Billings.

"There's no words on their bodies in these," Drake observed.

"No, I'll lay odds he did that when he dumped their bodies near the lighthouse," Booker commented.

"I'd say you're right, Miles," Ross said to the Crime Scene team leader. "But this is one big surprise," he added as the three of them moved on to the third set of photos, clearly being those of Donovan's intended third victim.

"Correct me if I'm wrong, but that is D.I. Morris isn't it?" Drake stared aghast at the photos.

"It is," Ross nodded in confirmation.

"That's how I knew her face," Booker realised.

Like Cathy and Hannah, Donovan had collected his own gallery of photographs of Detective Inspector Fiona Morris, like the others, all taken as she went about her daily life. Most disturbing were three pictures that showed the D.I. in her bedroom, in various states of undress as she obviously prepared for bed. Morris clearly didn't wear much when she climbed into bed at night.

"How the hell did he get these?" Drake was shocked.

"Telephoto lens," Booker replied. "You can tell by the angle these are taken from that he was slightly lower than his subject when he took these, probably perched in a tree or maybe on a nearby garage roof."

"From the way he was dressed, I've a feeling we got here just in time," Ross postulated. "All in black, and a bag filled with all he needed to carry out another attack, we might have missed him if we'd waited even another ten minutes."

"But what the hell was D.I. Morris doing, getting undressed with her curtains wide open so anyone could see into her bedroom?" Drake wanted to know.

"Police officer or not, she may be a secret exhibitionist," Booker offered in reply.

"Or maybe she thinks she can't be overlooked," Ross tried to think of some logical reason for her foolhardy behaviour.

"Either way, it's certain she was Donovan's next target," Drake correctly surmised. "Are you going to tell her?"

"No," Ross said, firmly. "I'm leaving that up to D.C.I. Agostini, or maybe even D.C.S. Hollingsworth. "I have one or two other comments to make about her handling of the first two murders. Those will be addressed to Oscar Agostini, and it'll be up to him if he takes it further."

"I take it you're not happy with the lady, Andy?" Booker observed.

"Let's just say she has a few questions to answer when this case is over."

By the time the search of Donovan's house was completed, the team, together with Miles Booker's crime scene techs had unearthed a large cache of pornographic DVDs, plus, perhaps more telling, a number of items of women's underwear, all of which pointed towards a sexually depraved killer.

"Where the hell did he get all these ladies knickers from?" Sam Gable commented.

"Look at them, Sam. They are not all brand new, and we know he didn't take away his victims' undergarments, so we are possibly looking at them having been stolen, probably from people washing lines," Sofie Meyer replied.

"Blood and sand, what a fucking pervert," Gable retorted.

"I think you are correct in your assumption, Sam," said Meyer.

In addition, a quick examination of Donovan's mobile phone, which he hadn't bothered to password protect, showed he'd downloaded a number of video clips from some rather extreme online pornographic sites. All in all, it seemed they'd moved none too soon in apprehending the double killer.

I'm looking forward to talking to Mr. Trevor fucking Donovan once we return to the office," Ross said, his face a grim mask of determination. As he and Drake were about to leave the house they were intercepted by Oscar Agostini, who was waiting for them on the threshold of the front door.

"Oscar, what are you doing here?" Ross expressed his surprise.

"Last time I looked, I'm still the commander of this team, am I not?"

"Of course you are. I just meant…"

"Oh, shut up Andy. I'm only pulling your leg. I needed to see this one concluded so I came down to offer you some moral support, on the ground, so to speak. You and your people have done a great job by the looks of it."

"Thanks, Boss, but you haven't seen anything yet. Let me show you Donovan's own murder gallery."

Ross left Drake to confer with the rest of the team for a few minutes while he re-entered the house, where a shocked D.C.I. Oscar Agostini took his time in perusing the killer's own record of his stalking, and the even more shocking photos of his victims, bound and half naked, both before and after being brutally raped, and ending with photos of their posed bodies, a sure mark of the killer's depravity. As they exited the house a few minutes later, Oscar Agostini looked visibly shaken.

"You alright, sir?" Drake asked, on seeing the look on his face.

"I'm okay, thank you, Sergeant. I guess I've been away from the sharp end a bit too long. Me and D.I. Ross have seen some pretty gruesome sites in the past, especially when we worked the streets together, but this is one of the worst things I've seen in a heck of a long time."

"We need to make sure this bastard goes down for a long time," Agostini said, and turning to Ross, added, "Make sure this case is watertight, Andy. I don't want some clever shit of a lawyer finding a single hole in our investigation, or in any evidence we present. Got it?"

"Loud and clear, Sir," Ross said, his own face a mask of determination. "Let's get back to headquarters, Izzie. I want to talk to Donovan sooner rather than later."

They left soon afterwards, leaving the residents of Beatrice Street bemused and bewildered by what had taken place in their street. His team had ensured there'd been no encroachment on the Donovan residence by the locals while the operation had taken place, a job they'd undertaken quietly and unobtrusively so as not to give Donovan any advance warning of the police presence in the street. Ross thanked them all before he and Drake departed, reserving a firm handshake and a big thank you to Inspector Brough for the help he and his officers had given in supporting the operation.

Before they could depart however, young P.C. Kumar came running up to Ross.

"Sir, sir," he was out of breath from running to catch the D.I. before he left.

"P.C. Kumar isn't it? What can I do for you Constable?"

"I just wanted to say, sir, it has been a pleasure working for you and your team and that I hope one day to have the opportunity to work with you again."

There, he'd said it. He'd been trying to pluck up the courage to speak directly to D.I. Ross throughout the operation and now he hoped he hadn't overstepped the mark.

"How long have you been a police officer, Kumar?" Ross asked him.

"Three years, sir."

"Then if you want to become a detective, you should apply. C.I.D. are always looking for good men, Kumar. You never know. If you have the backing of your senior officer, you might get lucky."

"Thanks a lot, sir. I appreciate you stopping to talk to me."

"No problem, Constable Kumar, no problem at all."

Chapter 31

A Wall of Silence

Trevor Donovan was possibly the most intransigent suspect Ross had ever interrogated in his career. By the time Ross and Drake arrived back at headquarters, Donovan had already lawyered up. The custody sergeant, Pat Newman had informed Ross of Donovan's request for legal representation as soon as Ross requested that the man be brought to Interview Room One. With no lawyer of his own, Newman had arranged for legal representation for their prisoner from the pool of on-call duty solicitors. Ross was quite pleased when he heard that the duty solicitor appointed to act for Donovan was Gina Thomas, who he'd had dealings with in the past. She was efficient without being belligerent towards the police, and most importantly from Ross's point of view, she was a woman, and perhaps more likely to be sensitive to the gravity of the crimes her client was accused of committing.

None of this was relevant however, if her client refused to speak and Gina was herself becoming exasperated by his refusal to say anything, even to her. As much as she'd attempted to confer with him, to try to give him a modicum of legal advice, after over an hour in the room the most Donovan had said had been to confirm his name to the interrogating officers.

Ross actually felt sorry for her. He knew she would do her best for Donovan under normal circumstances but, given the silence being exhibited by the man, she could do nothing for him. Ross would even have accepted an occasional 'no comment' from the man, but all Trevor Donovan did was sit staring at him, now and then switching his stare to Izzie Drake, at whom he looked as if sizing her up as a victim for his perverted lust. Izzie shivered each time he looked at her. She could almost feel the evil emanating from every pore in his body.

Ross admitted to himself that just being in the same room as this man, breathing the same air, gave him the creeps. What Drake felt, he could only imagine as they sat opposite was probably the most evil man they'd confronted in their time together as police officers.

He wondered if Gina Thomas felt the same way. After all, she was sitting next to the man, and was best placed to feel any vibes Donovan was giving off. For once, Andy Ross found himself feeling sorry for a defending solicitor.

"If you won't tell my anything about the murders, can you at least tell me what made you suddenly decide to copy the crimes you'd discovered your father had been responsible for?"

Again, his question elicited no reply.

"What about your photo gallery?" Izzie Drake tried this time. "It took a lot of patience, surely, following those women around, day and night sometimes, just to collect a few snap shots."

She hoped that by trivialising his precious gallery of horrors, by referring to it as 'a few snapshots,' it might at least raise his hackles enough to cause some display of emotion, a show of temper, anything to prove he cared about what he'd done or indeed what was happening to him at this precise moment.

Still, Trevor Donovan stared ahead, looking into Izzie's eyes without voicing a word. Once again, she felt that evil glare. She was in no doubt that, given the opportunity, he would happily rip her clothes off, perform some despicable sex act on her, before strangling the life out of her limp, abused body. The thought was enough to make her feel physically sick. Ross, sensing her discomfiture, decided that enough was enough. This interview, if that's what it could be described as, was getting them absolutely nowhere. He had little alternative but to give it up as a bad job. Announcing the interview was suspended for the benefit of the recording tape, he asked the constable who'd stood sentinel by the door throughout the session, to return Donovan to his cell, and the man was quickly led away in handcuffs to his place of incarceration.

"Well, Miss Thomas," he said the thirty something year old solicitor after Donovan had departed, "What do you think of your new client?"

"You know I can't answer that, Mr. Ross," she replied.

"I'm not asking you to betray any client confidentiality here," he said. "He hasn't spoken a single word since he was arrested and brought in, apart from to acknowledge his name, and that he was aware of his rights. Oh, and to ask for a lawyer. Don't you find that odd? Come on, off the record, just between us. Whatever you say won't be repeated outside this room. You have my word on it. I'm just interested in your first impressions of the man."

Gina Thomas hesitated for a few seconds. She looked as if she had the weight of the world on her shoulders, as Ross had already deduced as he'd watched the way she'd looked at Donovan as they'd attempted to question him and as he'd steadfastly refused to even acknowledge her, his own legal representative. Finally, she sighed, looked directly at Ross and spoke very quietly as if she was afraid of being overheard.

"Off the record, the man gives me the creeps, Mr. Ross. There's something unsettling about him, but I can't put my finger on it. I know I'm duty bound to represent him, but God knows how he expects me to mount any kind of defence if he won't speak to me. You're sure he asked for a lawyer when he was brought in?"

"Thank you, Miss Thomas. I just wanted to know if you felt the same sort of vibes that my sergeant and I have been feeling from being in close proximity to Mr. Donovan. I'm glad it isn't just us. I'm sorry you had to be the one to be on call when he asked for legal representation. Believe me when I tell you I consider this man to be a severe danger to women."

"I just hope he's more receptive the next time," Thomas replied.

"You'll be duly notified when we intend to interview Mr. Donovan again, Miss Thomas."

"Thank you," the solicitor said as she closed her briefcase and took her leave of the interview room. She actually felt dirty from having been in the presence of Trevor Donovan, for reasons she couldn't even explain to herself. As she walked across town to her own office, not far from police headquarters, she took the unprecedented decision to ask to be relieved from representing her new client. After all, it wasn't as if he'd actually spoken a word to her as yet.

Over the next two weeks, all attempts to try to engage with Donovan resulted in the detectives meeting with the same wall of silence. Gina Thomas had been replaced by a male solicitor, Gary Hopper, who found Donovan as uncooperative as his predecessor. In the end it was decided to subject Donovan to a psychiatric evaluation, but as he refused to speak to the psychiatrist appointed to examine him, it was impossible for him to be diagnosed as mentally ill. He was taken to be simply exercising his right to silence after his arrest. He spoke once and once only, merely to confirm his name at his remand hearing, and only when the magistrate threatened to have him jailed for contempt of court and brought back every week until he confirmed his name. Until then, he was told, his case would not be heard and his lack of cooperation would seriously hamper his cause. "I don't care if you spend the next two years in jail, being brought here week after week until you speak to confirm your identity. I am paid to be here, you are not. I will ask you once more, are you Trevor Donovan?"

"I am," he said, eventually, at the third time of asking.

Ross and his team were left with the task of gathering as much evidence as they could to ensure a successful prosecution, their task made easy by the fact that Donovan had taken no steps to cover up his actions. His home, the room containing his gallery of horrific photographs was a treasure trove for the detectives. They found a diary, not unlike that of his father, in which he described in sickening detail what he'd done to his victims. In the same drawer were notes he'd made from his father's diary, in which he'd recalled many of the intimate details of the original murders, enabling him to recreate his father's crimes, even without being in possession of the diary. Sam Gable, hardened by years of working in the Vice Squad, was actually physically sick after reading some of his words. By the time they'd concluded their investigation, Ross and his team were confident that Donovan would be going down for a very long time.

Meanwhile Detective Inspector Fiona Morris had been called to headquarters to see Detective Chief Inspector Oscar Agostini, together with her own boss, D.C.I. Mountfield. Morris was shown the photographs that identified her as Donovan's next selected victim and was of course both horrified and appalled. It was pointed out to her that she should be a little more aware of the potential for breaches of her private security by walking around her home in a state of undress, whilst leaving her curtains open, thus exposing herself to anyone determined enough to wish to observe her.

"Donovan must have watched D.I. Morris at some point during her investigation into either Cathy or Hannah's murder," Mountfield surmised," and become attracted to her as a potential victim."

"I've no doubt of that," Agostini agreed, "but speaking of the original investigation into these murders, it is my opinion and that of D.I. Ross, that your officer was less than diligent in her initial enquiries. She failed to fully engage with former D.I. Stan Coleman when he came forward after identifying the shocking similarities between murders of Cathy Billings and Hannah Lucas, and the murders in 1966. She was further remiss in not giving Mr. Coleman certain facts pertaining to the recent murders that could have led him to providing further information, such as he willingly supplied to D.I. Ross, and which could have aided her own investigation. She seemed unwilling to accept a direct relationship between those original Lighthouse murders and the recent killings to the extent that if left in charge, which thankfully she was not, she would in all probability currently be dead and lying on Doctor Nugent's autopsy table in the morgue."

Morris didn't know where to put herself and found it impossible to look Agostini in the eye. He went on, "It is my opinion that D.I. Morris acted unprofessionally and with a level of naivety not expected from an officer of her rank and experience."

By the end of the session, Morris was left wondering if she still had a career ahead of her in the police force. D.C.I. Mountfield was as supportive of his officer as he could be, but he had little choice but to agree with Agostini, and Morris felt herself lucky not to be demoted or fired. Instead, she got off relatively lightly with a reprimand which would be placed on her record and was instructed to attend a number of courses intended to improve her skills as a detective. If she refused to attend, she was told she would be demoted to detective sergeant and could expect to remain in that rank for a long time.

She accepted her punishment and had the good grace to apologise for her attitude and application during the initial investigation. The fact that she'd come so close to becoming the next victim of Trevor Donovan had a singularly sobering effect on her, and both Agostini and Mountfield were of the opinion that it was unlikely she'd make the same mistake again in the future.

Meanwhile, Andy Ross had Paul Ferris call former D.I. Stan Coleman to invite him to join Ross and his team for a drink later that night. Coleman was touched and delighted to receive the invitation and agreed to be at the pub at 8 p.m. as requested.

Doctor Christine Bland would be present, the profiler and forensic pathologist using the evening to say farewell to Ross and team before setting off for London the following day. Ross and his team all had the opportunity to say their farewells before Coleman arrived and though Bland offered to leave before he got there, Ross insisted she stay and join them for the evening.

"I wasn't really much help on this occasion, was I?" Bland had said, rather morosely as she sat nursing a gin and tonic.

"You gave us more than you know," was Ross's riposte. "You gave us plenty of pointers and everything you said made perfect sense. Please don't put yourself down. We all appreciate the effort you put into trying to help us on this awful bloody case."

"Here, here," Sofie Meyer said, raising her pint glass in Bland's direction.

"Here's to the doc," Tony Curtis added, and the others joined in, making Christine Bland feel that perhaps she had helped a little, after all.

By the time Stan Coleman arrived the party was in full swing, and the detectives were well on their way to feeling that alcohol-inspired feeling of happiness known by most police officers after the successful conclusion of a difficult case.

"Here's to you and your team," the former detective inspector said, raising his pint glass in a toast to Andy Ross and his squad members who were all present to take part in Ross's specially organised thank you to the man in charge of the original Lighthouse murders. "I must admit, when I came forward to bring the similarities in the two sets of murders to the attention of your colleagues I hardly dared believe you'd end up solving my original case as well as the new murders."

"Ha-ha, you don't know the boss when he gets going," D.C. Tony Curtis quipped.

"The bad guys don't stand a chance when we get going, eh lads and lasses?" Nick Dodds added.

"And let us not forget the heroic action of D.C. McLennan," Sofie Meyer raised her own glass in salute.

"You'll have to tell me all about that," Coleman pleaded, and Meyer quickly relayed to him the way Derek McLennan had rugby tackled Donovan to the ground as the killer had attempted to flee from his house on Beatrice Street. McLennan blushed, never comfortable being in the limelight, and his discomfiture grew when Sam Gable added,

"Yes, and he got to kiss Sergeant Meyer in the process."

"Really? Now that you just have to explain to me. Is this a new procedure in the manual of crime detection?" Coleman smiled as he spoke.

Izzie Drake tried explaining it in as professional manner as she could, but even her measured explanation did little to ease Derek's embarrassment.

To laughter all round, Andy Ross stood and addressed the small gathering.

"Okay, everyone. I want us all to raise our glasses in a big thank you to Stan Coleman, living proof of the old saying, *once a copper, always a copper*."

The rest of the team duly obliged, enough to almost bring a tear to an old man's eye. Stan Coleman actually blushed, unused to receiving such effusive praise. The ex-detective had another question however.

"You know, I'd never have thought of Pete Donovan as the killer, back in the day. He seemed so ordinary and gave no indication of having any criminal tendencies."

"To be honest, Stan, we wouldn't have caught on the him as the Lighthouse killer until the diary led us towards Trevor, in a roundabout sort of way."

"But why did he give up after three? There were plenty more women he could have targeted."

"We'll never know for sure, Stan, but I suspect you and your team must have got a little too close for comfort in your investigation, which probably scared him and caused him to back off."

"You think so? I'd like to believe that's true, that even though we never caught the bastard, we at least prevented him killing any more innocent women."

"And don't forget, we got the elder Albert Cretingham for the murders of his wife and her lover. All of it came about because you saw the links between the sixties murders and the latest killings and had the foresight to contact us."

"So, what happens next?" Coleman asked. "I understand that Donovan won't speak to anyone. How do you go on from here?"

"It doesn't matter whether he speaks or not," Ross told him. "We've done our job, gathered all the evidence and it's all in the hands of the lawyers now. The C.P.S. believe we have a watertight case against him, so he'll stand trial, whether he talks or not."

The Crown Prosecuting Service had taken one look at the evidence against Trevor Donovan and unhesitatingly recommended prosecuting the man. The prosecution had appointed one of the top barristers in the country, Sir Michael Trentham, to handle the case, in a show of legal force. They were not going to let this one slip. Of course, there was little Donovan's defence could do for him, due to his continued refusal to speak in his own defence.

"So you reckon he'll go down for a long stretch then?" Coleman asked.

"Wouldn't surprise me if he got life with a recommendation that he spend a minimum of twenty years before being considered for parole," Ross replied.

"I just wish life could really mean life," Tony Curtis added from the other side of the table.

"I agree with you, Tony," Sam Gable added.

"Well, let's wait and see, shall we?" Izzie Drake spoke diplomatically.

The evening continued amid plenty of back slapping and self-congratulations. As the time to call it a night crept up on the more than merry and of police officers, Stan Coleman showed his appreciation for them including him in the night's festivities by arranging for his own cab company to provide free rides home for every member of Ross's team, ensuring none of them had to risk driving over the legal limit. They could come back the following day to collect their own vehicles, and Coleman even promised anyone who needed it, a free ride back to the pub from their home in order to do so.

So it was that one of the Specialist Murder Investigation team's most harrowing and intensive cases to date came to its conclusion. Ross, in company with Izzie Drake had personally visited the still-grieving parents of both Cathy Billings and Hannah Lucas after Trevor Donovan's arrest and all that remained now, was the eventual trial and sentencing of one of the most evil killers the team had encountered. Many questions remained, chief among them the reason why Donovan had decided to 'celebrate' his father's death in prison by recreating his crimes of thirty-nine years previously. Unless or until Donovan decided to talk, any such questions would have to remain unanswered.

Ross and his team moved on, ready and waiting to tackle the next 'special' murder inquiry that would be passed on to them, although, the aftermath of the case of the Lighthouse Murders, mark two, wasn't quite concluded yet.

Epilogue

The trial of Trevor Donovan was a short but sweet affair as far as the police were concerned. Donovan continued to maintain his silence, even refusing to cooperate with his court-appointed trial barrister, Morton Howard. Due to the sensationalist reporting that had filled the press since Donovan's arrest, the trial was held in London at the Central Criminal Court, better known as The Old Bailey, named for the street on which it stands, and built on the site of the old, notorious Newgate Prison. Ross gave his evidence early on the first day of the trial and returned to Liverpool where he would await the result, of which he was in no doubt.

The sheer weight of evidence against him led to an inevitable guilty verdict on two counts of rape and wilful murder. The jury took less than two hours to unanimously convict Donovan of the rapes and murders after a trial that lasted three days, most of it filled with evidence from the police and forensic experts. The judge, Lord Justice Melville, sentenced Trevor Donovan to concurrent life sentences for the murders, and twenty years, also concurrent, for each of the rapes. Much as Ross had predicted to Stan Coleman, the judge also added his recommendation that Donovan should serve a minimum of twenty years before being considered for parole.

News of the conviction reached Ross as he and Drake were sitting in his office, where Izzie had arrived a few minutes earlier with some surprising news.

"I just received an invitation to a wedding, well, not quite a wedding, but our friend, Alex Sefton and her friend Lisa are entering into a civil partnership, and Alex was so grateful for the advice I gave her after she was brought in for questioning that she wants me to be there as a witness on her big day, as she calls it."

"Well, who'd have thought it, our Izzie, the agony aunt," Ross chuckled. "Seriously though, it's nice of her to invite you, Izzie. It's not often a member of the public feels such gratitude to a member of the force. You obviously made a big impression on her."

"All I did was treat her like a human being, and more importantly, like the woman she became after her gender reassignment, not as some kind of freak."

"I must admit, I was quite uncomfortable with her at first when she revealed her background to us, you know, not sure how to take her or treat her. You related to her far better than I did. I still have a lot to learn about such things, obviously."

"I could tell you were a bit unsure of her, and of yourself, come to that, when we first found out she was transgender. It's something we're going to have to get used to. There are probably a lot more people like Alex around than we know about since the operation became available."

"You're right, Izzie. Just look how I assumed worst about her when we first met her. I was ready to write her off as some kind of female impersonator, like a drag queen, a man posing as a woman. I don't mind admitting I was wrong and that we all, me included, can never stop learning and gaining new information and insights in order to be a better peace officer."

"That's a big speech, coming from you," Izzie smiled at him. "But you're not half as bad as you paint yourself. You were just taken by surprise when she told us the truth about herself, and you could have come to terms with it without me in end. What did amuse me though was poor Tony's reaction after he's been sent to drive her home. It proved how much of a woman Alex must be that he was almost drooling with admiration for her on his return. I'll never forget the look on his face when he learned she used to be a man. Now, *that* was something to see."

"Some things will never change, Izzie. Most men will always view people like Alex with slightly blurred perceptions I think."

"Sadly, I think you're right."

"Well, I'm pleased you were able to help her to see how things stood and that she acted on it. You did a good thing, Detective Sergeant Drake."

"Well thank you, kind sir," Izzie stood up and gave him a fake curtsy just as D.C.I Agostini knocked and entered Ross's office.

"Been elevated to the ranks of royalty, have you, Andy?" he joked.

"Just Izzie being facetious as usual," Ross replied. "Got some news for us, have you?"

"Guilty on all counts," Agostini reported and Ross stood and punched the air as he shouted a resounding, "Yes!"

Agostini gave Ross and Drake the details of Donovan's sentencing and left them to inform the rest of the team. As the D.C.I, departed, he was quickly replaced by Paul Ferris, who had more news for Ross.

"I know the case is over, sir, but I also know you don't like loose ends."

"Go on Paul. What've you got for us?"

"Teresa Moore, the former Edwin Cretingham, who you asked me to trace. Well, I found her eventually, and you can be sure we were wasting our time thinking of her as a potential subject."

"How so, Paul?"

"The reason nobody had seen her for a while was quite simple in the end. Teresa Moore has spent the last six weeks as a patient in hospital after a suicide attempt. Seems the last four weeks have been spent undergoing a psychiatric review. She was released yesterday. Best alibi I've ever seen I think, boss."

"You definitely get ten out of ten for perseverance, Paul," Ross complimented his sergeant. "I always know I can count on your thoroughness. How did Moore try to do away with herself by the way?"

"Slashed her wrists in the bath, landlord found her, when he called for the rent. He was only just in time apparently."

"I'm glad there wasn't another death during the course of the investigation," Ross said.

"Me too, Drake agreed. If she'd attempted suicide before we'd identified Donovan, we might have thought she was our killer as it was looking like at one time, and Fiona Morris might not be here today."

"Good point, Izzie," Ross agreed. "Still, it's all over now, time to move on folks."

* * *

The next couple of weeks after Trevor Donovan's conviction produced a period of calm for Ross and his team. Izzie Drake attended Alex Sefton's Civil Ceremony on the second Saturday, and Derek McLennan and his fiancée Debbie Simpson were busy putting the finishing touches to their wedding plans. While the whole team had been delighted to receive invitations to the wedding, which would take place just before Christmas, Derek had one more surprise to drop on one member of the team.

"You're serious? You want me to be your best man?" a surprised and delighted Tony Curtis was grinning from ear to ear.

"That's what I said," Derek repeated for a third time. "You were the first mate I made on the team when I was first appointed to the squad and we've worked together ever since. I can't think of anyone else I'd rather have by my side on the day."

"Cheers, mate," Curtis was grinning from ear to ear. I've never been asked to be a best man before. I might even forgive you for the invitation now," referring to the fact that his wedding invitation had been printed to show his real first name, Leonard. Nobody ever called him Leonard or Lenny and hadn't done since he first joined the squad and it was pointed out that he bore an uncanny resemblance to the famed movie icon Tony Curtis. The name stuck and nowadays the only people who used his real name were his parents and other family members. To everyone else he was simply Tony Curtis.

McLennan laughed and wriggled out of the implied criticism by insisting it had been Debbie who insisted that everyone should be invited under their correct names.

The final episode in the case of the Lighthouse murders came about a month later with the announcement on the news of the death of recently convicted murderer, Trevor Donovan, behind the walls of the Category A prison at Wakefield in Yorkshire. In grim similarity to his father, Donovan was murdered by a fellow inmate, eager to achieve his own brand of fame as the man who killed the notorious 'silent killer' as fellow inmates had quickly dubbed him. With his throat cut almost from ear to ear, Donovan was unable to say a word, even had he wanted to, as he bled out on the floor of the prison shower block with a group of some of the toughest inmates in the British prison system gleefully and silently watching his final death throes.

It was the rapes of course that had made him such a figure of hate. Under the prisoners' own code of conduct, rapists, child killers and molesters were regarded as the lowest of the low and fair game for anyone with the means to exact prison vengeance upon them. Nobody, least of all the members of Merseyside Police's Specialist Murder Investigation Team, would shed a tear for Trevor Donovan, unless one wished to count his widowed mother who, within a year, had lost her husband and her son, rapists and murderers both.

As the nights drew in, the evenings shorter, the leaves on the trees began their inexorable change from green, to russet and brown, and finally gave up their tenuous hold on the branches that held them. Derek and Debbie were busily making all the last-minute arrangements for their upcoming nuptials, Debbie finally having chosen her wedding dress after what, to Derek, felt like months of searching, rejecting first one, then another option for one reason or another. Tony Curtis, not usually the greatest sartorial member of the team had allowed Derek to assist him in selecting a quality suit for the wedding, and finally, the couple had selected the venue for their big day which would take place at the register office on Old Hall Street, with a small reception to be held at Croxteth Hall Park. Very soon, the clocks would be put back an hour as the country reverted from British Summer Time to Greenwich Mean Time and autumn would give way to the onrush of winter, with its early darkness, long nights giving way to shorter days and for the men and women of Ross's team, new depths of depravity and man's inhumanity to man would doubtless soon be raising their ugly heads once again. At least, for the moment, they had the upcoming nuptials of their friend and colleague to look forward to.

Dear reader,

We hope you enjoyed reading *A Very Mersey Murder.* Please take a moment to leave a review, even if it's a short one. Your opinion is important to us.

The story continues in *Last Train to Lime Street.*

To read the first chapter for free, please head to:
https://www.nextchapter.pub/books/last-train-to-lime-street

Discover more books by Brian L. Porter at
https://www.nextchapter.pub/authors/brian-porter-mystery-author-liverpool-united-kingdom

Want to know when one of our books is free or discounted? Join the newsletter at http://eepurl.com/bqqB3H

Best regards,

Brian L. Porter and the Next Chapter Team

Coming next in the Mersey Mystery Series – Last Train to Lime Street

As the late night Manchester Victoria to Liverpool Lime Street train nears the end of its journey, the driver of the train suddenly throws on the emergency brake as what appears to be a body drops from a bridge onto the track in front of his train. A sickening thud tells him he was too late to prevent the body being struck by his locomotive. With the line closed, Detective Inspector Andy Ross is called from his bed to attend the scene. Something about the scene doesn't look right to the uniformed officers sent to attend the incident. Sure enough, Ross and his team are soon inveigled into a complex web of mystery and suspense which begins with the simplest of questions, just who is, or was, the mutilated corpse now smashed into a bloody pulp by the impact of the fast moving railway locomotive? Was it an accident, or was it murder that sent the body of the unidentified man flying over the parapet of the bridge over the tracks? When at last the man is identified, Ross and the team must tread very carefully as their latest investigation takes them into some very murky waters indeed. Wealthy men often have powerful enemies, and Ross needs all his wits about him as the lucrative but seedy world of pornographic movie making rears its ugly head, in Last Train to Lime Street.

From International Bestselling Author Brian L Porter

The Mersey Mysteries

A Mersey Killing
All Saints, Murder on the Mersey
A Mersey Maiden
A Mersey Mariner
A Very Mersey Murder
Last Train to Lime Street (Coming soon)

Thrillers by Brian L Porter

A Study in Red - The Secret Journal of Jack the Ripper
Legacy of the Ripper
Requiem for the Ripper
Pestilence
Purple Death
Behind Closed Doors
Avenue of the Dead
The Nemesis Cell
Kiss of Life

Dog Rescue

Sasha
Sheba: From Hell to Happiness

Short Story Collection

After Armageddon

Remembrance Poetry

Lest We Forget

Children's books as Harry Porter

Wolf

Alistair the Alligator, (Illustrated by Sharon Lewis)

Charlie the Caterpillar (Illustrated by Bonnie Pelton)

As Juan Pablo Jalisco

Of Aztecs and Conquistadors

Many of Brian's books have also been released in translated versions, in Spanish, Italian and Portuguese editions.

About the Author

Brian L Porter is an award-winning author, whose books have also regularly topped the Amazon Best Selling charts, fifteen of which have to date been Amazon bestsellers. *A Mersey Mariner* was recently voted the Top Crime Novel in the Top 50 Best Indie Books, 2017 awards, while *Sheba: From Hell to Happiness* won the Best Nonfiction section and also won the Preditors & Editors Best Nonfiction Book Award, 2017. Writing as Brian, he has won a Best Author Award, and his thrillers have picked up Best Thriller and Best Mystery Awards. His short story collection *After Armageddon* is an international bestseller and his moving collection of remembrance poetry, *Lest We Forget*, is also an Amazon best seller.

Two rescue dogs, two bestsellers!

In a recent departure from his usual thriller writing, Brian has written two successful books about two of the rescued dogs who share his home.

Sasha, A Very Special Dog Tale of a Very Special Epi-Dog is now an international bestseller and winner of the Preditors & Editors Best Nonfiction Book, 2016, and was placed 7th in The Best Indie Books of 2016, and *Sheba: From Hell to Happiness* is a UK #1 bestseller, and award winner as detailed above. If you love dogs, you'll love these two offerings.

Writing as Harry Porter his children's books have achieved three bestselling rankings on Amazon in the USA and UK.

In addition, his third incarnation as romantic poet Juan Pablo Jalisco has brought international recognition with his collected works, *Of Aztecs and Conquistadors* topping the bestselling charts in the USA, UK and Canada.

Brian lives with his wife, children and a wonderful pack of eleven rescued dogs. He is also the in-house screenwriter for ThunderBall Films, (L.A.), for whom he is also a co-producer on a number of their current movie projects.

The Mersey Mysteries have already been optioned for TV/movie adaptation, in addition to his other novels, all of which have been signed by ThunderBall Films in a movie franchise deal.

Look out for the 6th book in the Mersey Mystery series, *Last Train to Lime Street*, coming soon.

See Brian's website at http://www.brianlporter.co.uk/

His blog is at https://sashaandharry.blogspot.co.uk/

A Very Mersey Murder
ISBN: 978-4-86747-100-5

Published by
Next Chapter
1-60-20 Minami-Otsuka
170-0005 Toshima-Ku, Tokyo
+818035793528
17th May 2021